Dear Diary,

What's new? Oh—right. You can't answer me.

Dear Pen Pal,

How are you? I am fine. Actually, I'm not.

# IN THE KEY OF

# DALE

## Benjamin Lefebvre

ARSENAL PULP PRESS
VANCOUVER

IN THE KEY OF DALE
Copyright © 2022 by Benjamin Lefebvre

ARSENAL PULP PRESS
Suite 202 – 211 East Georgia St.
Vancouver, BC V6A 1Z6
Canada
*arsenalpulp.com*

The publisher gratefully acknowledges the support of the Canada Council for the Arts
and the British Columbia Arts Council for its publishing program, and the Government
of Canada and the Government of British Columbia (through the Book Publishing Tax
Credit Program) for its publishing activities.

Arsenal Pulp Press acknowledges the xʷməθkʷəy̓əm (Musqueam), Sḵwx̱wú7mesh
(Squamish), and səl̓ilwətaʔɬ (Tsleil-Waututh) Nations, custodians of the traditional,
ancestral, and unceded territories where our office is located. We pay respect to their
histories, traditions, and continuous living cultures and commit to accountability,
respectful relations, and friendship.

Cover and text design by Jazmin Welch
Edited by Catharine Chen
Proofread by Alison Strobel

Printed and bound in Canada

Library and Archives Canada Cataloguing in Publication:
Title: In the key of Dale / Benjamin Lefebvre.
Names: Lefebvre, Benjamin, author.
Identifiers: Canadiana (print) 202202114OX | Canadiana (ebook) 20220211418 |
  ISBN 9781551529035 (softcover) | ISBN 9781551529042 (HTML)
Classification: LCC PS8623.E4469 I52 2022 | DDC jC813/.6—dc23

*For Jacob*

Chapter 1: Once there was a guy named Dale who lived with his mother and his stepfather and sometimes with his stepbrother. Dale felt bored and lonely, so he started writing about himself in third person and on second thought, I don't think this is working either.

Are you there, God? Oh, forget it.

## MONDAY, FEBRUARY 28

Dear Pa,

I read a book once about a character who kept "writing it out" in a diary, and when I rolled over and saw that it was three in the morning and I still hadn't fallen asleep, I figured I had nothing to lose if I started "typing it out" on my laptop. I tried a few different ways to do that, but none of them worked, so I decided to write you a letter instead. Writing to you makes sense since it's sort of because of you that I need someone to talk to. And even though you can't read this letter, I'm fine with that, because right now I need to talk to someone who won't talk back.

It's been seven years since you died. I was nine then, or as I liked to say in those days, nine and three-quarters. I'm sixteen now, about to turn seventeen. You probably wouldn't recognize me, or Ma, or anything about our lives if you could see us from beyond the grave. I'm not sure I'd recognize you either, in spite of the photos I have of you and the memories I play in my head sometimes.

Maybe you know (or maybe you're beyond knowing) that since last summer I've been working hard to perfect six super-complicated piano pieces—including a Chopin étude that I seriously thought was going to make one of my fingers snap off—to get ready for my practical exam at the Royal Conservatory of Music. Maybe you know the exam's usually held in June, but this year they moved it to February without telling us why. And maybe you already know that the harder I worked to get ready, the more Ma drove me crazy. Whenever she complained about having to hear me play the same pieces over and over, I'd plug my earphones into the electric piano, but then she'd grumble that wearing earphones so much was going to wreck my hearing. Or she'd sneak up behind me while I was concentrating and startle me by putting her hands on my shoulders. At one point I moved the piano so I could sit with my back to the wall, and she got annoyed that I'd done this alone, because apparently I could have hurt myself. And every time the exam came up at the dinner table, she'd look at me with a smile that was lacking in kindness—all mouth and no eyes.

But my hard work paid off, and yesterday morning Ma and I drove to the city for my exam. And I did okay! I don't want to jinx anything since I won't get the results in the mail for another month or so, but I know I did really well. Afterward I bumped into one of the judges in the hallway, and she said nice things about my technique and my expression, which totally made my day. As Ma and I walked out of the building and down the city streets, I played that compliment over again in my head, and I was just so proud and happy. All I wanted at that moment was to continue feeling good about myself for a little while and to daydream about the future.

Then Ma ruined it, with her usual two-pronged approach. First she told me she was glad all this was over now so that I could devote more time to my school work. I let that one roll off me since my grades are fine, but once we were in the car and I asked her what she wanted in terms of driving-away music, she unleashed part two.

"Honey, I want to talk about what happened the other night," she said, followed by pointed silence.

We'd barely left the parking garage at that point, but already the air inside the car started to crackle. I adjusted my seat belt to stop it from choking me and craned my head toward the window to watch the sky. This is what she does: she brings up a topic of conversation, then waits for me to jump in.

Except this time I didn't rise to the bait. I didn't even sigh to show her I was annoyed. I guess I was hoping that if I didn't react to what she'd said, my mind wouldn't absorb it, and I'd be able to continue enjoying the good feelings from my exam. But my head kept sinking, no matter how much I fought it, even as I tried to pretend I was somewhere else. I sensed that going over this again with Ma wouldn't solve anything, since it clearly hadn't the first time we'd had this conversation, and I knew full well that wasn't really what she wanted to talk about.

What happened was this: Ma walked into the kitchen one evening last week when it was my turn to load up the dishwasher and overheard me singing along to a pop song—I won't write down which one because you wouldn't know it anyway and because I don't want to admit to you that I knew all the words. The point is the song was a love ballad between a man and a woman, and I was singing the woman's part an octave lower. At first I wondered if Ma was upset by this for some reason, but soon it was clear that she was actually *excited* by the possibility that this meant something. And she just wouldn't stop with her questions. She even followed me from room to room as I tried to get away from her. I told her the truth: most pop duets are written for a male tenor and a female alto, and I can't sing the tenor line because I'm a baritone—my voice is too low. Singing the alto part an octave lower put it in my range. I wasn't trying to sing a love song with another man, and I don't see myself as a woman. And yes, I was sure.

None of this seemed to make any sense to her—she knows nothing about music except whether or not she finds it pretty—so she kept staring at me with this look of expectation on her face, like a new episode of her favourite TV show was about to start. And then today in the car, she turned to look at me even though she really should have kept her eyes on the road, and I saw that expression again.

I knew what she was fishing for, so I said nothing.

It drives Ma crazy when I stop answering her, although that's not the only reason I do it. I've learned the hard way that it's better to say nothing when you know full well that speaking will only make things worse. Ever since I told her my theory that Bach wrote his Toccata in F-sharp minor as a way to spite future generations of piano students from beyond the grave and she said I was just being dramatic, I've tried hard not to give her any reason to say that to me again.

I selected a love duet on my iPod in which the tenor is practically a eunuch, but she pressed the button on the steering wheel to turn the car stereo off before the vocal line started. So we drove in silence while I played some peppy music in my head to pass the time.

Soon the signs for Guelph came up as we headed west on the highway, and suddenly I remembered.

"Ma," I said, sitting up straight again, "since we're driving past Guelph, could we stop at the cemetery on the way home?"

When Ma didn't reply, I turned in her direction and saw a look in her eyes like she was no longer seeing the road, and I felt my eyebrows skew together, but then she seemed to shake herself out of it.

"Oh, honey," she said, "it's been a long day. I'm really tired. Why don't you go next weekend? You have your driver's licence now—you can borrow the car."

"But we're driving right by it, and the anniversary of Pa's death is today," I said. I thought I was being logical. I mean, hey, I could have pointed out that if Ma thought *she* was tired, she might try imagining what the day had been like for the one who'd had to get up on that stage and be evaluated by a panel of judges after a year and a half of work, but I didn't.

Ma said nothing, so I stared out the window and tried to think of something else. But soon enough my eyes filled with tears that streamed down my face while I pretended not to notice. This hadn't happened since maybe a few years after you died. I don't know if it counts as crying—it's like my eyes are faucets and I've walked away without making sure the taps are fully closed. But it's awful because I can't seem to do anything except wait for it to stop on its own.

I watched the scenery whiz by—trees and the remains of snowbanks and a couple of ancient farmhouses here and there—as I thought about all kinds of things I could have said but didn't. But soon I felt the car lurch into the right lane and sensed that we were heading up the overpass to Highway 6, at which point Ma drove us north, toward Guelph. She said nothing, and I said nothing, and eventually she turned into the main entrance of the cemetery and parked. "I'll give you ten minutes," she said in a tone I didn't recognize.

I got out of the car. The sun was still shining, but the wind had picked up, so I bundled up and marched through the pedestrian gate and down the gravel path. Even though I hadn't been to the cemetery in a couple of years, I figured it was just a matter of time before I recognized some landmarks that would guide me straight to your grave.

Except I didn't. I stood at an intersection and didn't know which way to turn. I didn't know what to do. I closed my eyes and tried to remember the day of your funeral, but when I felt my heartbeat climb up my throat, I shook the memory away. I still don't understand how this happened—it's true that I've visited you only once or twice since Ma married Helmut and we moved away from Guelph, but I used to bike here all the time.

"Where the hell are you, Pa?" I called out, but of course you couldn't answer me.

But then, in the silence that followed, a bird flew over my shoulder and landed on a gravestone nearby. I know dick all about flora or fauna, so the only thing I can tell you about this bird was that it was bright red with a black patch around its beak—that's what made it so noticeable against the grey landscape. It danced and hopped and looked at me, its head bobbing this way and that like it was keeping its guard up for predators.

So I stood there, breathed, and watched for clues. In the distance, a truck backing up beeped in E-flat.

After a while the bird flew away and landed on another grave in the distance. By that point I figured my ten minutes were up, so I turned around and headed back to the car, which Ma had kept running. I thought about pointing out how bad that was for the environment, but instead I thanked her for stopping, said nothing about her being so pissed off at me that she wouldn't get out of the car, put my seat belt back on, and found some instrumental music on my iPod that hopefully Ma wouldn't object to. She didn't ask any follow-up questions, which was just as well, because I never would have admitted to her that I hadn't been able to find your grave. So we drove home in silence, all my questions trapped inside my head.

I don't know if it would horrify you to learn that Ma got married again, but she did—three years ago. I like Helmut. He doesn't try to be my dad or anything, and he loves to cook, so there's always something interesting on the dinner table. He's a lawyer who specializes in slip-and-fall cases against the city, so it's hard to win an argument with him, but we get along okay.

Helmut has a son who's a couple of months younger than I am. His name is Gonzales, but he's always been known as Gonzo for some reason. We're not exactly friends. Helmut and his ex-wife have joint custody, so Gonzo lives a week with us and a week with his mother. I've only seen Iliana from a distance, but she seems nice.

Helmut was in the kitchen putting the finishing touches on supper when we got home. He asked me how the day had gone, but Ma started with her own answer as though I wasn't even there. So I poured myself a glass of water and moved as though to head downstairs to my room, but as soon as I closed the door at the top of the stairs, I sat on the steps and figured that eavesdropping was the only way I'd get to understand what was really bothering her.

She had a whole laundry list of complaints. First, I was sullen. I was moody (I forget if she used the word "pouting" or just implied it). I wouldn't open up to her. All of which Helmut brushed aside as me being a typical teenager. But Ma said I was also manipulative—I used tears and guilt about the anniversary of your death to get what I wanted, even after she'd said no. I had no respect for boundaries or for her feelings. She said nothing about the exam, not even whether I thought it had gone well, except to say that at least it was "done," as though all that work had been more of an ordeal for her than for me.

There was no further talk about the exam when we sat down to dinner. Instead, Ma got on my case about the state of my bedroom and about being way overdue to get my teeth cleaned, which apparently reflects badly on her because she's a dental hygienist. I just sat there and pushed food around my plate. It was too bad, because Helmut had made all my favourites, including this glazed chicken that's practically a symphony of flavours.

After supper I called Rita, who's been my piano teacher since I moved here, to let her know I thought I'd done okay. It was also a chance for me to thank her for everything, given that I'll need to find a new piano teacher now because at this point I've apparently outgrown her. "Don't wait too long before you start contacting people on the list I gave you," she said. I'm sure she meant to be kind, but at that point my fingers still ached from the Debussy piece that to me has always sounded like a barrel rolling merrily down a steep hill, so I said something vague in response.

I texted Jordana after that because I really needed someone to talk to. You'd remember Jordana, Pa. We've stayed friends the whole time she's been at her fancy-pants performing arts school in Boston, but she's hard to pin down sometimes. Whenever I text something like *Hey, we should chat sometime,* all I'll get in response is *Definitely—sometime.* And when I ask point-blank if she's free to chat, often I don't hear from her until days later, if at all. As I was getting ready for bed, I heard my phone buzz and grabbed it, hoping Jordana had texted me back, but it was a notification that my phone was going to die unless I plugged it in.

I don't know. This is probably pointless. I'm writing a letter that can't ever be delivered—I'm pretty sure that's called a dead letter, which is fitting—because I don't have anyone else to talk to. I mean, I remember getting along with you when I was little, and I have some nice memories of us spending time together, playing music. But would I be talking to you like this if you were still alive? Or would you be like Ma and Helmut, nagging me about my homework instead of saying you're proud of me for doing well on my piano exam?

Anyway, it's almost four o'clock in the morning and my eyes hurt from the glare of the screen, so I'll hide this file in my system preferences folder and try to get some sleep.

Your loving son,

Dale

## FRIDAY, MARCH 4

Dear Pa,

I just reread the letter I wrote you a few nights ago. I thought I should add an update in case I come across this file years from now and can't remember what happened next, even though it's not much of an update. Tonight at the dinner table, Ma told Helmut—and me, I guess, since I was sitting right there—about a patient with a bad gag reflex who was so uncomfortable she started swatting at Ma like a cat. Ma wasn't particularly amused by the way I reacted, which was to burst out laughing, but at least it broke the five days' worth of tension that had been building between us.

Gonzo does his weekly "switch" every Friday after supper. Either Iliana drops him off here or Helmut drives him to her place. They've been doing this for so long that I don't think it's occurred to either of them that he's old enough to take the bus. Even so, there's always an adjustment period when he arrives or leaves, like the house is different depending on whether or not he's around as a buffer.

Right now he's moping in front of the TV in the family room because he wanted to go to this big party but wasn't invited, or a girl he likes was going to be there but now she isn't, or some key member of his circle of friends has a pimple or a broken leg. I looked in on him when I went to get a bowl of chocolate-chip ice cream, but I left before he had the chance to tell me to get lost. I headed back to the basement, where I have my bedroom and what I like to call a combination sitting room / music room that doubles as the home gym Helmut never uses. No one else ever comes down here, besides Gonzo to read sometimes, which is fine except for the dirty socks he kicks off and leaves me to deal with.

I'm sitting at my desk, listening to music, specifically a weird orchestral piece by Camille Saint-Saëns. A year and a half ago I made a list of about seventy-five composers from the last four hundred years—the usual suspects as well as some people who are so obscure even I'd never heard of them—and now I spend a lot of time listening to whole orchestral compositions on YouTube and rating them in an old binder. Ma thinks it's nice that I have soft music playing in the background while I do my homework. What she doesn't get is for me, the homework is in the background while I listen to the music.

But it's Friday night and I don't want to think about homework for at least a couple of days. In case you're wondering, yes—I hate school. Well, "hate" is probably too strong a word. I just sort of despise it. Gonzo and I go to this preppy all-boys' school where everything's this big game of King of the Mountain, and I've never been able to stand any of it. I've seen guys in my class get into fist fights over who was voted class president—guys who weren't even running. Gonzo fits right in. He's nowhere near the top of the pile, but I've definitely seen him trying to elbow his way up.

The uniform's okay—navy blue pants and jacket, white shirt, striped tie with the school colours—but what makes my school especially unbearable is that we're not like most high schools, where you make up your schedule and go from one class to another till the day ends. We're more like an elementary school for teenagers, which means you're in the same group of twenty-five guys all day and it's the teachers who roam from class to class. That means I'm stuck with the exact same twenty-four douchebags all day, without even the benefit of variety. They say organizing classes this way has to do with class spirit, but it's just a way to increase the sense of competition.

One of my classmates for the third year in a row is Gonzo. You'd think it'd be awkward for two stepbrothers to be in the same class, especially when they don't talk to each other any more than they have to, but fortunately for us, no one at school seems to have any idea that we're related.

Still, something out of the ordinary happened today. I'll probably get in trouble if anyone else finds out, but I guess telling you is a safe bet.

When we moved to Waterloo three years ago, I wasn't crazy about going to a school that didn't have a music program, so part of the deal—both with Ma and with the school—was that they'd allow me some time to practise. They weren't about to buy a piano for me, so that left the violin. So every day during the winter term, while the rest of my class toddles off to gym, I go play violin in an empty room in the basement with a little window that looks onto a poorly lit hallway. In exchange I'm supposed to swim for an hour at the community pool every Saturday. Usually I work on something I'm recording or grab some old repertoire from when I was a kid and play that for fun. As long as I play something, I figure they don't need to know I haven't taken a violin lesson in years.

Still, even though the school made a big deal about their willingness to adjust my schedule, they've made it clear all along that this is a privilege they can revoke for any reason. Every once in a while the vice-principal wanders by to make sure I'm there. He's so suspicious. I find it hard to believe he doesn't have anything better to do.

Usually this isn't a problem since his shoes are so loud he could probably tap dance with them, but today I didn't hear him. It's been an off week for me, not only because of what happened on Sunday with Ma but also because of the unexpected boredom I felt when I thought about what I wanted to work on next on the piano now that my exam's done. I was starting to feel a bit better about all that—sometimes when I'm down it just takes a while before I can resurface—but this morning the asshole who sits behind me called me a name I'm not going to write down and it dragged me under again. So by the time I was faced with having to practise, I just couldn't scrape together the energy needed to pick up my violin, let alone play it. So I played an old recording on my phone and sat in a corner of the room with my eyes closed, hoping the mood would pass.

That's how the vice-principal found me. He barged in and jumped into lecture mode with both feet—I guess he wasn't concerned that he'd found me curled up in a ball on the floor—about how he'd known all along that I wasn't really practising, and he was going to call my parents, and this just proved he'd been right to object to making special accommodations or whatever he called it.

And through it all my recording of the solo violin in Ralph Vaughan Williams's "The Lark Ascending" accompanied him like a descant.

If I'd continued feeling down, I probably would have just sat there and let this guy lecture me to death. But thankfully some resentment bubbled up after a while. It pissed me off that he was barking at me, given that this was the first time in two and a half years I'd been caught goofing off. He's never even noticed that I eat my lunch in that room every single day instead of in the cafeteria like I'm supposed to. So as soon as he paused for breath, I jumped up, turned off the recording, and pointed to some random sheet music I'd left open on the stand. I told him I'd been struggling with this piece for weeks, and so I'd recorded it to help me figure out what I was doing wrong. Then I looked him in the eye and asked if he could help me with it.

It was a risk, because if he knew anything about music he'd call my bluff, and I'd be boiled alive for insubordination. But he backed away from me like I'd started foaming at the mouth and left the room. When I heard his footsteps pause outside the door, I picked up the violin and started playing a Clementi sonata I'd learned in grade five, making up the parts I couldn't remember. And after he'd left for good, I kept playing because I genuinely felt better.

That's the thing about high school. If you obey the rules like they expect you to, you have to let them walk all over you. But when you push back—not too much, but just a little—their power crumbles into a pile of dust.

This sounds like a recent discovery, but it isn't. I figured out that the whole high school experience was going to suck about five minutes into grade nine. By the end of my first morning I'd vowed never to speak to *anyone* at that stupid place—*ever*. And for the most part I still haven't. Sometimes some dude in my class will ask me a question or make some asshole comment, and I'll just stare him down till he walks away. I even write a note to my teachers every year explaining that my voice instructor has me under strict orders to preserve my vocal cords while my voice finishes changing, even though I'm not taking voice lessons and I was already a baritone by the time I turned thirteen. No one's ever questioned this. No one seems to wonder why I'm going through the slowest puberty imaginable, and when Ma goes to parent-teacher meetings, no teacher ever mentions to her that they've hardly ever heard me speak. The fact that I get good grades, I don't give my teachers attitude, and I'm not a bad influence on the douchebags in my class seems to be all that matters.

It's funny, though. You'd think my cone of silence would make me feel lonely, but having been picked on so much at my old school, I still think it's the best idea I've ever had.

My ice cream has melted into a lumpy swamp and my Saint-Saëns album is done, so I guess I'll end here. I don't think I like him all that much. He's a romanticist writing in a classical style, and it's really boring. I think I'll go look for YouTube clips of old TV shows about former teenage outcasts who go to their high school reunions and feel better about themselves, and hopefully they'll help me dream about the future.

Your loving son,

Dale

## SUNDAY, MARCH 6

Dear Pa,

I played the organ at church this morning, which is a lot of fun—the organ-playing part, I mean. There are two keyboards called manuals that you can set to different sounds, and there are pedals for your feet—it's like playing the piano, except you're doing a little dance while you sit. It's awesome. I don't understand most of the services, which isn't surprising since before I started this job I'd only ever been to church for weddings and funerals, but it's not like anyone's going to quiz me.

The people who go to Eastwood United are a pretty mixed group in terms of age and background. I see people in suits having friendly conversations with people with multiple body piercings, which is great. When I started working there last fall the only person I knew was a woman in her late twenties named Jenice, and that's because we recognized each other from a choir we're both in. I don't know how they came up with her name. I'm guessing one parent wanted to name her Janice, the other one wanted to name her Denise, and this is how they compromised, but that may not be true. Jenice and her girlfriend, Sophie, are great: down-to-earth, genuine people who talk to me like I'm a human being instead of a kid. Even though I rarely tell them anything about me and they rarely ask, they totally get me. They're both working on PhDs at the university here, one of them in women's studies and the other in cultural studies, although their work is so similar I can never remember who's doing what. I've learned so much from them— about composting and protests and getting involved in things. They're also talented musicians and vocalists, and sometimes they sing together during the service.

Every Sunday people stick around after the service for coffee and doughnuts, and after working there a few months I started joining them. It seemed rude just to lock up the organ and bike home. Today, when I was sitting with Jenice and Sophie and a few other people in the church basement, which probably hasn't been repainted in my lifetime, we spent half an hour talking about their wedding in a couple of weeks. One thing I've noticed is that Sophie tends to be the peacemaker and Jenice tends to zero in on things more. Jenice, for instance, is really into crystal-based healing. Judging by the way Sophie's lips purse whenever this comes up in conversation—which it does surprisingly often—I sense that she does *not* share this interest, but I've never heard her say anything about it. They took turns telling the rest of us about the bridal shower their families had thrown for them. They weren't correcting each other, but you could tell that they go through life differently.

Sophie: "It was so nice. All the women in our families were there. It was this beautiful expression of sisterhood and belonging."

Jenice: "Both our families are heavily committed to traditional gender scripts. When my cousin got married last year her bridal party made her a T-shirt with *The Future Mrs. Her Husband's Surname* written across the front *and* the back. No one thought to ask her what she'd decided to do with her surname—they all assumed she'd take her husband's. Which she did. Sophie and I sent everyone an email letting them know we're both keeping our names, just so they'd know not to do that with us."

Me: "Where were all the men in your family?"

Jenice: "They weren't invited. I guess they went to hang out at the hardware store."

Sophie: "The tradition in our families is that there's a bridal shower for the bride and a bachelor party for the groom."

Jenice: "So in our case they killed two birds with one stone. I personally would have preferred a shower with everyone there, but I had a pretty good time."

Sophie: "At most of the other bridal parties I've gone to, the bride spends most of her time spilling dirt on the guy she's marrying, and the other women give her advice on how to 'manage her man.' Most of what I know about heterosexual sex comes from these things. Obviously we weren't going to do that, especially since we were both in the room, but we found other things to talk about— it was fine."

Jenice: "Sophie's sister is the most loving, most generous woman alive. I honestly don't know where she gets all her energy. And yeah—I get that she was in completely new territory with the prospect of Sophie marrying another woman. But she rolled up her sleeves, did her best, and made it work. Everyone seemed perfectly comfortable, even after we told them we're going to walk down the aisle together, rather than one of us being dragged by her father like a piece of livestock trading owners."

They've asked me to play the organ and to perform at the reception—they decided to gather all their musical friends for a coffee house as a way to cut back on speeches. They also asked me to play something on the piano when they sign the register, giving me a list of songs to choose from. I'm planning a surprise for them: rather than just play the piano live, I've pre-recorded the piano part and some backing vocals, and on the day of the wedding I'm going to stand up and sing instead. Last summer I signed up for a free audio production course online and learned how to do all this. It's not that complicated, but it's super time-consuming. I ended up bombing a math test because I spent so much time trying to get everything right.

Sophie and Jenice both love music, and sometimes they like to sharpen their academic knives to talk about it. A couple of months ago, the topic of boy bands came up—I forget how or why—and it turns out they have this weird theory about them. I think one of them or both of them went to a conference where boy bands were talked about as a phenomenon. I'd never have guessed there could be such a thing as Boy Band Studies, but there you go. I don't understand all of what they said, but basically what they seem to find fascinating about boy bands is that their music is mainstream and countercultural at the same time: mainstream because there's rarely anything innovative or even that interesting about the music or the lyrics and countercultural because most of the songs are pretty vague as to who they're about. Most of the singers in boy bands are straight, so when they're singing about love and kisses and heartache and all that mushy stuff, people mostly assume they're singing about either one girl or a bunch of girls. But all their lyrics are addressed to "you," or "darlin'," or "baby," so it's actually pretty open-ended in terms of gender.

Also, the fact that there are usually five members in a boy band is supposedly a critique of monogamy, but I didn't ask them what they meant by that.

Jenice kept waving her arms and using terms like "homoerotic pentagon" and "implied woman" and "shared narrative I," which I also didn't get, but apparently the fact that the vocalists each take turns singing the melody is super significant, and even though most of these bands are designed to appeal to ten-year-old girls, the fact that their videos show five boys singing love songs to *each other* is countercultural because it makes it okay for people to think about same-sex love and not get too freaked out about it. I don't know if I buy that. All I know is that a lot of boy-band songs are super catchy—once I was up half the night because I couldn't get one out of my head—and, with five boys singing together, there are usually some pretty cool and complex harmonies.

Anyway, this conversation inspired me to plan another surprise for their wedding. I won't tell you what it is, though, because I'm not sure yet if I'll have the guts to go through with it.

Both Sophie and Jenice come from large families. I've always found their stories about aunts and uncles and grandparents and second cousins three times removed kind of fascinating, since it sounds so different from my family. Today, as we were bringing our coffee cups back to the kitchen, Sophie told me about this boy she used to babysit when she was in high school. Apparently she had a no-nonsense way of bribing him to be good: she rewarded him with sugar. As long as he behaved himself pretty well, she'd let him take the can of whipped cream, aim the nozzle at his mouth, and press it before going to bed. Apparently they called this *bjjjjjjjjjt*.

I should get going. I have a bit of reading to do for school tomorrow, so I think I'm going to try out this CD that Sophie and Jenice loaned me. It's supposed to be this weird fusion of '70s folk, '80s electronica, and '90s ska. So far I've listened to the first track, and the rhythm sounds a lot like a dryer full of towels—in a good way. The image on the jewel case is of two elephants fornicating while a peasant boy looks on, but apparently some of the later songs are pretty good.

Your loving son,

Dale

## SUNDAY, MARCH 13

Dear Pa,

Oh, God. This weekend's been filled with dinner parties, and the contrast between them would be enough to drive anyone insane. On Friday, one of Helmut's colleagues came to dinner and spent the whole time stuffing his face, complaining about his soon-to-be-ex-wife, and trash-talking everyone else he works with. I stared at my plate for the entire meal in case he decided to turn on me next. Then, late Saturday afternoon, just as I'd finished setting up to continue remixing a song I'd recorded, Ma came downstairs to remind me—or to claim she was reminding me, since I had no memory of her mentioning it the first time—that we'd all been invited to Burt and Beverly's for supper.

Well, if you want to get all technical about it, she appeared in the doorway to my room and let out one of her irritated sighs. "Why aren't you ready yet?" she asked, like this was a terrible blow to her.

"Ready for what?"

Which prompted her to let out another irritated sigh. She'd just come home after discovering that no one else in her book club had liked her most recent selection, so it wasn't the greatest set-up for me.

We were both in a pretty foul mood by the time we made it to the car. My mood sank even more when Ma announced to Helmut in this bright, theatrical voice she uses when she's annoyed that I was sulking. So I turned to the window and watched the houses go by without really seeing them.

It also didn't help that I can't stand Burt and Beverly. Let me clarify: I like them well enough in general, but there are specific things about them I can't stand. Like how Beverly will always ask me the same open-ended question about how school's going and then ignore me for the rest of the visit. Or how she'll insist I play piano for them after supper as a way to get me out of her hair, forgetting I'm sixteen instead of six, but then she'll want to keep talking while I play, so she'll shout.

Then there's Burt. He's still big into hockey, and that's all he ever talks about. He wears that same toupée that looks like he's glued a golden retriever to his head and always tries to entertain me with internet videos he thinks teenagers would like, mainly of random people's Ski-Doo mishaps. He's also an anxious host whose feelings are easily bruised, even more so since the last time you saw him. If I'm not inhaling food and drink every second I'm there, he starts to panic. And if I ever turn down something he offers me, *without fail* he'll follow up with "You sure?"

Sometime last year I started to wonder if the problem was me—if there was something about the way I answered him that made him think I didn't know my own mind and all I needed was some coaxing. One time I answered him in a flat tone that left no room for misinterpretation. But he kept at it to the point that I wanted to bang my head against the table till I passed out, and then Ma gave me a lecture on rudeness the entire drive home.

Now that I think back, I'm starting to wonder if maybe I secretly resent them because it was at their dinner party that Ma and Helmut met—Burt and Helmut used to hang out in their university days, apparently—and so it's because of them that my life changed so much. Not that I minded moving to Waterloo, since it meant saying goodbye to the idiots who'd tormented me in elementary school and getting to live closer to Grandma and Uncle Scott and Uncle Joe. Still, no one ever asked how I felt about any of it. Then again, I remember thinking Burt and Beverly were ridiculous people even when you were alive, so maybe not.

Anyway, Beverly let us in, and I'd barely taken off my coat before Burt wandered into the front hall wearing an apron with the words *Master Chef* on it and carrying two glasses of wine, which he handed to Ma and Helmut in turn. Then he looked at me.

"What about you, young man? You want a pop or something?"

"No, I'm good. Thanks, Burt."

"You sure?"

"Yep."

They marched us through the house so we could see all their recent renovations—the kitchen backsplash, the new ceramic tile in the master bath, the faucets, the bedspread that looks like something your great-grandmother quilted but has state-of-the-art ventilation so you're comfortable no matter how hot or how cold it is. Ma made all the appropriate *ooh* and *aah* sounds, but I knew from the look on her face that she'd have a lot more to say about it in private.

Next, we sat in the living room on couches that had recently been reupholstered to match Beverly's eyes. She asked what was new with all of us, looking at me with an encouraging nod. "Oh," I said, like there was so much exciting news I couldn't figure out where to start. I shrugged and made a deferring gesture toward Ma, and by the time she and Helmut had finished with their updates— none of which included their kids or any recent Royal Conservatory examinations, by the way—it was time to move on to something else.

I can be pretty smooth sometimes.

While the adults were talking about friends of theirs who hate their time-share and are trying to get rid of it, I studied one of their side tables whose legs look like hoofs and tried to figure out what the fuck was up with those. Then Misha, one of their high-end cats who always looks like she's frowning and whose coat reminds me of an expensive handbag, came over to inspect me. She nudged me with her paw until I looked down at her, but as soon as I moved to scratch her neck, she made a point of turning away.

I don't know why I keep trying with her. But I do.

Eventually Burt brought out enough appetizers for twenty people. He kept interrupting the conversation to offer me liquids and solids and asking me if I was sure because I kept saying no. After each refusal he looked thoughtful, like he was trying to figure out the magical combination of food and drink that would finally make me crack. He even offered me some mixed vegetables once we'd made it to the table, even though the platter was right in front of me. *No, thanks—the idea of broccoli makes me want to hurl. You sure? Yes.* I tried to act like I was engrossed in Ma and Beverly's discussion of some scandal involving municipal politics that I couldn't manage to follow.

Then, when it was time for dessert, the unthinkable happened.

"Dale, you want some ice cream with your cake?"

"Yes, please."

"You sure?"

"No."

Burt put the ice cream scoop down and stared at me like he didn't know what to do. I didn't either, so I just said, "Yes, please" again, like I hadn't said it the first time, and the smile returned to his face.

Later on, as I was helping Burt clear the table while Ma and Beverly and Helmut headed back to the living room with more wine, he startled me by straying from our script.

"So, you're what—seventeen now? You got a girlfriend yet?" he asked as he rinsed out bottles of Perrier for some reason before putting them in the recycling bin. He even winked at me as he asked the question, like this was some kind of male bonding. I wondered if we'd have to go through the rest of our lines. *No. You sure? Yes.*

So I just said, "I'm still sixteen for a couple of months, and um—no. I don't have a girlfriend. I don't even—I don't *date* girls."

"Oh." And then all these wrinkles snuck onto his forehead, and his eyebrows started to skew at an angle I'd never seen on anyone outside of a cartoon before. "What do you do with them?"

I involuntarily snickered but tried to make it sound like a cough. "Nothing. I'm not dating anyone. But just for the record, it's not girls that I'm not dating—it's boys. If that makes any sense."

"What?"

I didn't know how to make it any clearer than that, so I looked at him, raised an eyebrow, and waited for the other shoe to drop.

"*Oh.* You mean you're—"

"Gay. Queer. Sure. But I'm still single."

"Huh."

I braced myself for him to ask how it was possible for me to be gay by myself, but instead, he started telling me about a guy on the hockey team he coaches who came out last year and how they all worked together to keep going as a team and blah blah blah blah blah. I didn't contribute any more to the conversation than "uh-huh," but I didn't mind. Since I never let on that Ma and Helmut didn't know, I figured Burt would tell Beverly and Beverly would mention it to Ma, so that was one more thing I could strike off my list.

Ma was more relaxed on the drive home than she had been on the way there. I'm sure the wine helped, but mainly it's because Ma and Beverly have been best friends since they were in high school and they don't see each other as often as they'd like. Then again, I've often thought but never dared say out loud that they'd probably end up strangling each other if they spent more time together. At one point Ma brought up Beverly's granite countertops and pointed out that she and Burt have too much money to spend because they don't have any kids—just their ridiculous cats. (If that's true, maybe next time I should mention that their honorary nephew could really use a new mixing board. Tempting, but risky.) And I remembered that at one point I'd caught Burt and Beverly giving each other a knowing glance after Ma said something about the dentist at her office who enrages her by referring to the hygienists and the administrator as "the girls," which made me think they have a lot to say about Ma behind her back, too. But Ma and Beverly are still there for each other. I guess one of the reasons I get sad when Ma forces me to go over there is it reminds me that at the rate I'm going, I'll never have friends I've known since high school.

I thought about texting Jordana, but I didn't have my phone on me, and anyway, she hadn't responded to my last attempts to reach out to her, so my heart sank again.

"What were you talking about in the kitchen with Burt for so long?" Ma asked, turning around to look at me from the passenger seat as we pulled into the driveway.

I stared at her for a second before replying. "His hockey team. Apparently one of his guys came out of the closet last year."

"Why would he tell you that?"

"Oh, you know Burt—he just talks and talks and talks." And with that, I got out of the car, made a beeline for the front door, and used my key to get inside.

Tonight's dinner party was by far the most enjoyable of the three. Jenice and Sophie invited me for dinner as an advance thank you for playing the organ at their wedding. I didn't realize till I got there that they'd also invited Reverend Heather and her husband, Albert, whom I'd never met before. At first I felt a prick of disappointment in my eyes over the fact that they hadn't seen me as enough of a dinner guest on my own, but I didn't want them to think I was sulking, like Ma had on the way to Beverly and Burt's.

So I forced myself to smile until I was having such a great time that I wasn't forcing myself anymore.

We talked about all kinds of things, none of which had anything to do with church. I told them I was listening to the work of Sergei Rachmaninoff, which I like, even though he's the king of long-drawn-out endings, and about my favourite TV show, *Ranting and Raven*, about a cop named Joe Ranting who gets a bird as his new partner. Albert told us about bumping into an old friend from Hebrew school whom he hadn't seen in a couple of decades, and Sophie told us about some dude in her PhD program who likes to smoke a pipe and wear a lot of scarves but is surprisingly unpretentious once you start talking to him. It dawned on me as I was laughing at something Heather had said that this is what it'll be like when I'm an adult, once all the nagging at home and all the misery of high school have ended. I can't fucking wait!

Heather and Albert left early, but Sophie and Jenice put on another pot of tea, so I stayed. At one point the conversation turned to their wedding guests in a way that seemed a bit too smooth, and soon enough, I realized why they'd invited me to stay behind. "It'll be nice to see Jonathan again," Jenice said, and I understood this as a move on their part to ruin the surprise. I'd fully expected Jonathan would be at their wedding, given that they're the ones who introduced us—of course, now that I look back, I'm starting to wonder if maybe it wasn't a coincidence that Jonathan just happened to be at that coffee shop at the same time as us. Now they were looking at me pointedly, so I smiled and said something like "Uh-huh." And I kept smiling. My strategy all along has been to say nothing so that if he ever inquires whether I've asked about him, they'll have to say no.

I mean, Jonathan and I weren't really dating. It was more like an extended bad idea. The only reason I went through with it was because he was cute and a bit older and because I thought it would help me confirm which way the wind was blowing, and it did. But I found him exasperating, especially whenever he played music for me on the phone like that was his idea of a conversation. I knew for sure it wasn't going to work out when he brought up Emmylou Harris's gymnastics career, but I ended up letting it drag out a while longer. And because, in the end, he broke up with me before I could break up with him, I guess I have the advantage of being the wronged party, so I don't have to explain myself. Besides, as much as I appreciated the heads-up, it doesn't really matter, because the prospect of seeing him again doesn't fill me with dread at all. I'm aiming to be pleasantly cold.

This time I've been listening to an album by a pop duo I'd never heard of but that apparently was insanely popular in the '70s. I thought it strange that they had songs called "It Can't Be You," "Maybe It's You," and "Baby It's You" on the same album, but it turns out I was listening to a greatest hits compilation, so I guess that makes it okay.

Your loving (and future-thinking!) son,
Dale

## WEDNESDAY, MARCH 16

Dear Pa,

A funny thing happened at school today. At least, it was funny to me. Nobody else would understand, so I might as well tell you.

When we first moved to Waterloo, Uncle Joe asked me if I'd like to sing in the choir he's part of. I tried it for a couple of weeks and found it fun and challenging, so I stayed. No one minds that I'm the youngest member by far. Uncle Joe and I can't sit together because he's a tenor and I'm a baritone, so that's forced me to make small talk with people I don't know. Which is fine, but I don't like how people react when they find out Joe's my uncle—they seem to find it strange, I guess because Joe's Black and I'm white. I'm pretty tired of explaining to curious strangers that no, I'm not adopted, and he's my uncle by marriage, because then they want to know about my aunt, who of course doesn't exist. I get that Uncle Joe and I are of different backgrounds, but I've known him all my life. He's always been my uncle, even though he and Uncle Scott didn't get married till the summer after I turned nine.

And then there are the choir members who can't be bothered to learn people's names, including two women with asymmetrical haircuts who once referred to Joe as "you know—the Black tenor" just as I walked by them. I thought that was an odd way to describe a person, so I tried to smile.

"Actually, his name's Joe," I said with a shrug.

"Oh? Do you know him?" one of them asked as they exchanged a look.

"Well, yeah. He's my uncle," I explained. They stared at me like I'd raised a leg and let one rip in their direction, and then they walked away.

Uncle Joe picks me up every Tuesday evening for rehearsal and brings me home afterward. We don't usually have any trouble finding stuff to talk about. But last night he was acting weird, asking me open-ended questions about bullying and teasing and whether I'm having a hard time at school. He does this every once in a while: he assumes I'm unhappy at school, which is true enough, but not the way he seems to be thinking. Part of me wonders if he hopes I'll break down one of these days and whisper that sometimes it feels like I barely exist, just so we'll have that to bond over. But I can't lie just to make him feel better. Instead, I adjusted my seat belt and unleashed part of the truth.

"Not really. I've managed to make myself pretty invisible at school."

"But—so the boys in your class don't give you a hard time?"

"No. They barely pay any attention to me."

"R-really?"

I happen to know, because I once overheard Uncle Scott talking to Ma, that Uncle Joe *was* teased and bullied when he was young. I think both of them were, but with Uncle Joe it got pretty bad. I often wonder if that's why he can't stand even good-natured teasing. Sometimes I watch Uncle Scott and Uncle Joe together, and Uncle Scott starts kidding around because that's what he does, and for a while it's fine, but then a line is crossed and it gets to be too much.

Uncle Joe tried to pump me for more info, but I just shrugged because I knew he'd repeat anything I told him to Uncle Scott, who isn't the best at keeping secrets. So when Uncle Joe pulled up in the driveway, I didn't linger in the car like I do sometimes. But I kept thinking over the conversation as I was getting ready for bed last night and this morning as I was shaving, and I decided it was time to put my cone of silence to the test.

First, this morning I sat at the very back of the bus, in the row that *everyone knows* is reserved for the oldest, coolest kids in school, and pretended to read a biography of Yo-Yo Ma—no one paid any attention to me. When I got to school, I walked through the crowd of smokers in the outside stairwell known as the Dragons' Den—no one said anything. During homeroom, I wrote myself a text message while the class president made an announcement about some school activity I wouldn't be caught dead at, and I spent most of English class with my head on the desk, staring blankly—no one seemed to care if I was dead or alive. Later, at lunch, I darkened the door to our cafeteria for the first time and took a seat at the end of a busy table where a bunch of guys were horsing around and knocking each other out of their seats—they didn't even look my way.

I must be the most successful loner ever.

And so, as I sat at my desk waiting for fourth period to begin, I wondered if my cone of silence would allow me to observe my classmates without being noticed. I kept my eyes darting from one side of the room to the other so that no one could catch me staring, but I probably didn't need to bother. After spending the bulk of three years ignoring everyone in school, it was weird to pay close attention to how they acted around each other. It was like watching a live documentary about teenage douchebags.

I watched Cyclops, whose eyes are a little too close together, chatting up our class president, Captain Doucheberry, who was trying to come across as aloof, except every once in a while his face would change for a split second, like he couldn't repress his interest completely. Freckles 'n' Fur, who has fire-engine-red hair up and down his forearms, was showing something on his phone to Sniffles, who has a perpetual cold that never seems to get any better or any worse. Two best frenemies whom I always think of interchangeably as Snooty Dorkelson and Snotty Pompous-Face were making small talk like nothing was the matter, even though, from what I've pieced together, they're trapped in this weird love rectangle with two girls who are double cousins. And finally, Preppy McPrepperton, who wears so much product in his hair that a paper airplane once got stuck in it and whose horrible acne makes him look like a cross between a Muppet and a tennis ball, was telling Gonzo about that insane party Gonzo didn't go to, and I could see Gonzo gritting his teeth as he listened to the juicy details. A bunch of people around me were reading magazines or doodling on their desks, but Blondie Hairwall, who sits to my left, just stared ahead vacantly.

Oh, they all have names. I even know most of them: Gabe, Varesh, Rusty, Spiros, Langdon, Mario, and two guys named Dave. But I find it more bearable to think of them this way.

It was fascinating to watch them like that. And kind of sad. I don't know if I'll do it again.

Last night after supper I borrowed Ma's car and drove to Sophie and Jenice's house to go over some last-minute details for their wedding. I played them both versions of the Carpenters song I'd prepared for the signing of the register: first the regular version with me at the piano, which they said was very nice, then the version with me singing along to a pre-recorded accompaniment I made that includes several tracks of backup vocals, which made them both burst into tears. Awesome!

Ma was still up when I got home. We were talking in the living room, and she mentioned that she'd heard something on the radio about the piano competition I used to take part in when I was a kid. She sighed and recalled how cute it apparently was when my eight-year-old self got up in front of the crowd of people and announced, "My name is Dale Scott Cardigan and I'm going to play 'Serenade for the Doll' by Claude Debussy." She remembered the auditorium, the adjudicators, the ribbon I won for second prize that's now in a box somewhere in the back of my closet. I told her I remembered how vague and patronizing one of the adjudicators was—she called my selection "a very musical piece" and told the girl who'd played before me to think of a trill as "a decoration, like a necklace—a sparkle in the music," or something like that.

I waited for Ma to keep going with the story, but then she got up and said it was past her bedtime. So I sat alone in the living room and went over the rest of the memory in my head. I remembered the three of us going out for lunch right before I was supposed to perform. The waiter accidentally spilled my glass of chocolate milk on you, and it went all over your shirt, and you had to spend the whole afternoon smelling of spoiled milk, wearing an old raincoat we'd found crammed in the trunk of the car.

Do you remember any of that? Or, rather, *would* you? I guess I'll never know. I'd forgotten all about it until Ma brought it up, but then I remembered how much the three of us had laughed, how much I'd felt loved by both of you. And the fact that Ma wouldn't remember any of those parts of the story out loud made me incredibly sad.

Then my sadness morphed into something else when I went to my room and found a shopping bag on my unmade bed. It was from the clothing store Ma and I went to a few weeks ago to buy me a new suit for the wedding, and there was a note with it written on an index card: *Just in case you change your mind. Love, Ma.*

A peek inside the bag confirmed my suspicion of what it was: a dress shirt the colour of a pink highlighter and a tie that looked like someone had barfed up pink and yellow flowers on it. I sat on my bed, feeling my blood pressure start to rise as I replayed some key moments from our trip to the store, like when she kept steering me toward ruffled shirts and glittery jackets and seemed annoyed when I wouldn't try them on. "But honey," she'd said, sounding exasperated, "I just thought now that you're getting older, you might like designs that are a bit more …" And she did this vague hand gesture, as if that explained what she meant by "a bit more." "There are so many options to choose from now—so many ways for you to express yourself."

"And the options I like best are blue and grey," I said. Ma wouldn't stop sighing as she paid for my clothes and drove us home, whereas I couldn't seem to stop shaking because I was so angry. I *knew* what she was doing—or at least what she thought she was doing—and it pissed me off. And now I'm even angrier to discover she went back to the store and bought me that pink shirt "just in case" I changed my mind. I don't know what else I can say to convince her that I wouldn't be caught dead wearing that shirt or that tie. At least the receipt's still in the bag, so I won't have to bury the shirt and the tie in the backyard.

As part of my musical odyssey into the work of Franz Liszt, I've been listening to some selections from his Catholic devotionals phase while I type this out. Everything's called "Ave Maria" or "Benedictus," but it commits the sin of being really dull. Still, it's pretty good homework music.

Your loving (and invisible) son,

Dale

## SUNDAY, MARCH 20

Dear Pa,

Sophie and Jenice's wedding was yesterday. March weddings are apparently a roll of the dice since there might easily have been a snowstorm, but they told me it all boiled down to math for them: (modest budget + two large families) × off-season rates = their wedding.

Overall it went well, although I needed a nap this afternoon to recover from it. Ma dropped me off at church super early—thankfully without saying anything about the fact that I hadn't put on that garish shirt she'd bought me against my will—so I chatted with people as they came in. Both brides were running around, greeting their guests, adjusting each other's flowers and hair. They both looked so beautiful, and so happy, and so *calm*. It wasn't at all like weddings I've seen on TV. Even Ma was more frazzled the day she married Helmut, and they had only four guests.

About fifteen minutes before the ceremony was supposed to start, I took my spot at the organ and read through my copy of the program to make sure I had everything in order. My name was listed—*Dale S. Cardigan*—and I felt so proud to be there. I mean, maybe they would have invited me to the wedding even if they hadn't wanted me to play the organ for them, but you never know. I played a few random pieces as the last of the guests arrived, partly to warm up, partly to set the mood. I kept my eyes peeled for

Jonathan so that the sight of him wouldn't throw me, and he didn't notice me when I spotted him, which was a bonus.

Once I got the signal that everyone was ready, I launched into "Nun bitten wir den Heiligen Geist," by a seventeenth-century German composer named Dieterich Buxtehude. (I have my copy of the program in front of me in case you're wondering how I know how to spell all that.) That's not a typical wedding processional, but Jenice and Sophie told me they wanted something that didn't sound remotely like Wagner's wedding march. I know the Buxtehude piece fairly well, so as I played, I was able to catch a few glimpses of the procession: Sophie's sister, Jenice's two brothers, a woman I found out later was Sophie's ex, a few of their closest friends, and a handful of nieces and nephews.

And then—and I have to admit I nearly lost my place when this happened—the brides emerged through the double doors and headed up the aisle, hand in hand. They looked radiant. They both wore dresses, but not conventional wedding dresses. I can't figure out how to describe them—I think one of them was peach and the other one lime, but maybe I'm confusing them with some of the desserts. Both dresses rustled—I don't know if that helps you to visualize them. But in any case, what they wore suited them well.

Finally the ceremony got under way. There was a mix of readings and hymns, and when the brides joined hands and proclaimed their vows I could barely keep my eyes off them. Soon it was time for them to sign the register and for me to get up and sing. I'd hooked up my iPod to the church's sound system, and the track was programmed to give me fifteen seconds to get in place in front of the altar before it got going. At first I started to worry that I hadn't cued it properly or that the volume would be out of whack, but once I heard the opening bars, I relaxed and looked out into the crowd of people, all of whom seemed delighted for my friends, so full of love for them.

And then, in one of the middle pews, I spotted Rusty Friesen—otherwise known as Freckles 'n' Fur—looking back at me like he was just as surprised to see me as I was to see him.

I nearly missed my own cue, but I made myself concentrate on the music and did fine. I'm not always comfortable singing in public—I never know what to do with my hands—but this time I just sang, my arms by my sides, trying not to act like a crooner. The church has great acoustics, so I hadn't bothered to set up a microphone. Years of singing in choirs have trained me to project my voice, so that's what I did. I would never say this to anyone but you, but I think I sounded pretty fantastic, especially when all the backup Dales came on, enveloping me like a warm draft.

There was some scattered applause after I'd finished, including from Sophie and Jenice. But I thought it'd be dumb to bow at someone else's wedding, so I darted back to my spot behind the organ and hid for the rest of the ceremony. Then, after a few more hymns, Reverend Heather introduced "Sophie and Jenice for the first time as a married couple"—and everyone cheered! For ages! Usually on TV people clap politely, like they would at the end of a performance that was good but not great, but here the applause felt like a collective cheer that had welled up in everyone until it spilled out, and then it kept building and building until Jenice and Sophie couldn't help but laugh. I joined in, of course. I was, and *am*, so proud and happy for them.

For a recessional I played "Festival Toccata" by Percy Fletcher, another one of my favourites, and kept going until the church was practically empty. Then I locked up the organ, put all my music away, smiled and nodded politely when a few people stopped to compliment me on my singing or whatever, and headed to the parish hall, where people were waiting in line to congratulate the married couple. When I'd been over at Sophie and Jenice's house on Wednesday, they'd asked if I could drive them from the church to the reception in their car, so I figured I'd save my congratulations for later.

I swept past Jonathan without acknowledging his presence and stood in the middle of the church hall, drinking a glass of water and peering at this woman who was about Ma's age. She had feathery hair dyed completely white except for long jet-black bangs hanging over her face. She looked like she was from the future. Her outfit or whatever you want to call it looked like a cross between a bib and a tablecloth. Unlike her hair, it was a single colour—this bright bluish-greeny-reddish brown—and since she was a bit turned away from me, I could see exactly what it was covering and what it wasn't. Just as I was reminding myself not to stare, I sensed movement in my peripheral vision, and then a voice asked, "Who's the lady with the side boobs?"

I burst out laughing, choked on my water, and turned to see Freckles 'n' Fur grinning at me. Since I was too busy wiping my mouth with my sleeve to answer his question, he kept talking.

"Hey—you're that guy in my class who never says anything, right?"

My face responded by turning a gruesome shade of red. I know I blush easily. I've never understood why some people feel the need to point it out to me.

"Yeah. I guess so."

"I'm Rusty," he said. I guess he figured that since I've never spoken to another student at school I wouldn't know his name. Except I did.

"Dale," I mumbled as we shook hands. His hand was soft and warm, and I noticed that we were pretty much the same height, that he had friendly green eyes, and that he was wearing a brownish-orangey suit that brought out the red in his unruly hair. All these details made me decide I could talk to him, in spite of the fact that he's in my class. "So how do you know Sophie and Jenice?" I asked him.

"Sophie's parents live next door to me. She used to babysit me back in the day." Immediately the word *bjjjjjjjjt* and the smell of whipped cream filled my head, along with the image of Rusty as a hyper seven-year-old being chased around the house by a teenage version of one of the brides. "You?" he asked.

"I know Jenice from a choir we're both in, and I've been filling in for the organist here since the fall." I started to tell him about how the organist wants to retire but also doesn't want to retire, so the compromise he's reached with the church elders is that he picks out the hymns and I play them for a fraction of his pay. Even I found that boring, though, so I stopped.

"Cool. Yeah—that was some pretty radtastic playing there." I swear on your grave that he used the word "radtastic." Although I don't think it really is a word. "You're a kick-ass singer, too. I had no idea."

"Thanks. That's why I don't go to gym class—I have to practise."

"Is that why? I figured you had some sort of debilitating disease."

I couldn't tell if he was joking or not, so I did what I always do: I tossed the conversation back to him, like a birdie over a net.

"What about you? Are you into music?"

"A bit. I don't play anything, and I couldn't carry a tune if my life depended on it, but there are a couple of bands I like. I guess I'm more of a film kind of guy."

"Uh-huh," I said, or something like that. We shot the shit a while longer about fairly inconsequential stuff, like last week's math test and how neither one of us knows what we're supposed to be doing in our media studies course. I found it surprisingly easy to talk to him, almost like I'd known him for years.

All this time we were standing in a corner of the parish hall, and I guess I had my back turned to the rest of the room, because only when Rusty's parents joined us did I notice that hardly anyone else was left. Rusty's father was holding a baby girl in a frilly white dress with a fair bit of drool on it, and as soon as she saw me she heaved herself toward me with a giggle and outstretched arms.

"Who's your new friend, Maisie?" Rusty's dad asked with a laugh. I was still trying to make sense of the fact that I was now holding this slobbering child, so I blurted out the first thing that came to mind.

"I'm Rusty Friesen," I said. After I'd finished smacking myself mentally, I added, "No—Rusty Friesen is this guy. I'm Dale—Cardigan. Um—I'm in his class at school."

Rusty's parents didn't say anything about the fact that I'd mistaken myself for their son and introduced themselves as Pam and Mitch. They seemed friendly—at least Pam did. They complimented me on my singing and asked me how long I'd been playing the organ, and then thankfully we moved on to something else. The way we were all acting, you'd never have guessed that I already knew Pam as Ms. Friesen, my extremely pregnant biology teacher from last year, who was now hearing me speak for the first time.

Finally they said they had to go. I assured them that I had a ride to the reception, even though my heart had already sunk to my stomach when I'd realized that Sophie and Jenice must have left without me. I mean, this was supposed to be one of the happiest moments of their lives, so I couldn't blame them for forgetting about the organist, but it still sucked. I walked down the street to the bus stop and glanced at the schedule, even though the venue was out in the country and no bus was going to take me within walking distance of it. I dug through my backpack for my cellphone, but just as I was dialling home the battery died.

No sooner had this happened than a car slowed to a stop in front of me. I thought I recognized Maisie in her car seat, but still I stumbled a bit when Rusty emerged from the other side of the car, looking confused. "Uh—need a lift?"

I glanced at the amount of change I'd dug out of my pocket, at which point my liver and my kidneys decided to start functioning in reverse. "Uh—yeah," I said. I mean, it was the truth. I didn't have enough money for a taxi, nor a way to call one, which didn't matter anyway since I only vaguely remembered what the venue was called. But their car was blocking a lane of traffic, so I grabbed my bag.

Rusty held his door open for me, so I had no choice but to go in first. That meant I was literally pinned between his thigh and Maisie's car seat, not to mention weighed down by all the crap in my bag. "It must be a bit of a squeeze back there," Pam said sympathetically as we drove off.

"It's fine," I assured her, even though that was a lie. I tried to buckle my seat belt, but doing so would involve brushing my hand against part of Rusty's leg that deserved to be left alone, so I decided to take my chances and force myself to act more upbeat than I felt. "Thanks for stopping. I did have a ride to the reception, but it looks like there was a change of plans."

We rode in silence until Rusty nudged me with his elbow.

"Do you like bubble tea?"

"Bubble tea is the spawn of the devil."

"You don't like it," he said, shrewdly enough. Only much later did it occur to me that he'd probably meant this as an invitation.

Then Mitch mentioned that the reception wouldn't start for a couple of hours while the brides were busy with the photographer, so they were heading home. "You're welcome to join us," he added, like he meant it. "Any friend of Rusty's is a friend of ours." At that I sensed Rusty's head turn in my direction, but I didn't dare look back at him.

"Thanks—that'd be great," I said. What I was thinking, though, was more along the lines of *Fuuuuuuuuuck.* "Wasn't that a great ceremony?" I asked, then leaned back in my seat and fell silent as Rusty's parents commented on everything under the sun: the brides' dresses, the wedding party, the flowers, the church, Reverend Heather's sermon, and some major-sounding life updates about people I didn't know. I was super aware the whole time of Rusty's leg pressed against mine, how warm it was getting in the car, how long I should wait to ask one of them to crack open a window, the way Maisie kept staring at me like I was her long-lost brother returning to the fold. I tried to concentrate on my breathing, but Mitch and Pam kept pulling me back into the conversation. Don't get me wrong—it was nice of them to include me or whatever. But every time I leaned forward to talk to them and then leaned back, the amount of space between Rusty's leg and his sister's car seat seemed to shrink.

Eventually we pulled into the driveway of a house about five blocks away from mine and headed inside. At first I figured we'd hang out and make small talk, but Mitch went to put Maisie down for her nap and Pam said she had some stuff to do, so when Rusty motioned toward the family room downstairs, I didn't have any choice but to follow him.

The thing is, I've always been a loner. Ever since the first day of kindergarten, when I apparently returned home and announced to you and Ma that all the other children in my class were stupid and dumb, I've had this weird, unexplainable hate-on for everyone else my age. I don't think I've ever wilfully gone to a friend's house to hang out, let alone to "play," except to Jordana's. An afternoon at her house consisted of us playing music, having a snack, then playing music again. So all this was reminding me of the few times you and Ma had forced me to go to some other kid's house, either because it was easier than getting a sitter or because one of you thought it was for my own good. I was standing there, feeling the shag carpet under my socks, wearing a suit, my bag still slung across my shoulders, and I didn't know what to do, what to say, or how to act. Rusty sat down on the sofa and stared at me like he couldn't figure out what to do with me, either.

"So," I said. Then, as I always seem to do, I blurted out the first coherent sentence that came to mind. "Um—so Maisie's, like, way younger than you, right? Do you and she have different sets of parents or something?"

"No. They just like to space things out, I guess," Rusty said with a shrug.

My mind drew a blank after that, so I asked him where the bathroom was. I locked myself in, dumped my bag on the washing machine, and stared at my reflection in the mirror.

I felt like I was overheating. There's no other way to put it.

I knew I couldn't stay there forever, but I figured a few minutes alone would help me get some of the static out of my head. Finally I flushed, even though I hadn't gone, washed my hands for the sake of appearance, and decided that I needed to figure out some kind of activity, even if that meant playing Hungry Hungry

Hippos. So when I found Rusty sitting on the floor in front of the TV, silently holding out a console, I reached for it eagerly and tossed my bag aside. He was playing a game that Gonzo has—one that mimics all these seasonal sports I have no interest in trying in reality—and I let myself relax a little. Playing video games is one of the only things Gonzo and I do together, mainly because we don't have to talk, so I knew I'd be pretty good at this one. Rusty apparently isn't the silent type when it comes to gaming, though. For two solid hours, as we went through level after level, he kept up a one-sided commentary on everything we were doing.

"Ugh—this part's brutal. It's literally epic."

"Watch the tree!"

"Oooh—I'm going to get you for that, fucker!"

I didn't mind, though. He clearly wasn't expecting me to respond, so I didn't.

Eventually we headed back upstairs, where I met Rusty's grandmother, who was going to stay behind with Maisie. She asked Rusty who his "little friend" was, and he hesitated for so long I wondered if he couldn't think of a diplomatic way to admit we weren't friends at all or if he'd blanked on my name. I forced myself to keep smiling, because I couldn't think of anything else to do. And then, pushing it all over the edge even more, Pam asked if "you boys" were ready to go. The idea of Rusty and me as a pair made me flinch.

Anyway, it's getting late and my fingers are about to fall off, so I'll stop for now. I've been listening to an album of crooners that I can only describe as "old lady music," which makes sense, since it's a CD I inherited from Grandma. But now the crooners have worn themselves out, and so have I. To be continued—at some point.

Your loving (and sleepy) son,

Dale

**MONDAY, MARCH 21**

Dear Pa,

I had a hard time falling asleep last night, despite how tired I was. I guess I was worried about whether Rusty Friesen would try to talk to me at school today—not so much because of what happened at his house but because of what happened later, at the reception. But he didn't. He smiled, nodded, even offered me a friendly thumbs-up in the hallway before class, but that's it. All morning I was on my guard, ready to back away if he tried to come near me, but it never occurred to him to do that. And so, me being me, I spent most of the afternoon wondering why.

Now that I think back on it, I was worrying even on the way to the reception about what would happen now that my cone of silence had been so unexpectedly shattered. I started dreaming up ways to make him turn against me somehow or want to stop talking to me, even though that seemed pretty extreme—not to mention impractical, since his parents were in the middle of giving me a ride. Plus I was sandwiched again between Rusty's leg and Maisie's car seat, even though this time it was empty. But I'd managed to buckle my seat belt before he sat down, so at least I wasn't taking my life in my hands again.

So by the time we got to the reception, I was pretty annoyed at the situation I'd found myself in. And the fact that it was a situation that wouldn't make sense to anyone else made it a quadrillion times worse.

The reception was at a country club I'd never been to before. I forget what it was called—Shady Pines, Twin Peaks, Blue Lagoon, Plum Creek, Silver Lake, or something like that. As soon as we got out of the car I saw Pam nudge Rusty and tilt her head in my direction, at which point Rusty let out a breath and said, in a tone that was totally lacking energy, "Hey—let's go check out that pond or whatever." I told him I'd be playing at the reception and needed to set up. It was sort of a lie; all I needed to do was take my music books out of my bag and put them on top of the piano. But I felt pretty frazzled by everything, and all I wanted was to find a small room where I could close my eyes and breathe again for a few minutes.

That proved to be impossible, though. A bunch of people from the wedding stopped to talk to me, ask if I had any CDs to sell, and blah blah blah. It was nice and flattering and all that, but after a while my temperature seemed to be rising and I just wanted to shout at them, "Look—I'm a kid! Why don't you go fuck yourselves!" even though I knew perfectly well that that was a bit much. Finally, when I saw Jonathan heading my way, I ducked out a side door and wandered across the lawn to where Rusty was standing with his hands in his pockets near a pond with a bunch of crap floating around in it. We were standing under a canopy of trees, with no one else in sight—it was the kind of setting you'd see in a period drama.

He turned to me as I approached and looked like he was trying to smile. "Did you see the seating chart? Looks like Sophie and Jenice put us at the same table," he said. I didn't respond right away, so he added, "Not with my parents. I didn't recognize any of the other names."

"Huh," I said finally. Or did I? Maybe I said something else.

Anyway, I turned back to the pond. It was a nice day, surprisingly warm for March. The water was this beautiful Windex colour. After a while I glanced at Rusty, whose eyes were squinting a bit. I had no idea what he was aiming to ask me, so I jumped in before he could do it. "Oh, hey—um—look at those geese and their, um, their—little geese?" I said. That's right, Pa—your son can be a total doorknob sometimes.

Rusty looked at me, surprised, then turned back to the pond. "You mean goslings, right?"

"Goslings! Yes! *That's* the word I was looking for."

"Oh. Well—those are ducks."

"Huh."

My eyes glazed over as he told me about their migration patterns, but eventually he interrupted himself, nudged me with his elbow, and pointed with his chin at something in the distance. "See that cardinal over there?"

"The what now?"

"Um—that striking red-coloured bird." He pointed in the distance, where hanging out on a branch was the same kind of bird I'd seen at the cemetery a few weeks ago.

"Oh. Is that what those things are called?"

"Are you for real?" But the way he asked made him seem curious, not incredulous, so I didn't mind.

I told him I'd been seeing those birds everywhere lately, although I didn't mention where I'd noticed the first one. He started telling me all about them, and at first I was bored, but then he mentioned the superstition that cardinals symbolize people who have died and are watching over you. I said something vague like "Oh, that sounds fun," but inside I could feel myself smiling with the thought of you.

Eventually we made it to our table, where I discovered that Rusty was assigned to the seat at my left. This would prove to be unfortunate—because I'm left-handed and he's right-handed, we ended up knocking elbows repeatedly over the next two hours. Sitting with us were five people in their early twenties who all seemed to know each other but were total strangers to me, as well as Jonathan, much to my chagrin. I guess we were the Miscellaneous Young People table. Jonathan looked pretty much the way he always looks, with that handsome, scowling face I once found so appealing for some reason. To my right was a young woman who assured me in the first fifteen seconds of small talk that she and the guy with her weren't serious, that it was "a good arrangement for now," whatever *that* meant. Beyond that she ignored me, which was fine. On Rusty's left was another young woman who offered Rusty a nice smile until he responded to her question that he was sixteen and still in high school, and at that point she turned away. Rusty and I seemed doomed to have to keep talking to each other throughout the meal, which probably would have been fine, but after Jonathan nodded at me across the table and flashed me a discreet A-okay sign with his hand, I ran out of things to say. Plus the seam in my underwear was caught in my butt crack and I was trying to figure out a way to readjust it without everyone else noticing. I kept my head low as I ate my salad, nodded a few times at what the others were saying, and enjoyed the food.

By the time we got to the main course, things took a turn thanks to the asshole sitting across from me, to Jonathan's right. I don't know which happened first—recognizing him as someone who'd graduated from my high school the year I'd started or figuring out that he was an asshole. He started to get fixated on the fact that I wasn't drinking alcohol, maybe because he was already drunk. There were two bottles of wine on the table, and everyone helped themselves. That was fine—I kept saying stuff like "I'm okay— thanks" and no one thought anything of it. But this guy wouldn't let it go. He did that thing that assholes do where they'll say things that are supposed to be jokes, but no one's laughing. "Hey! You pregnant or something?" and "Hey! You're not at the kids' table anymore." Finally he reached across the centrepiece, poured some red wine into my glass, and set the bottle down on the table with a thud. "Dude, I *guarantee* you'll thank me for this later. *Trust* me."

But I didn't trust him. By that point I kind of hated him— not only for being such a dick over something so stupid, but also for making everyone else around the table stare at me in silence. I glanced at Rusty, but he turned away. I looked around the rest of the table and saw that nobody was going to help me—not even Jonathan, whose face sported a sympathetic smirk. I felt my cheeks flame up, which is always a dead giveaway, and stared at my wine-glass like it might tell me what to do.

"Drink it," the asshole commanded.

I picked up my glass. I didn't want to do anything that would embarrass Sophie and Jenice, so short of eating the rest of my dinner outside, I figured the only thing I could do was to sip some wine and hope he'd back off. I tried to reason with myself: I wasn't driving, and one glass wasn't going to ruin me. But then I thought of you, and I realized I didn't have to do anything sneaky to get out of this—all I needed was to tell the truth.

"My father was killed by a drunk driver when I was nine," I said.

Then I suddenly became aware of everything: that I'd managed to speak without letting my voice shake too much, that the insides of my stomach had turned toxic, that my blood sugar had fallen off a cliff and caused my hands to quiver, that gasps had sounded from around the table. We sat together, all of us frozen in the moment. Then something shifted in my mind and made time move forward again. I set the wineglass down, reached for my fork, and resumed eating, not because I could taste the food but because I couldn't stand to see everyone staring at me. When I looked up again, the asshole had turned clammy and ghostlike. I couldn't resist, so I added, "Also, you're an asshole."

Then he got up and never came back.

Needless to say, that brought all conversation at our table to a screeching halt. I turned around and clapped at the end of every speech, but I didn't hear anything because my mind had filled up with static. I wanted so badly to talk to Ma. Or to Uncle Scott. Or to anyone who would understand, not just sympathize. But I knew my phone battery had died, and then, as I thought it over, I remembered how weird Ma had acted the day she hadn't wanted to stop at the cemetery, and that became a new layer of sadness to sift through. Whenever I turned in the direction of someone giving a speech, I was aware of Rusty next to me, but I didn't think about him much. All I could do was try to smile and wait for the static to melt away.

By the time dinner was over, I was more or less okay again. At one point I saw Rusty about to say something, but before he could spit it out, Jenice invited everyone who was playing music to come forward, so I grabbed my bag and headed toward the group of people huddled together at the front of the room with binders and instruments. Even though all these people were strangers, their energy changed me. It was like these friendly-looking people managed to brush the cobwebs from my mind just by standing there. One guy with a beard and a newsie cap grinned at me, called me "buddy," patted my shoulder, and said something nice about the Carpenters song I'd sung during the ceremony, and that made all the difference. Sophie made up a list of what each person wanted to perform, and when she came to me, I shrugged. "Let's see how it goes," I said.

First I sat at the piano for several songs, accompanying Sophie and Jenice either separately or together. Then I got off the stage and listened to some of their friends perform—such a wide range of people and musical styles. I recognized some of the songs—one was by Tracy Chapman—but most of them were new to me, and if there's one thing I enjoy in this life, it's listening to a fantastic song for the first time. I was hiding in the wings, sitting on a chair behind the heavy curtain, listening with my eyes closed, and enjoying the effect that good music nearly always has on me. It was calming, yet reviving. It grounded me. It welcomed me home. For the rest of the night, I didn't think about that asshole at my table a single time.

At one point Sophie and I were chatting while a friend of hers was setting up her guitar, and I said something like, "Wasn't that last song about a couple breaking up? It was great, but I figured we should stick to music that's more—you know—*weddingy*."

"Oh, we don't care," Sophie said with an easy hand gesture. "We love music. Sing about death if you want."

"Really," I said.

So when it was my turn to perform on my own, I sat at the piano and decided to sing two songs to test the waters with the crowd: "Blue" by Joni Mitchell, followed by "All by Myself" by Eric Carmen. They seemed to go over pretty well. I looked at Sophie behind the stage, and when she gave me a friendly thumbs-up sign, I announced in the microphone that I'd need a minute to set up my final song. I pulled my iPod out of my bag, asked someone how to plug it into the sound system, and moved my microphone away from the piano so I could stand behind it, at centre stage. "Um," I said, looking out into the crowd in front of me, "as you saw at the wedding, one of the things I like to do is fiddle around with recording techniques and basically create my own karaoke tracks. So, for my last song, I'd like to sing something meaningful to Sophie and Jenice. I hope you enjoy it."

This was the surprise I was telling you about! This new boy band from Niagara Falls called Climax is playing on the radio incessantly. Some of the guys in my class make fun of them, even though they seem able to recite all their lyrics from memory. Which is no small feat, because their lyrics are atrocious.

> Baby
> What you done to me?
> Darlin', can't you see?
> Baby
>
> Momma
> How you did me wrong
> I just can't go on
> Momma

I don't know. Maybe it's code.

About a month ago I picked their song "Bedroom Eyes" from their latest album, *Woke Up from a Dream*—which I downloaded illegally because I wouldn't be caught dead buying it—and ran it through this program that separates a song into individual parts. I took out all the strings, slowed the melody down, transposed it to a key within my range, added some piano, and recorded all the backing vocals myself. Basically I transformed it from bubble-gum pop into a fairly mellow ballad. As for the lyrics—well, there wasn't much I could do about those. I wanted the song to be familiar and new at the same time.

As the piano intro started, I could sense some of the people in the audience tensing up, like they sort of recognized the song but weren't sure what it was. The second I started to sing the first shitty lyric there was a bubble of recognition and applause, and then, as I made my way through the first verse, I couldn't help but notice the whole room staring at me. Even though I normally hate being the centre of attention, I don't mind it when I'm singing.

I happened to watch Rusty as I started the refrain and all the backing vocals jumped in. His face broke into a grin and he shook his head a little, but in a good way. I know this'll sound silly, but I was half pretending I had four best friends singing behind me onstage, even though it was just me overdubbing myself.

I got through the second verse and the second chorus. My version didn't include the bridge, where all five Climax boys sing the words "yeah," "nah," and "baby" over and over again—I just couldn't make it work with the new tempo. But for the final refrain, which echoed the term "bedroom eyes" several times, I'd added more and more vocals, letting it build and build until there were about twenty voices singing—plus me onstage.

When the song ended, the audience burst into applause. They wouldn't stop clapping. It kept increasing instead of dying down. For a while I just stood there. I didn't know what to do. Finally I stepped away from the microphone stand and bowed, a small surrender of gratitude to all these people for liking what I'd done. Then I fled from the stage into the wings, reminding myself to breathe. But Jenice grabbed my arm and pushed me back onstage. "They love you! Play something else."

"I could play all night," I said, because at that moment I could have. Over the next hour or so, alternating with more of Jenice and Sophie's friends, I sat at the piano again and played the theme song from *The Simpsons*, "A Song for You" by the Carpenters, "Downstream" by Supertramp, "Daffodil Lament" by the Cranberries, and one of my favourite pieces by Debussy. I also sang a spontaneous duet with the woman in the wedding party who was Sophie's ex, while her husband, the bearded guy in the newsie cap, played along on his guitar. They asked me if I could play "Bridge over Troubled Water," so I played piano while they sang and played guitar, and then everyone who'd played in the coffee house joined us for the last refrain, and we wrapped up the song in the most elaborate way we could think of.

The coffee house ended at that point, and after that they served the cake. A bunch of people came up to me before I even had a chance to put my music books away and get off the stage, but I was still riding the high of all that music, so I didn't mind. Someone asked me how much I charge to play at events, and when I shrugged, she explained that she was organizing a reception in a few months—I forget for what—and she wanted me to play background music or something. And one of Sophie and Jenice's friends asked if I was interested in starting a band. I know they were just being polite, but it felt nice.

Rather than hire a DJ, Sophie and Jenice had set up a playlist of MP3s on Sophie's laptop, which they plugged into the sound system. They asked me to keep an eye on it throughout the dancing, so I sat on the floor of the stage, ate my cake, fiddled with the order of the songs, and watched everyone else cut a rug. The smirk never left Jonathan's face as he danced, which I found fascinating. Rusty kept waving me over, but I pointed at the laptop and shrugged as if the music wouldn't play unless I sat by it the whole time.

Finally, just at the point when my performance high had deflated and I was starting to think it was time to go, Ma appeared in the doorway. I saw her look of delight as she took in all the people and the decorations. She spotted me on the stage and waved, so I checked that there were lots of songs left on the playlist, grabbed my bag, and headed her way. "Hi, Ma," I said, giving her a hug, even though I hadn't done that in public in years.

"Hi, honey. I didn't know what time you'd want to go, but it's nearly midnight and you have an early day tomorrow."

"Thanks. I'm glad you're here. My phone battery died again."

"I figured. How did your music go?" Ma asked.

"It went fine," I said.

"It was sensational," Jenice said behind me. I turned to see her and Sophie standing there, their faces flushed from the dance floor. I introduced them to "my mother, Susan," and the three of them made small talk for a few minutes. Finally, just as Ma and I were leaving, I glanced around to wave goodbye to Rusty, but he was too busy dancing to notice.

All day today I felt kind of meh. After the amazing experience of performing at the wedding, algebra class was pretty underwhelming. I tried to block out what I was doing and recreate that feeling in my mind, but all I could manage was a shitty photocopy of it. After school I lingered in front of my locker and watched some of the guys in my grade horsing around and laughing together. I didn't like any of the things they were talking about, but it dawned on me that they seemed a lot happier than I was feeling. Then I noticed Rusty by his locker, and for a split second I wondered what would happen if I walked up to him and started to shoot the shit the way normal people do. But I couldn't. If he'd wanted to talk to me today he would have, but since that never happened, clearly he didn't want it to.

I've been trying to get through Björk's latest album. It's a little bit exasperating. You can't really sing along to it because it's missing things like melody and cadence and a beat. But I guess it's the music of the future, so I'm trying to get used to it.

I'm tired. Not just sleepy—another kind of tired, too. But I don't know what to do about it.

Your loving (and tired) son,

Dale

## THURSDAY, APRIL 7

Dear Pa,

I guess it's been a couple of weeks since my last letter to you. There didn't seem to be much worth writing about for a while, except maybe the weather. It's a gorgeous day out, apparently. I got my piano exam results in the mail a few days ago, and I did really well, but somehow I didn't care all that much—partly because I knew no one else cared. So I decided to hide the letter in my desk drawer and wait to see if Ma ever brings it up, even though I know she won't.

The other night I dreamed I was in the hospital because my tonsils had grown back for some reason and I had to have them removed again. But this hospital paired patients by procedure rather than by age, so I was stuck in a recovery room with a bunch of kids who openly made fun of me for having to go through this a second time. To get even, I tried to scare them by telling them about a made-up disease that was a cross between syphilis and chicken pox and caused people to lose their sanity temporarily, but no one believed me. When I turned my head, I discovered that I'd teleported to another room where people spoke Danish, and since the only Danish word I knew was the equivalent of "thank you," everyone was perplexed when that's all I could say in response to their questions about why I was walking around in a hospital gown that wouldn't close properly.

I wouldn't have bothered writing you just about the hospital dream, but something random happened at school today, and a thought popped into my head: *I'll have to tell Pa about this.* Just for a second, I think for the first time in these seven years, I forgot you were dead. And when I remembered again, I fucking lost it. I'd always thought "bursting into tears" was a figure of speech, but that's exactly what I did. It was like I puked, but through my eyes. And the more I tried to stop, the worse it became. My whole body was shaking, and I kept hearing these awful heaving sounds coming out of me. Before I could calm down, I looked up to see every single douchebag in my class staring at me, along with my teacher, Ms. Montrose, who demanded to know not if I was okay but what had happened in *her* class to cause this outburst. I looked inside my desk for a tissue and didn't say anything, but when she kept badgering me, I finally broke my three-year vow of silence.

"Why can't you just mind your own business?"

A few guys let out audible gasps, probably because I'd thrown in an F-bomb—for emphasis or whatever. Anyway, I had to go downstairs to the office, where they gave me a three-day detention and added a note to my file. But I *still* wouldn't tell anyone what happened, so technically I win.

And the worst part is I don't remember anymore what it was that I wanted to tell you.

Everyone avoided me like the plague after that. When the final bell rang, I went back to the main office to ask about making an appointment with the school counsellor, but before the administrative assistant could answer my question, the principal spotted me, stormed out of her office, and started yelling at me about getting to detention. Now I wouldn't go back there if it was the last office on earth.

So I don't know what to do. I can't say I'm surprised that my school is useless, but I really think I need to talk to someone. A little while ago Rusty Friesen called—apparently Sophie gave him my number—to ask me something about our media studies quiz, even though it's a week away. And, naturally, I made a total ass of myself.

"Dale? It's Rusty Friesen calling."

"Oh. Hey. Fine—and you?"

"What?"

"Huh?"

I braced myself for him to ask me about this afternoon—*So like, you crying in math class for no apparent reason? That was pretty radtastic*—but he acted like it had never happened. Instead, he told me a bit about this sketch show he likes—he didn't call it radtastic, but he did use the term "scandalicious" at one point, although I forget in reference to what. I said it sounded cool, even though it didn't, and then we wrapped things up.

Weird.

Besides that it's been a pretty boring week. Choir practice got cancelled on Tuesday because Marty, the director, is out of town for something—I forget what, but it's not remotely interesting. I haven't been making much progress with all the orchestral music I've been listening to—I got stuck recently on Isaac Albéniz. There hasn't been anything good on TV, and even my dreams have been reruns.

Oh, but something happened yesterday at Gonzo's basketball game. The rule in our family is that everyone goes to my concerts and recitals and to Gonzo's games—period. Which I guess is surprising given how weird Ma is when it comes to me and music, but Ma likes to think she's treating Gonzo and me the same out of fairness. Except we're not the same. No one thinks Gonzo will ever be good enough to play professionally or to get a sports scholarship or anything, not even Gonzo. For him, basketball is just something to do in the time between more important things, like studying and work. I wonder sometimes if that's why Ma's upset with me: because with music, I want to go far beyond where Gonzo's going with basketball, but she sees it as a distraction from what's really important, like my last algebra test.

The weird part is that Ma, Helmut, and I will sit at one end of the bleachers, and Gonzo's mother will sit by herself at the other end. Sometimes she and Helmut wave to each other, but we don't ever talk to her. I can't understand why. I mean, I don't get the sense that she and Helmut hate each other or that their marriage ended because one of them did something unforgivable. One time I asked Gonzo why his parents don't talk much and he grunted and unleashed this tirade about both his parents. Then he said—I remember this so clearly—"The whole divorced parents thing sucks. You're so luck—" And then he bit off the rest of his sentence.

I knew what he was about to say. "You're so lucky that your parents aren't divorced." Even though he can be a jerk to me sometimes, I'm sure he just forgot temporarily that one of my parents is dead. And I do feel bad for Gonzo sometimes. I don't suppose it's any fun to have to keep moving between one parent's house and the other's, never feeling totally at home. And sure, in that way I *am* lucky: this house where I live with Ma and Helmut is always my home. But it seemed like such an odd thing for Gonzo to think, let alone say.

Then again, I know how quickly things can change. If Ma had been in the car with you, I guess I'd be living with Uncle Scott and Uncle Joe now. And that would've been fine, too. If Ma died now, I'd probably go on living with Helmut. I know Ma updated her will after they got married, but I forget what it says.

Anyway, usually at Gonzo's basketball games we wait around for him outside if it's nice or in the foyer of the arena if it isn't, but never close enough to Iliana that I can get a good look at her. Gonzo's at his mother's this week, so after he got out of the locker room he waved to us and walked out with her. Helmut handed me some mail that Gonzo had received about his driver's licence and asked me to run it over to him before they drove away. I caught up with them in the parking lot, handed him the envelope, and smiled at Iliana.

"Hi," I said. "I'm Dale. I'm Susan's son." It seemed a better thing to say than the alternative: *I've been your son's stepbrother for nearly three years, yet somehow we've never met.*

"Dale, it's so nice to meet you finally," Iliana said, shaking my hand. "Gonzo's told me so much about you."

I was taken aback by how friendly she was. She really seemed to mean what she was saying. And I realized I was dying to get acquainted with this woman, who'd been such a mystery to me for so long. The trouble was, I couldn't think of anything to say. *So—you used to be married to my stepfather. What was that like?* I'm not that stupid. So I complimented her on her car instead.

Somehow that broke the ice, because soon the three of us were having a fantastic chat about school, basketball, the weather, Iliana's work (turns out she produces a local news show), and upcoming summer plans. I think Gonzo and I exchanged more words in those fifteen minutes than we have in all the time we've known each other. Iliana even gave me a hug before I managed to drag myself away.

When I got back to Ma and Helmut on the other side of the parking lot, Helmut asked me what had taken so long. "Oh, I was talking with Gonzo and Iliana. She's awesome. I can't believe it's taken this long for me to meet her."

Helmut smiled at me in the rear-view mirror and drove off. Ma sat there and said nothing, but the *way* she said nothing was incredibly loud.

I don't know what her problem is. Actually, I think I do. But I don't *get* what her problem is, so I didn't ask her about it.

Once we got home there was some sunlight left, so I decided to go for a bike ride. I didn't have a destination in mind. I just rode through the streets in this neighbourhood that's become home. And somehow, because of the combination of the setting sun and the wind and the fact that my thoughts weren't fixed on anything in particular, I had these vivid flashes of memory of the way things used to be when I was a child, like my old room and kids at my old school and my curiosity about everything, and the fact that I was happy then. The feeling was gone almost as soon as it started, but I missed you so much in that moment. I looked around for the cardinals, but I guess it was their night off.

When I got home I texted Jordana a funny cat video from YouTube that I thought she'd like. I could see that she'd read the message, but I haven't received a reply yet.

Just now I let my mind wander for a minute, and for some reason the memory of the day you died popped into my head. But I don't want to think about that, and I'm finding the symphony I'm listening to pretty exasperating since it's basically "I'm a Little Teapot" in a minor key, so I'll stop here.

Your loving (and apparently shit-disturbing) son,

Dale

## WEDNESDAY, APRIL 13

Dear Pa,

Last night I had a dream that was considerably more memorable than the one last week about having to get my tonsils out again. I was back at the house in Guelph where we lived when I was little, but I was the age I am now. And Ma was there. And you. You were alive, sitting in a chair on the front porch, smiling at me. And I was sitting next to you, holding your hand. I could feel it—warm and strong, with hair on the knuckles like I'm starting to have on mine. And I was crying. And I said to you, "I know you're dead, but I'm so glad to see you, because I've missed you so much."

I woke up—and I wasn't crying. I remembered that today would have been your birthday. You would have been forty-four. I don't know what verb tense that is: *would have been*.

It occurred to me as I was packing my lunch this morning that I can't remember the sound of your voice. In my memories of you, those in my mind and those that are helped along by photos, there's no sound. Just now, as I looked up at the photo of you on the wall above my desk, I tried to pinpoint how you used to speak to me, but the sounds I imagined didn't fit.

The dream scared me, I think, because it reminded me that I've also started to forget what you looked like when you moved or what your face looked like when you weren't posing for the camera. When I look at old pictures, I see glasses and smiles and angles, but they're all without movement. Which I guess makes sense, because you're likewise without movement, since you're dead.

All day I thought about doing something special to mark the occasion. Not baking a cake or singing for you, but something to acknowledge you, at least. But I didn't know what I could do. At some point during dinner it dawned on me that Ma had forgotten. She wasn't doing the *I just won't say anything unless he says something first* parenting routine she's so good at. She laughed easily, as if something was funny. She expressed concern about a colleague who's going through a terrible breakup and gave us an update about some minor scandal involving one of Beverly's nephews. She talked about looking forward to spring weather and taking out the patio furniture.

So after dinner I went down to my room and lit a tea light I swiped from the kitchen. It's burning in front of me as I write this, and I'm playing some music I found online that's so lulling that you really shouldn't play it when you're driving a car. It isn't much, but it's all I could think of.

This morning as I was walking down the hallway before my first class, I noticed Rusty Friesen sitting by himself. People were standing around him and talking, but he just stared into space, his hands clasped together, his bushy eyebrows aquiver. I wonder what he was so pissed off about.

Your loving son,

Dale

## SATURDAY, APRIL 16

Dear Pa,

Today turned out to be such a weird day. I couldn't shake the feeling that if I waited too long to write you about it, I wouldn't be able to remember all the details. But I'll try.

Most Saturday mornings I head to church for a couple of hours to practise the organ, and then, if I feel like it, I drive to the community pool in a half-assed attempt to meet my gym requirement for school. I say "half-assed" because most of the time I can't be bothered to go. If organ practice goes too well or not well enough, or if I'm sleepy or hungry or anxious or horny or bored, or if it's too hot or too cold outside, I skip it.

But today the stars lined up, and for once I'd packed my gym bag before leaving the house, so off I went, expecting it to be like any old day at the pool. I found a quiet corner in the locker room, changed into my swim trunks, put on my goggles, and followed the smell of chlorine till I got to the pool. I made my way to an empty lane, stretched, dove in, and did laps for half an hour. Swimming has been my sport of choice for years, by the way, ever since one of my teachers at choir school recommended it to Ma as a way to help me develop my lungs. It's pretty much the only sport I have patience for outside a video game—there's something soothing about going back and forth, arm over arm, again and again, at my own pace, not giving a flying rat's ass about what's happening on either side of me.

At the end of my set I was bobbing like a cork at the end of my lane, debating whether to get out and pee or just pee in the pool, when I noticed a pair of feet standing above me. I peeled off my goggles and panned up the hairy legs attached to those feet to discover Rusty Friesen in swim trunks. It turns out he has even more freckles and fur than I'd previously thought.

"Hey, what's going on?" he called out, and then he jumped over me and into the water, feet first. I think he assumed he was jumping into the shallow end, because when he broke the surface, his arms were flailing and he was sputtering. Needless to say, I was pretty surprised to see him, but somehow, the fact that I was suddenly trapped between him and the edge of the pool didn't cause me to panic and drown. While swimming laps I'd been focusing on my arms and my legs and random thoughts in my head, but now someone real had literally jumped into my reality, and I wanted to talk to him! Yes, that's right: *me*!

We stayed where we were at first, treading water, until my arms got tired and I remembered that we were in a lane meant for laps. So we got out, grabbed our towels, and jumped back into the section of the pool that was a big free-for-all. Mostly we just stood around in the water and splashed each other and kept talking—just guy stuff. We went over everything that had happened in class over the last few weeks, *except* for my crying fit. And we didn't talk about that asshole trying to force me to drink wine at Sophie and Jenice's wedding reception so much as we talked *around* that moment. It was so unexpectedly nice that I barely noticed anyone else in the pool.

It was only after a while that I thought to ask what he was doing there. Apparently his mother had signed Maisie up for something called Baby Aqua Fitness, and since Rusty had nothing better to do, he'd decided to tag along. "Oh, cool," I said, or something like that. Then we started making up names of baby classes that aren't likely to exist: Baby Hot Yoga, Baby Kickboxing, Baby Self-Defence, and Baby Body Shred. It was a lot funnier than I'm probably making it sound.

At one point we spotted his mother with Maisie, so we got out of the pool and headed over to them, still laughing. "Dale!" Pam exclaimed when she saw me. Maisie spun around in her mother's arms and reached out for me. I took her from Pam and held her, and then Rusty started to tickle her chin. To do that he had to stand awfully close to me, and at first that was fine, but when I realized I could feel his bare skin against mine, I turned away. "How was Baby Aqua Fitness?" I asked Pam.

"I found it terrifying, but Maisie loved it," Pam said, adjusting her bathing suit straps. I think her suit was orange and green and blue and purple or something, and it was either one piece or two—or three. We shot the breeze until Pam said it was getting past Maisie's lunchtime.

"Oh," Rusty said. He turned to me with his eyebrows skewed together, like he was imploring me to do something.

So I explained that I had Ma's car and offered to drive Rusty home if he wanted to stay at the pool a little longer. Pam shrugged like she didn't care one way or the other—or, to be all fancy-pants about it, she *acquiesced.*

"Since you'll be driving Rusty home, why don't you stay for lunch?" she said.

"Yeah," Rusty said, like this idea had just occurred to him, "and maybe you could stick around for part of the afternoon. We still have a few more levels to try on *Virtual Sports for Couch Potatoes VII*."

I figured I didn't have anything better to do at home except some homework, so it was my turn to acquiesce. Pam left with Maisie, and Rusty and I jumped back in the pool. I suggested we do some laps, and at first he was game, but since he's not that strong a swimmer, he was wiped out before he'd made it across once. He waved for me to continue, and I did for a while, but I couldn't stay focused when I knew he was watching me.

Once we decided we'd had enough swimming for one day, we headed back to the locker room. Rusty gestured to the sauna with his thumb and an uncomplicated-looking smile, but I said something about hunger and video games and kept walking. We ended up showering in stalls next to each other, which was fine but kind of weird. I watched his feet under the partition between us, moving around like he was doing the latest dance craze. But that seemed strange, so I started playing Handel's *Messiah* in my head—specifically an aria called "How Beautiful Are the Feet"—while I shampooed my hair. It's not the most riveting aria, but it still fit the occasion.

Once I was done, I opened the door to my shower stall, my towel wrapped around my waist and my balled-up trunks in my hand. A second later Rusty emerged from his stall the same way, his wet hair practically brown and going every which way. We just stared at each other until I shrugged. "I guess I'll see you in the lobby?"

"You bet," he said. He followed me out of the shower room, and I figured we'd go our separate ways at that point, but when I reached my locker he was still standing behind me. "Oh, weird," he said, stepping past me to the locker right next to mine. He looked at me, his Adam's apple bobbing up and down. "I—I picked this locker because of the number," he said, gesturing to *619*. Apparently his birthday is the nineteenth of June.

"Oh, cool," I said, because I couldn't think of any other reply. "Mine's in May."

And then—well, the conversation died, like someone had pulled the plug on it. I thought about making a joke about spring babies, but it got caught in my throat and I had to swallow it back down. I reached for my padlock and struggled with the combination. I felt my ears heat up, like I'd been wearing headphones for a while. And then my stomach started to churn, but not only because I was hungry.

I got my door open, and when I stepped back from my locker, I could see that Rusty had started to dry his hair with his towel.

I tried not to look. I really did. I didn't know what to do, but then my mind went into overdrive: this is just what happens when you have a friend and you go swimming with him. I told myself to stop being such a chicken, cued up Mozart's "Regina Cœli" in my head, dropped my towel, and forced myself not to run away from him as I dried off and found my clothes.

I'll spare you the details, but let's just say I had no idea how apt the nickname Freckles 'n' Fur was until this moment.

By the way, I'd never in a million years tell you any of this if you were alive. But at this point I don't think I have to worry about shocking you. While writing this letter I've looked up periodically at the framed photo of you on the wall above my desk, and you're still smiling. So whatever.

I think the whole situation would have been less awkward if Rusty and I had kept talking. But it was as if the air in the locker room had done something to our vocal cords. Somehow we got dressed and left the building. It was only once we were in the parking lot that I managed to get us going again by pointing out that a shrub was covering part of the building's sign, so from where we were standing it said *Community Poo*. At least it made him laugh.

Oh, that's weird. My iPod is on shuffle. I have 1,300 tracks on it, and yet it just played three Joni Mitchell songs in a row. I wonder if the universe is trying to tell me something.

When we got to his house I figured I should call home to let the folks know that both the car and I were fine. My cellphone battery had died again, so Rusty told me to use the phone in the living room while he rummaged through the fridge for some lunch. So I called home, hoping I'd get Ma or Helmut, but it was Gonzo who answered.

"Oh, hey," I said, trying not to sound annoyed. "Could you do me a favour? Tell my mother I'm spending the afternoon at a friend's house."

At first I wondered if the line had gone dead. "I'm sorry— what?" he said.

"Tell Ma I'm at a friend's house."

"No—I heard what you said. I just don't get what you mean. A friend's house. Seriously. *You?*"

I could see the humour in this even as I started to get mad, so I shrugged. "Just fuck off and tell her I'll be home for supper—thanks," I said before hanging up.

When I turned around Rusty was standing in the doorway holding a red bell pepper and a knife. "Everything okay?"

"Yeah. My stepbrother likes to give me a hard time," I explained before I remembered that Rusty knows Gonzo from school but doesn't know we're connected to each other. I joined him in the kitchen, where he'd set out bread, lunch meat, hummus, and vegetables on the counter.

"So which one of your parents do you live with?" he asked as we assembled our sandwiches.

That seemed like an odd question, but, thinking I might have heard wrong, I told him I lived with my mother and my stepfather.

"Do you see your dad often?"

I stopped what I was doing—I was so confused that the term "flabbergasted" would have been fitting. I felt my eyes widen as a different kind of faintness from what I'd felt in the locker room started to take over. "Um—no. He's dead. He died in a car crash when I was nine."

Rusty dropped the knife he was holding and put his hand to his mouth. He looked horrified. "Holy shit," he said. "You mean that was *true?* I'm so sorry, Dale—I didn't know. Well, I *did* know, but I didn't—I thought that was just something you—with that guy at the wedding reception who—"

"It's okay," I said before he could get tangled up any further. And after a while, I guess it was. It ended up opening the door to a fairly intense talk about death and life and parents as we sat down at the table opposite each other and started to eat in the homey quiet of his kitchen. Rusty told me all about this super-complicated belief system about the afterlife and hierarchies of angels and having the choice between reliving your own life without the ability to change any of your actions or being reincarnated as your own nemesis—or something. But the volume of detail surprised me given that we barely know each other. I mean, maybe he's the kind of guy who has no problem sharing that level of personal thought with every stranger he meets, but I'm not. Which I guess is why I can't bring myself to write down any of the things he told me.

As for my side of the conversation, I stuck mainly to platitudes and vague ideas about life after death that I've picked up from Reverend Heather's sermons about forgiveness and grace and crap like that. I ended up revealing next to nothing about myself—I seem to have a knack for this. And the whole time I kept glancing at his striped shirt, distracted by the memory of his skin and his freckles and his fur, even though I tried not to be.

Then Rusty's dad had to walk in and ruin everything.

"You said you were going to wash the car this weekend," Mitch said, even though it was barely one o'clock on Saturday afternoon. "And I hope you're not planning to leave all these dirty dishes."

"We're still eating," Rusty pointed out. "You remember Dale from the wedding, right?"

Undaunted, Mitch started to lecture Rusty or maybe both of us about chores and grades and responsibility and character and whatever. Rusty continued to eat his sandwich, nodding occasionally but not paying much attention. I followed his lead, filling up on olives until Mitch gave up on us and left the house.

"Don't worry about him," Rusty said as we filled up the dishwasher together. "I just smile and nod a lot."

"Hmm," I said.

I don't like Rusty's father. There—I said it. It's not that he isn't friendly—exactly—and I know I've met him only twice, but he has this irritating alpha male personality, which means he has to know everything *and* he always has to be right. It's not a good combination. He's the kind of guy who sees himself as being in charge and can't bear the idea of giving up that role. I can picture him as a Boy Scout leader, going on and on about trees and woods and stars and knots, insisting that everyone in the pack listen to him with rapt attention and not tolerating anyone talking back or fidgeting. Basically, he's a middle-aged version of the typical douchebag at school. I found out later that he's a history teacher at the private school for girls that's supposed to be our "sister school." Somehow that didn't surprise me.

I didn't tell Rusty what I thought about his dad—it seemed kind of rude, especially since I was standing in their house—but when he mentioned that both his parents had been born and raised here in Waterloo, I couldn't help myself. "What high school did your dad go to?" I asked.

Rusty stared at me as he put away some leftover slices of bread. "Ours. Why?"

"Oh, no reason," I said, trying not to grin with smug self-satisfaction. That's a phrase I read in a book once, and I couldn't figure out before what it meant. But I knew at that moment, because I had to repress it.

I hadn't thought there was much else to say about Mitch, but Rusty parked himself down next to me at the table and started telling me all about how his dad drives him bananas by nagging him about chores one minute and trying too hard to be his pal the next. "It's like he woke up the other morning and realized he's in his late thirties and he doesn't have any friends. And somehow that just leaves me. But it's like, you can't invite me to hang out with you and play video games and then start lecturing me about how I'm spending my allowance. It's like, pick a lane!"

We started comparing notes about the social lives of the adults we know well, and then he looked at me like he was pondering something, then decided to go for it. "What about your father? Did he still have friends?"

At first I was so stunned that after a few seconds of silence he tried to take it back. But I waved that away. "No—it's just—no one's ever asked me about my father since we told everyone who needed to be told that he'd died." So I put my thinking cap on and studied the wallpaper on the opposite wall, wishing I still had something to do with my hands as I pondered Rusty's question. "Well, let's see. There were three friends in particular that my father was still pretty tight with: Mike 1, Mike 2, and Gary. They all went to high school together—I think. Maybe one of the Mikes was from work. I haven't seen any of them since the funeral, so I don't remember."

"Why Mike 1 and Mike 2? Was one of them older than the other or something?"

"Oh, God—I don't know." But Rusty seemed so genuinely curious that I forced myself to figure out an answer. "Mike 1 bought me a toy magician's set when I was six or seven, and it was my favourite thing. He remembered the names of my stuffed animals and talked to me like I was a person, rather than some annoying kid who was always in the way. Mike 2? I guess I liked him well enough—and Dara, his wife, was nice, too—at least until she became too religious. But his idea of conversation was to tell me something ridiculous with a straight face—like his house had burned down, or his niece had entered a convent, or they were giving Big Bird his own spinoff show—and then roar with laughter when I believed him. One time he told me that they fill up a box of Cheerios by throwing two live ones into the box, waiting for them to reproduce until the box was full, then sealing the bag so all the Cheerios suffocated." When Rusty snorted with laughter, I said, "Yeah, I know—but I was seven! I remember looking at him wide-eyed as he told me this and just not being able to figure out if he was joking or not. So that's probably why I gave him lower billing."

The afternoon itself wasn't that eventful. We went to the family room and played video games, one of which had this super-complicated premise: Player A causes all sorts of natural disasters to befall a bucolic community, while Player B has to pick up the pieces—and every ten minutes the game makes you switch roles. It was weird, but the music was pretty catchy. After a few hours of that we hung out in Rusty's room, which was even messier than mine, and listened to some music that blared from an external speaker that looked like a hockey puck. Rusty sat on his unmade bed and made room for me, but I opted for the chair at his desk. I gathered from the posters on his walls and the objects strewn around that he likes cars, fishing, and baseball. Which means we have dick all in common.

I guess I'm making it sound like I had a horrible time. I didn't. But after a while there wasn't much to talk about, so I started to get bored. I'd ask him about some object in his room, receive a one-sentence answer, and move on to something else. He didn't ask me any questions, which was fine, because what on earth would I tell him?

*My choir is working on Gabriel Fauré's* Requiem *and I'm singing two solos—in Latin.* No.

*I listen to every piece of music by this list of composers that I keep in a binder and rate them—this is my idea of fun.* Nah.

*I've started writing letters to my dead father because I don't have anyone to talk to.* I don't think so.

As soon as it was reasonably close to supper time, I got up and told Rusty I had to go. I was taken aback when he asked me what I was doing tomorrow. Except for music afternoons with Jordana when we were younger, I'd just voluntarily hung out with a friend for the first time, and it had gone on for five hours. I figured I'd need most of Sunday to recover. So I told him I had to play at the church service in the morning and do chores and homework in the afternoon. "But I'll see you at school on Monday," I said, which I guess was a dumb thing to say, since the only time I've spoken to anyone at school recently is when I mouthed off to my math teacher.

Once I got home, I had more bullets to dodge at the supper table, because Ma was insanely curious about these developments. I did what I always do: I offered a "kind of, sort of" truth. "Oh, he's someone from school I bumped into at Sophie and Jenice's wedding, and he happened to be at the pool this morning with his mother and his baby sister," I said with a shrug.

"Do I know him?" Gonzo asked me across the table, like it was an innocent question.

"I don't think so," I said, trying to sound thoughtful. "Helmut, how did you make this delicious gravy?"

Thankfully, the conversation moved on. Ma told us about an argument she'd had a few days ago with a patient who didn't like flossing his teeth because it made his gums bleed. Apparently he hadn't bought her explanation that if only he flossed more often, his gums wouldn't bleed anymore. He'd retorted that it might be more effective to give up flossing entirely. I waited for the lull after her story, then asked her if I could ask her something, even though that's always seemed to me like a pointless question.

"For some reason, I was thinking today about Pa's friends—Mike and Mike and Gary. I was trying to think if we ever saw them again after Pa died, and somehow I'm just drawing a blank. We did see them again—didn't we?"

Now that Rusty had broken the seal about you as an acceptable topic of conversation, I saw no reason anymore to tiptoe around you or to use library voices or to never mention you at all. But as soon as I heard the clang of silverware hitting Ma's plate and saw the ashen look on her face, my heart sank, because I realized that even though *I* was ready to have an open conversation about you, *Ma* most definitely wasn't. She looked in my direction, but her eyes weren't quite making contact with mine, as though she'd been badly frightened.

"I don't remember, honey," she said. "It was all such a long time ago."

And with that she rose from the table and went upstairs, even though we hadn't finished eating. After a few minutes, Helmut said something I can't remember exactly, but basically it meant I shouldn't ever bring you up again. "Don't you remember how hard all that was for her?"

I could tell from his tone and from the way he glared at me that he was trying to shame me into silence—because that's what people do, apparently, when someone brings up something they don't like. But for once, that made me angry rather than ashamed. I jumped out of my seat—I swear I never react to things this way—and leaned across the table toward him.

"He was *my father*, Helmut. And you weren't even there!"

I started to march away, then came right back to grab my dinner plate and bring it with me downstairs. Part of me thought for sure someone would follow me down so we could talk it over, but no one did. So I sat in my room, put on an album by Ludovico Einaudi, and decided to write to you before today's events fade from my mind.

As for Rusty, part of me wonders what will happen next, and another part of me dreads it. I mean, today was fine, but I don't know if I can spend time with someone regularly. Well, wait—I think I *could* do it, but I'm not sure I particularly want to.

You know what? I'm jumping to conclusions again. Rusty probably just wanted to hang out with me some more because we like the same kinds of video games. He'll find someone else to spend time with sooner or later and forget all about me. So I should try to relax. At any rate, this'll be good practice for when I make a *real* friend. Till then, there's not much else to say, except good night. And that's a relief, because while writing this letter I've discovered how oddly stressful harpsichord music is. The last piece I've been listening to might as well have been called "L'Exquise des Jangled Nerves," so it's time to put it away.

Your loving son,

Dale

## WEDNESDAY, APRIL 20

Dear Pa,

I know I told you I was looking forward to a recovery day after spending all of Saturday with Rusty, but then I seemed to come down with a case of the Sunday sads. I stayed up late that night finishing the last book in the Merciful Unravelling series, which meant I had this weird book hangover at school the next day. Then Monday night after supper I plugged my cellphone in and went online. Soon enough my phone beeped to let me know I had a text, which turned out to be from Rusty.

*I'm bored. What are you up to?*

I was in the middle of watching amateur storm footage of trees falling down, trampolines blowing away, and hail pellets the size of golf balls denting car hoods, so I texted back, *Looking up bands I like online.* When I realized that was hardly enough to keep the party going, I sent another one: *You?*

First he asked me what bands I was looking up, then told me he had the perfect name for a band: Precarious Employment. I asked him what kind of music that band would play, and he wrote back, *Some kind of ska-country-reggae fusion.*

That led to us brainstorming unlikely band names, which then prompted us to dream up lists of unlikely names for a bunch of other things. I'm going to give you some of the highlights, not only because I laughed so hard I nearly peed my pants, but also because I need to set the scene for what happened at school today.

Unlikely band names: So-and-So and the Whatevers. Condiments for 100. Gory Hand Job. (Wait—is "hand job" one word or two? I'll have to look it up.) Combative Vegans. Creed by Committee. Sounds Like Tuberculosis. Aching Testicles. Tacos in Bed.

Unlikely video game titles: Apostle's Apoplexy. After the Rapture. Red Tape. Hell Bus Ride. Vasectomy City. Ménage-à-Six. Plague of the Mullet. Plastic Surgery. Zombie Pool Boy.

Unlikely cat names: Carol. Donna. Steve. Doug. Hypotenuse. Ms. Montrose.

Unlikely dance routines: The Wolf Scat. The Mad Cow Disease. The Nutjob. The Gutsy Burglar. The Bad Gemini Moment. The Bro Code. The Angry Intestine.

Unlikely sequels: *Superman VII: The Flaccid Years. Sweet Valley Retirement Home. Cinderella V: Gus-Gus's Revenge. Little Red Riding Hood* from the point of view of the picnic basket. *The Hardy Boys in the Mystery of the Mid-Life Crisis.*

Unlikely breakfast cereals: Sugar-Frosted Garbage. Nuts 'n' Things. Buckets o' Crap. Pig Trough. Most of the others were so gross that they don't need to be recorded.

Unlikely names for a baby born into royalty: Cody. Amber. Rhoda. Bucky. Chester. Linda.

And when Rusty said "radtastic" again, we held a contest for new merge words, or what Google tells me are called "portmanteau words." We started with some pretty tame ones—like vomitrocious, scandalicious, ginormagantuan, screambarf, and tabootastic—before things degenerated into ways I'd never admit to anyone alive: wank-idextrous (the ability to masturbate with either hand), newdity (the novelty of seeing someone naked for the first time), and Zephyrillis (an STI you catch on a ship). When Rusty mentioned that all the street names in his grandmother's neighbourhood refer to parts of the solar system, I suggested a neighbourhood where streets are named after sex terms, and this made us come up with Bi-Curious Drive, Fellatio Court, Aphrodisiac Avenue, Polygamy Place, Side Boob Boulevard, and Premature Ejaculation Crescent.

We stayed up late until I couldn't take it anymore. Probably for the first time in my life I fell asleep laughing, and I'm pretty sure I woke up laughing, too. But that isn't as fun as it sounds, because it meant I couldn't stop. Even sitting myself down mentally and say-ing, *Okay, Cardigan—that's enough now* only made everything come flooding back. I managed to shake it off by lunchtime, at which point I was looking forward to a tame afternoon of math and media studies.

You probably know where I'm going with this.

Ms. Montrose called the class to order and started to write the day's math lesson on the board. Suddenly the fact that one of us had come up with "Ms. Montrose" as an unlikely cat name proved too much for me. I bit down on my lower lip. I tried to think about something else—*anything* else—like angry nuns and roadkill and Mozart's dead body being tossed into a pauper's grave. I took deep breaths. But then my head pivoted in Rusty's direction across the room, and he looked back at me and grinned, like he was thinking the same thing, and the funny just became bigger than me. I burst out laughing—literally. It was like a rerun of my crying episode, but with the emotions reversed. It happened when Ms. Montrose's back was turned, so I knew she'd assume I was laughing at her. I wasn't, but there was no way I could explain that I was laughing because her name would be so ludicrous for a cat.

After what seemed like an eternity, I got all the funny out of my system. I looked up and saw Ms. Montrose staring at me in silence, marker in hand, with the same expression my grade seven teacher had had when I'd defined "incongruous" as "Suzanne Vega's pop song about child abuse." Then I glanced around and noticed the other guys in the room staring at me wide-eyed like we were all at a funeral that had just taken a weird turn. So I sighed and did the only thing I could think of. I stood up. "I'm sorry. Do you want me to go down to the office?" I asked.

Now there was dead silence. I couldn't figure out from Ms. Montrose's face if she thought that I was mocking her or that I'd gone insane, but finally she let out the breath she'd been holding.

"No—just—just sit down," she said, sounding more concerned than angry.

I suddenly felt deflated and overheated, and all I could do for the rest of the afternoon was stare at my desk. Once the final bell rang, I thought about trying to find Ms. Montrose to apologize, but I couldn't shake the feeling that that would make things worse. So I went home. I didn't say anything to Uncle Joe when he picked me up for rehearsal, since it would have been such a stupid thing to explain.

But do you know the worst part of all this? Rusty stopped texting me. I guess I scared him away.

I've had my iPod on shuffle all this time, and just as I typed out that last paragraph, a song came on by a band called Phornicatrix, whose backup singers sound like lowing cattle. The lead singer has a hint of baby voice, which I don't usually like, but hers has a certain maturity to it, if that makes any sense. Still, it doesn't fit the mood I'm going for, so I'll stop for now.

Your loving (and possibly insane) son,

Dale

## SATURDAY, APRIL 23

Dear Pa,

It's Easter weekend, which means I've been at church more than usual because of some extra services, but since I get paid by the hymn, I don't mind. The highlight today—or, maybe more accurately, the thing that marked a break in my routine—was that I drove over to see Jordana, who's home from Boston for the long weekend.

She'd emailed me a couple of weeks ago to let me know she'd be free to get together, but when I wrote back and she didn't respond, I'd shrugged and figured that was that. Then when I got home last night, Ma told me Jordana had called our landline to summon me to a restaurant called the Chew Chew, located in an old train car on an abandoned track in downtown Guelph, today at noon.

Sometimes, when I haven't just seen her, I tell myself that the great thing about me and Jordana is that we can pick up where we left off, even when we haven't been in touch for months. Like Ma and Beverly, except that Ma and Beverly like each other. But I don't like Jordana anymore. I don't like what she's become. And I don't like how *I* become when I'm with her. Yet I hang out with her sometimes when she's home and try to stay in touch with her when she's not, I guess because I like the idea of our friendship. I thought I was having a good time while I was there, but I ended up sighing a lot on the drive home.

I got there a few minutes after twelve. Jordana hadn't yet arrived, so I got a table, sipped some water, and tried to ignore the pangs in my stomach whenever the cute waiter came by to ask if I needed a few more moments to make up my mind. To pass the time I pulled up my pant leg, played with my leg hair, and wondered if Ma had got the message wrong and Jordana had actually wanted to meet at midnight instead of at noon.

Finally Jordana breezed in, her eyes fixed right on me as soon as she entered, as though she'd known all along where I'd be sitting. I stared at her all-black outfit and her side ponytail and her "cultural studies glasses," as Sophie and Jenice would have called them, and tried to shake off the sudden wave of weariness that hit me. I stood up and tried to look game for anything.

"Dally."

"Jordi."

I hate those nicknames. They bring back memories of kids calling me Dilly Dally, which infuriated me when I was eleven. I tried to figure out from Jordana's body language whether she expected me to hug her or not. In the end, she held my hands across the table like we were at a seance, and then she asked if we could switch places because the seat I was in would allow her to have a better energy flow.

In a way, the fact that we've been friends for so long is part of the problem: we know how to push each other's buttons. As soon as I sat down again she made a crack about sideburns that made it abundantly clear she found mine idiotic, and to get back at her I ordered the eggplant parmigiana because I remembered she'd once told me even the word "eggplant" made her want to gouge her eyes out. Thankfully the waiter kept calling me "buddy" and "fella" as he took our order, and that made me feel better.

Jordana has changed a lot since the last time I saw her. She's grown into an intelligent, articulate young woman. Which is one way of saying she spent most of the time talking—about what she's been playing on the cello, her friends, her classes, the boy she's been "hanging out" with (that's the phrase she used), and what it's like to live in a boarding school full of artsy teenagers where the students outnumber the adults thirty to one. Apparently she's gone New Age, which means she had a lot to say about her chakras. She'll be traipsing off to Vienna this summer—as much as it's possible to traipse while lugging a cello—where she'll attend a week-long string orchestra workshop that's apparently so intense that quite a few people have died from it. She told me she went online and diagnosed herself with oppositional defiant disorder, and because of her school's student-centred approach to health, now she can pretty much do whatever the fuck she wants with total impunity. Or do I mean immunity? You know what I mean.

Normally I'm only too happy to keep the focus off me in a conversation, but with Jordana I didn't even have to try. She reminded me of Burt, except she had more than one trick in her playbook.

"My eye swelled to the size of a golf ball because I'd been wearing a super-old contact lens. I made the mistake of googling it and for a while I thought I had oracular herpes. No! I mean *ocular*. God—was that a weird Freudian slip or what!"

"We call her Greasy Bangs because she has greasy bangs."

"He was becoming ridiculously high maintenance with his super-toxic energy, so I had to cut all ties with him."

"A woman in a green woollen Victorian cape frowned at me, and I burst out laughing for no reason."

"She was trying to redefine herself. I don't know how successful she was. I listened to the first track and it sounded okay. I thought the bridge happened too soon. I don't know about the rest of it."

"I mean, I know he's supposed to be her boyfriend, but he's, like, so gay. Like—*soooo gaaaay*. It's like, face the facts, sweetheart!"

"Like, whatever happened to Billy Ocean? Did he drown?"

Her phone buzzed a couple of times a minute, too, which meant she kept interrupting herself to read and answer text messages. One time, she glanced at her phone, her eyes widened, and she placed it back on the table right away. When I asked her what was wrong, she made a face and told me she just couldn't even.

I'd wanted to tell her about playing the organ, about Sophie and Jenice's wedding, about living in Waterloo—hell, even about what's been going on with Rusty. But every time I tried to jump into the conversation, she skilfully steered it back to herself. Once she even did it while in the middle of asking me a question.

Every once in a while she'd pick up her sandwich, bring it to her mouth like she was going to bite into it, leave it hanging there for a few seconds, then return it to her plate. She kept doing this, like it was a type of physical exercise. Eventually I started interjecting random things when she paused to sip her water, but she didn't seem to hear me. It was strange—like we were talking *at* each other, not *with* each other.

We ended up staying for three hours. That was how long it took her to finish her lunch because she literally would not stop talking, and even then she had to pack up part of it. The whole time we were there, I couldn't help but remember what had happened right before she'd left for Boston almost three years ago. Basically she told me she'd always been crazy about me and started sucking my face off. And I was kind of into it, which you'll probably find surprising, even though you're dead. I wonder if she remembers that.

What am I thinking? She can't possibly have forgotten. And yet we've never spoken about it. It's this weird *thing* between us now.

I did manage to tell her a bit about the coffee house at Sophie and Jenice's wedding reception. When I tried to describe the wedding, she cut me off to tell me lesbian weddings are all the rage at her school and apparently you're not considered cool until you know someone who's been to one, which led to this long explanation about all the things you can do at her school to show people how cool you are. Later I told her about the woman who'd asked me to perform at an event coming up—I forget if I've mentioned this to you yet, but she got in touch with me and wants to set something up for July. Jordana's response, or at least the thing she said after that, was how happy she was to have her scholarship so she could focus all her energy on music without having to—I forget the exact way she put it, but it was something like "prostitute her art." I was halfway home before I figured out she'd meant that as a dig.

Eventually she threw out hints about me going to visit her in Boston at some point, which made my eyes widen. Judging by the number of unanswered texts on my phone, I'd honestly thought our friendship was in the last stages of dying. But I didn't ask her why it seemed so hard for us to keep in touch—in the end, I realized I didn't want to know. She seemed disappointed that I wasn't more enthusiastic about visiting her, but the idea of being trapped with Jordana in a strange city for more than a couple of hours made me want to kick the table in self-defence.

Our lunch depressed me, so when Jordana invited me to spend the afternoon with her, I said I couldn't because my mother needed the car. Instead I drove to our old house, parked across the street, and looked at it for ten or fifteen minutes. Then I drove to the high school I would have attended if we hadn't left Guelph—a red-brick building I hadn't seen in years—and played a game I invented called What If as I sat in the otherwise empty parking lot. What would my life have been like if you hadn't died? If I'd gone to school here, would I have had a friend my own age by now? If we'd stayed here after you died, would I have found it comforting or upsetting whenever I bumped into someone who knew you? If you hadn't died and we'd stayed here, would I have been happy?

It was a relief to visit our old house and my might-have-been school without needing to ask anyone to take me there or to explain to anyone why I wanted to go. Like Ma. Especially Ma. I thought about heading to the cemetery next, but I didn't want to be late for supper. So I drove home and listened to a lot of sad music. I have a playlist on my iPod called "Gut-Wrenching" that usually does the trick. And oddly enough, I felt better.

One thing Jordana told me was how competitive her school is—and not always in a good way. Apparently there's such limited opportunity and attention that the super-aggressive students do whatever they can to stay on top. It sounds even more cutthroat than my school, and that's saying a lot. Sometimes I think it's just as well I didn't get in.

Your loving son,

Dale

## SUNDAY, APRIL 24

Dear Pa,

It never rains but it pours. No—that doesn't really capture what I want to say. I can't think of a better turn of phrase, though, so I'll just tell you what happened.

Today's Easter Sunday, and since we've had a bunch of nice days in a row recently, we celebrated by spending the afternoon doing yardwork. Gonzo and I are usually in charge of the lawn, whether that means raking it, fertilizing it, mowing it, putting a tarp over it, or rolling the tarp up and putting it away. I like mowing the lawn—it has to be done, and I have two arms, so I do it. I'm less thrilled about raking the dead leaves that the snow forgot to decompose over the winter since it basically involves stirring up leftover death, and today I was annoyed that Gonzo was out with Iliana and his grandparents for Easter dinner, because it made more work for me. But I had reason to be thankful for his absence later on.

Helmut doesn't like it if I listen to music with headphones while I'm working in the yard. He's afraid that if the lawn mower decides to turn against me or a satellite falls out of the sky, I won't be able to hear it in time. Thankfully he can't control what I think, so when I'm working outside I daydream about something I've seen or read or listened to, or if I'm desperate, I think about homework, and that helps pass the time.

I was about halfway done raking the front lawn when Rusty jogged by. I had my back to him, and when I turned in frustration because I couldn't get the stupid yard waste bag open, there he was, like he'd appeared out of nowhere, much like that time at the pool. And—well—I doubt I'd ever tell this to anyone who's alive, but I kind of felt a rush of something when I saw him and that toothy grin of his. It was like my heart rose in my chest and sank at the same time. And I think I've finally figured out what's happening.

In a way, it's pretty simple and straightforward: I was happy to see him. I like him.

But in another way, it isn't. Because I realized for the first time that I was *very* happy to see him—that I *really* like him. And that's bound to cause some problems if we're going to be friends or whatever.

I forced myself not to think about that as I tossed the rake aside and joined him on the sidewalk.

"Oh, hey," he said with a laugh, pulling his earbuds out. I couldn't help but notice that the cord disappeared somewhere inside his shirt. "I didn't know you lived here."

"That's right," I said. It wasn't something I could deny, unless I claimed to be working as a chore boy at someone else's house. "Have you just started jogging?"

"This year—yeah. I usually go to the park near my house, but it's still too soggy." He was out of breath, and his cheeks had started to match his hair. I can't say I hated the effect.

"Neat. What are you listening to?"

He started telling me about this band I'd never heard of called Diabolical Clutches. From the way he described them they sounded decent enough, and when I hummed with mild interest he offered me one of his earbuds and stuck the other one back in his ear. At first I took a step away from him—this was such a Jonathan thing for him to do—but soon we were standing on the sidewalk listening to the song, facing each other, our heads linked by a short wire, and that's when it dawned on me how much I like him. You know. Physically. Sexually. I am sexually attracted to him. Or should that be "I am attracted to him sexually"? Either way, it's like his body was a magnet and was drawing me closer and closer.

I guess I'd kind of known but hadn't known before, if that makes any sense. But at that moment, I knew—oh, boy, did I ever. At one point he lifted his sweaty T-shirt to scratch his belly button and I thought I was going to puke—*in a good way*.

As we stood there listening to the song, I could feel his breathing slow down. Soon I started to get this uncontrollable urge to put my arms around his waist and kiss his cheek, consequences be damned. I let myself enjoy that feeling for a few seconds, then forced myself to think about kittens and state capitals and the hypotenuse of right-angled triangles until it went away.

Because of course it's impossible.

And that's when I noticed that the song we were listening to was about an impossible love. I'm not sure what made it impossible— the lead vocalist wasn't big on consonants, so I'd need to listen to it again to find out—but it was like Rusty had read my mind and this was his diplomatic way of saying, "Yeah—don't even think about it."

I ended up pulling the earbud out and stepping away from him halfway through the final chorus.

"Oh, there's another one on here I think you'll like," he said, pulling his iPod out of his pocket and scrolling through his songs before I could say anything. "It's literally the best song ever. Ready?"

I shrugged and put the earbud back in. "Sure. I guess the lawn can wait a few more minutes."

The second song was by a band called Fox in the Snow, I think. In many ways it was a pretty standard power ballad, a couple of notches above the average Climax offering. It started with a simple guitar riff, some minor piano in the background, and a single vocal track. More and more layers were added as the song progressed: a drum line, more piano, some backing vocals, even horns and strings. The piano started to double the lead vocal line, then did something else. My eyes closed of their own will, and soon, without any effort on my part, I ceased to be aware of anything except the music and the lyrics, the cool spring air, and the warmth of Rusty beside me on the sidewalk. The singer was telling someone how difficult it was to express how he felt and inviting the person to step into an alternate dream state where they could be together and forget the world. I'd need to listen to it again to get it fully, but right there on the sidewalk I was so moved that by the time it was over I'd started to cry a little. I opened my eyes, and all I could see was a blurry Rusty smiling at me. When he saw my reaction, he reached over and touched my arm. "Dale," he said.

I can't describe exactly how he said it. The word "tender" comes to mind, but that makes him sound like a steak.

"I'm fine," I said, shaking my head. "Music does this to me sometimes."

Then I heard another voice. "Dale? Are you okay?"

I turned and saw Helmut several paces away from us on the front walk, staring at us like we were up to something obscene. "Oh, hey," I said, pulling the earbud out and stepping away from Rusty. "We were just listening to music."

"On the sidewalk?"

"Well, yeah. I think I'm allergic to all these dead leaves. This is—um—this is Rusty, a friend of mine from school. Rusty, this is Helmut, my stepfather."

Rusty marched right up to Helmut and held out his hand. "It's a pleasure to meet you, sir."

I thought about being mortified, but it was too funny to watch my stepfather start off stern and skeptical and then melt like a bowl of ice cream in a microwave. I think something about being called "sir" mollifies him, even though he really is a likeable guy. "Rusty, is it?" he said as they shook hands.

"That's right, sir. It's short for Russell."

"Fuck," I said. Fortunately they were too wrapped up in each other to hear me.

They kept talking, and after a while I started to wonder if they'd forgotten I existed. Just as I was about to pick up the rake again, though, Helmut turned to me.

"Dale, when you're done raking the leaves, would you mind helping your mother get the patio furniture out of the shed? I think she'd also like to meet your friend here."

"Would she," I said flatly.

"Yes, she would," Ma said pleasantly as she approached us from the side of the house. She didn't even look my way. "Hello there. I'm Susan, Dale's mother. You must be Dale's friend."

"Um—sure. I'm Rusty Friesen. It's nice to meet you, Susan."

I couldn't help but notice that Ma referred to him as my friend, singular, like it was so unthinkable that I might have more than one. Which I guess it is. All I could do was watch as the three of them made small talk about the weather and the neighbourhood. It was like I was becoming a spectator in the drama of my own life.

"Honey, there's a pitcher of lemonade in the fridge," Ma said to me once she'd remembered I was there. "Why don't you invite your friend inside for some?"

I think I let out a slightly strangled sound. I don't know why—it's not like Gonzo was home. Rusty looked at me and squinted.

"Thanks very much, Susan, but I can't stay. Our algebra homework has been driving me crazy—I should probably get back to it."

"Oh, well, Dale's been doing well with algebra," Ma pointed out almost hopefully, her voice rising several octaves higher than usual. I looked at her, wondering where she'd got that impression—it's not like I ever talk to her about school work—but she had eyes only for Rusty. "Maybe you boys could do your homework here together sometime. I'm sure Dale would be glad to help you. Wouldn't you, honey?"

My head turned to Rusty and then back to Ma. I tried to figure out what diabolical scheme she had up her sleeve, but I couldn't read anything between the lines. She just seemed glad I'd made a friend. I turned to Rusty, trying to act neutral, though I probably came across as robotic. "Yeah—or whatever."

The corners of Rusty's mouth curved into a smile before he looked away. "Okay—maybe," he said. And after a few more rounds of pleasantries, he took off.

Ma and Helmut watched him jog away. They even had their arms around each other, like that was helping them savour the moment. I turned to Ma, trying to figure out what I was supposed to say to her.

"What a nice young man," she said finally. I couldn't tell if she was talking to me or to Helmut or to herself. Then she saw me looking at her, at which point her brow creased. "What is it, honey?"

Now that Rusty was gone, I felt this weird wave of anger ripple through me, almost like an internal earthquake. This whole interaction was reminding me of the few times she'd tried to arrange playdates for me with other children when I was little, which meant toys and sports and board games and sharing, and which ended with someone—usually but not always me—in tears. It finally dawned on me that her perception of me hasn't changed. She always assumes that if I don't try to make plans with someone, it's because I'm shy, not because I don't fucking want to. But I knew there was a lot she wouldn't understand and I had no intention of explaining any of it to her, so I forced myself to dial it back.

"Nothing. It's just—I know you meant well, Ma, but I can manage my own time," I said, feeling a rattle in my throat in spite of myself.

"I don't understand. Your friend needs help, and you'd rather sit around in your room doing nothing?" she said.

And there, in a nutshell, is the difference between us. She's a people person—a doer—someone who likes to keep busy. If there's something that needs to be done—yardwork or staying late at the office or making food for an elderly neighbour or trying to talk Beverly off a ledge—she plunges in without hesitation. She reads books and the newspaper and watches the news every night, but the idea of sitting around an empty room contemplating the secrets of the universe holds no appeal for her. Probably she thinks that when I'm in my room with the door closed I'm brooding or masturbating, and she doesn't want to know about either activity. The fact that we're different isn't the problem—it's that she can't fathom anyone perceiving the world differently than she does. She can't understand that when I'm sitting in my room listening to music for hours on end, I'm not brooding—and I'm not masturbating either, at least not most of the time. I *want* to sit and read and listen to music by myself. What I listen to and think about isn't the background—it's the focus. It's the rest of my life right now that's in the background.

As we faced off on the lawn I realized there wasn't anything else to say, so I exhaled the rest of my frustration and picked up the rake again. By the time I'd turned around, both she and Helmut had disappeared.

Dinner tonight was a bit of an ordeal, given that Ma and Helmut had to do all the talking. Ma told us a funny story about a colleague of hers who'd cracked a tooth while gnawing on a finger-nail and refused to get it fixed, even though he's literally a dentist, but I just stared at my plate. Fortunately I've had several years of experience making myself invisible, so no one seemed to notice when I helped myself to a third serving of ham and scalloped potatoes.

This has happened before—me liking another guy. Usually all I do is wait it out until it goes away. Of course, except for Jonathan (sort of), this is the first time I've been attracted to someone I've actually spoken to, someone I could feasibly be friends with if we wanted. But otherwise, it's nothing new. Back in grade seven there was this boy on the bus—for months I couldn't keep my eyes off him. I didn't know anything about him except that he was a year older than me. And then, when I started high school, I did find one of Gonzo's friends particularly fetching, although I'm not going to say which one on the off chance Gonzo goes snooping on my computer when I'm out. (*That's right, Gonzo! I'm on to you!*) And there's a man at church in his early twenties, I think, who has a goatee and an eyebrow ring and eyes that are the hottest shade of green—I've never dared go near him. And there've been others.

Shit—I just thought of something.

Since this afternoon I haven't been able to stop thinking about what Ma said after Rusty had jogged away. "What a nice young man." I'd found it irritating; Gonzo has friends here sometimes and she's never made cracks like that about any of them, whether she thinks they're nice or not. But it just hit me: she *did* say something like that last fall, when Gonzo started hanging out with this girl he'd met at a dance with our sister school. "What a nice young lady," she'd said then, as she watched her and Gonzo walk away. (I forget where they were going or why I was there to see them off, but I remember that her name was Gwennifer, that she was awesome, and that I couldn't imagine what she and my stepbrother had to talk about.) So—what? Does that mean she

Sorry for stopping in midsentence. My phone just beeped to let me know I've received a Facebook friend request from none other than Russell Friesen.

I've been sitting here for the last couple of minutes, muttering obscenities under my breath. I don't know what to do! I really like Rusty, and clearly he wants to be friends with me. I want to be friends with him. With most people this wouldn't be a problem. *Is* this a problem? I mean, the fact that I secretly have the hots for him? Facebook makes it seem so official: *Do you want to be friends with him? Yes or no? Decide now.*

Well, for starters, I don't think I've ever had a friend before. Jordana and I hung out when we were younger because we both loved music, but all that's left of that now is memories and the occasional torturous lunch. Sophie and Jenice like me and I like them, but we've never spent time together outside church except when it had to do with wedding plans. I don't think I know how to have a friend. Or how to *be* a friend.

No! I need to follow the same advice I gave myself last weekend in the locker room. Stop overthinking everything and stop being such a fucking chicken! I barely interact with people on Facebook. I use it to get news about bands I like. The only friends I've added recently are some of the people I met at Sophie and

Jenice's wedding, and we never talk to each other. Rusty and I have seen each other naked, so what's the harm in letting him be my friend on some stupid website?

So I hit the "accept" button, and then I started reading through his status updates. Some of them are pretty clever—I like that. And then, within minutes, I got a notification that Rusty had posted on my wall. What he wrote indicated that he, too, hadn't wasted any time browsing my profile. He must have gone straight to my photo album as soon as I accepted his friend request, because his post said, *I didn't know you played the violin.*

And then, a few minutes later, I got a text from him: *Unlikely ice cream flavours.* That's all it said, but it led to a back and forth that kept going until I had to tear myself away: Hellish Hash, Candy Floss Pink-Eye Swirl, Bear Patty, Prunes and Ipecac, and Pralines and Bed Bugs.

I once read something about Pandora's box, but I couldn't figure out what it meant. I still don't exactly, but I have a funny feeling I've just enacted the online version of it and I'm about to find out what the consequences will be.

Your loving son,

Dale

**FRIDAY, APRIL 29**

Dear Pa,

I started to write to you a few times this week, but there didn't seem to be much to tell you about. It occurred to me today that something *is* happening, though.

It's Rusty. Somehow, I have a friend! And it's all happening electronically!

There was no school on Monday because of the Easter holiday, so I went to church in the morning to practise the organ. There are a couple of pieces I've been working on as postludes for May and June, and I'm trying to pace myself. While I was there, my phone beeped to let me know I had a Facebook message that read *Unlikely salad dressing flavours* and a text message that read *Unlikely Christmas carols*, both from Rusty, sent within seconds of each other. I gave it some thought before answering them one after the other: Raunchy Ranch and "This Christmas I Despise You All." Not my best work, but pretty good for the Monday morning of a long weekend. Then, minutes later, he sent me his own answers: Balsamic Meth and "Cram It Up Your Chimney."

We ended up texting each other so much that at one point Reverend Heather came out of her office wondering if the organ music starting and stopping so abruptly over and over again was my way of signalling for help.

It petered out by midafternoon. I figured the ball was in my court after that, so after loading up the dishwasher I sent Rusty a text that read *Unlikely tea flavours.* We spent the evening swapping answers and a bunch of emoticons and initialisms that indicated that we were rolling on the floor laughing. Honey Lemon Ativan, Sleepy Toxic Slime, Stinging Nettle (although I found out later that's an actual flavour), Dishwasher Sludge, Rotten Broccoli, Sour Cough Drop, and Runny Nose were some of the highlights.

We spent the rest of the week keeping this up between classes, with a list of unlikely stripper names (you'd be amazed how long it took us to exhaust that one), unlikely workshops at a hippie music festival (like Unleashing Your Inner Rage, Fist-Bumping Your Inner Bro, and How to Make Your Enemies Pay), unlikely gum flavours, unlikely fashion trends, unlikely smartphone apps, unlikely game show premises, and unlikely hyphenated surnames (like Belchy-Burpee and Frost-Knipping). Not all of our answers were gems, and thankfully I didn't have any more unexplainable outbursts of emotion in class, but our game sustained a mild state of hysteria between us throughout the week.

Then it started to get ridiculous.

When I woke up this morning, I checked my phone and discovered a text I'd sent Rusty in the middle of the night, referencing Crotchisil, in response to his question about unlikely medication names. I had no recollection of doing this.

And all this time, Rusty and I seemed to have this unspoken gentlemen's agreement that we weren't to acknowledge each other at school. I was glad of this, since my cone of silence isn't something

I want to mess with any more than I have to, but I didn't understand it. This afternoon, as I was standing in front of my locker cramming my umbrella into my backpack, I sensed someone standing behind me, and there was Rusty, holding up his phone and offering me his answer to my challenge about unlikely children's picture books: "*They're Called Chickens and We Eat Them*," he said with a triumphant laugh, like he was proud of his wit, before walking away.

If he'd stayed, I probably would have asked him if he wanted to hang out. I'd never done that before, but it can't be too hard if everyone else on earth seems to manage it just fine. But he didn't stay. I followed him to the bus stop, where he was talking with someone about our media studies teacher, and I felt like such a chump. Not because Rusty had done anything mean or because he seemed pissed at me—in fact, I ended up getting a text from him about unlikely university majors as soon as I got off the bus—but because it all seems so impossible. Even if he did want to hang out, what would we do? Sit around and make more lists?

Your loving son,

Dale

## WEDNESDAY, MAY 4

Dear Pa,

Yesterday, on the bus ride home from school, I was feeling kind of bummed out about everything—mainly about Rusty, who was sitting five feet away from me, texting on his phone. I do appreciate that he hasn't tried to talk to me at school—it's almost like he gets me—but that doesn't give me any freaking idea of what to do next. I tried to act like I was just looking in his direction, but no one was paying any attention to me anyway, which was depressing enough.

Then Rusty turned and looked right at me and held up his phone, without any change in his facial expression. When my eyebrows skewed together in confusion, he indicated the phone with his eyes before turning away. At this point I was dying of curiosity, so I dug through my backpack for my phone, turned it on, and felt my mouth water when I saw four texts from him.

The first, sent at 12:10: *Were you at the pool on Saturday? I couldn't go.*

The second, sent at 12:58, right before afternoon classes had started: *Unlikely cake flavours.*

The third, sent at 1:35, during math class: *Fuck I hate math!*

And the fourth, sent moments earlier: *Help me with algebra? All those Xs and Ys make me want to mutilate myself.*

I suppressed a smile, looked up at him and nodded, then texted back, *Yes. My place? Now?* Or at least that's what I meant to text. I ended up typing so fast that what I actually sent was *Yes. My place now!*

It was his turn to grin and nod. He snapped his phone shut and put it away, which I guessed was his reply. Ten seconds later I rang the bell for the driver to pull over, got off the bus, and turned to see Rusty standing behind me. It felt like we were spies. I waited until the bus had vanished around the corner, then smiled.

"Hey," I said.

"Hey. Thanks for being willing to help me."

"No problem. Did you text me from math class? That was ballsy, don't you think?"

"Why? If Ms. Montrose had caught me I'd have just told her I was using the calculator on my phone."

"No wonder you're having a hard time with algebra," I said.

Fortunately he found this funny rather than insulting. As we headed down the street to my house, I tried to bring to mind the current state of my bedroom before deciding to set up shop at the dining room table. I had a few reasons for suggesting we go to my place instead of his. First, Ma wouldn't get off my case about the fact that I'd had lunch at his house, so now it was his turn to be invited to a meal at mine. According to her, once a person invites another person to do something, proper etiquette dictates that this start a chain reaction of follow-up invitations that presumably continues until one person attends the other's funeral—otherwise it's incredibly rude. Second, I liked the idea of inviting him over when

I knew I'd have to leave for choir practice with Uncle Joe as soon as we finished eating.

Helmut was already making dinner by the time we got home. His hands were covered in egg and raw beef, so he and Rusty did that routine people sometimes do where they reach out to shake hands, then withdraw at the last second and make this "gotcha" sound, like they're the first people on earth to have dreamed up something so witty. Helmut was in a good mood—his latest case got thrown out after he unearthed CCTV footage that showed the plaintiff wilfully throwing himself down a flight of stairs, and this also explained why he was home so early. He was in a chatty mood, too, so it was clear we wouldn't get any work done in the dining room. I put together a snack for Rusty and me and led the way downstairs.

I guess part of me was secretly hoping that algebra was a pretext for us to hang out together, but it turned out that Rusty was genuinely confused about every single aspect of it. As soon as we sat down at the table downstairs, he loosened his tie, dug out his textbook, and spent the next five minutes eating cookies and complaining about variables and quadratic equations and how stupid they all were. My way of helping him was just to go over some of the problems with him and repeat what our teacher had shown us, but somehow it seemed to sink in.

"Oh! I get it now!" he said, sounding relieved as he scribbled away. "Thanks, guy. It's finally making sense. Somehow when Cassie explains it—"

"Cassie?" I said. "You mean Ms. Montrose?" The fact that he'd just called our math teacher by her first name was the most hysterical thing I'd heard all day.

It turned out Rusty's known her all his life. "She and my mom are super-good friends—they went to university together. She's over at my house all the time." Then he looked at me like he was assessing my face. "If I tell you something, can it stay in the vault?"

"Absolutely," I said. The truth is, I was far less interested in the actual secret than in the fact that he was entrusting me with one. I guess it's not surprising that he trusts me, since I literally never speak to anyone at school unless an adult compels me to, but still, parts of me started to tingle in anticipation.

"Ms. Montrose hates teaching," Rusty half whispered. He leaned closer in my direction as he spoke, even though we were alone in the room. "Big time. Apparently she always has. At first she figured it was because she was new, but then the novelty wore off and she still hated it. Then they offered her a permanent contract, and since the job market for teachers is vomitrocious she couldn't bring herself to turn it down because she'd beaten the odds. She's not even forty yet, and she's trapped in this job she despises, counting the years till retirement."

I studied his face throughout: the way his eyes lit up, the way his mouth curved into a smile as he spoke, the way his head kept bobbing toward me. At one point, his knee brushed up against mine under the table and stayed there. At first I liked the warmth and I didn't want to move. But then it almost felt like my knee was burning, so I dragged my leg away.

"Fuck," I said sympathetically. "She *told* you all this?"

"Of course not. I pieced it together from years of eavesdropping."

"Huh." I leaned back in my seat and thought it over. "That really sucks. I have to give her credit, though—she doesn't let it show. She's a good teacher, too. I've always kind of liked her. Not that I've ever spoken to her or anything."

I glanced at him with a minor avalanche of panic, realizing that I'd indirectly referenced my cone of silence, not to mention my crying and laughing fits, both of which had happened in Ms. Montrose's class. He might think I wanted to talk about them. So I kept going with whatever popped into my head next—which, as always, was idiotic.

"My uncle Scott's the same way," I said. "He works for some massive insurance company, which by itself isn't exactly a barrel of monkeys."

"Barrel of monkeys? Where do you *get* these weird expressions?" Rusty asked with a laugh. I forget how I responded to that.

"He works in this building that looks like a giant photocopier surrounded by parking lots. There's some issue with his boss— apparently the guy never does anything—and his boss's boss doesn't care that my uncle is constantly covering for him because she has too much of her own work to do. Every time we talk he gives me the latest instalment, like when you keep missing your favourite TV show and someone else has to fill you in. One time I said, 'Hey, Uncle Scott—if you hate your job so much, why don't you look for a new one?' He stared at me like I'd actually said, 'Hey, Uncle

Scott—why don't you moon your boss and see if that helps?' I think in his case he secretly likes the drama too much to do anything about it."

"That must suck for your aunt," Rusty observed.

"Oh. I don't have one."

"Really? Maybe we should set him up with Ms. Montrose," he said with a grin.

"No—trust me—they wouldn't hit it off."

I turned away, kind of embarrassed that I hadn't said more about Uncle Scott—like the existence of Uncle Joe. Somehow it felt like if I even acknowledged that I knew people who were gay, it would blow my cover about liking Rusty the same way. Then I figured that was stupid, since it's because of Sophie and Jenice that we started talking in the first place. But by then it was too late. We turned back to our homework, or at least I pretended to, and later I asked if he wanted something to drink and then left him alone while I went upstairs. As I poured two glasses of ginger ale, I asked Helmut if I could invite Rusty to stay for supper, and he seemed pleased. He likes to cook for an audience, I guess.

So I went downstairs and did just that—although, now that I think back on it, it probably sounded more like I was informing him that we wouldn't fight him if he stayed—and he called home and got the go-ahead from his mother. I have a feeling that he would have been given a hard time if his father had answered the phone instead, although Rusty didn't say anything about it.

Then, if my memory is accurate—and sometimes it isn't—we ran out of stuff to talk about after that, so he asked to see my room.

I couldn't see the harm, so I led the way in and made the bed. When I noticed him looking at stuff on the walls and on my shelves I felt another wave of panic, since my room wasn't set up for public viewing. He was smiling, but I couldn't tell if he was amused or pleased or appalled. The thought running through my head again was that we had nothing in common except for video games and lists of unlikely things. But that turned out to be all right, too.

"So—Joni Mitchell, huh?" he said, picking up a book on my nightstand.

"Yup," I said. "She's awesome. Her work takes some weird turns starting in 1975, but her early stuff kicks ass."

Oddly enough, it turned into a rerun of our conversation in his room a few weeks ago, except that he was asking me questions and seemed interested in the answers. But even though we were on my turf, I felt just as awkward as I'd felt in his room. I didn't know what to do with my arms or my legs. We were standing for the longest time, until finally Rusty sat down on the edge of my bed. I mean, it made sense since he was closer to the bed than I was. But it felt funny—almost gross.

Anyway, I did tell him about my upcoming solos—in Latin!—in Gabriel Fauré's *Requiem*. He wanted to know more about the overdubbing I'd done for Sophie and Jenice's wedding, so I booted up my laptop and showed him a few things I'd been working on. He seemed to think it was pretty cool, and that was fine, but then he asked me to sing the song from the wedding reception. Not *for* him, obviously, except there was no one else in the room. I really, *really* didn't want to, but he talked me into it. I would never have guessed

I could be so easily manipulated by those teddy-bear eyes of his and by the sound of his voice saying "Aw, come on," but I lost any willpower I possessed.

I turned back to my laptop to search for the right file. By the time I got the song going and turned around again, Rusty was *lying on his stomach on my bed*, grinning at me. I nearly died, but I managed to shut off that part of my brain because it was time for me to sing. Rusty looked like he was having the time of his life. At the wedding I'd sung the song seriously, but this time I worked in some lame boy-band hand gestures and basically hammed it up, partly to cover for the fact that I hadn't warmed up my voice and partly to make him laugh. Right before the bridge, I even tried a spin, but I only managed a three-quarter turn.

And, of course, it was at that point that I noticed Ma standing in the doorway, her eyes wide, like she couldn't fathom what on earth I was doing. Even though there wasn't much ambiguity: I was standing in my bedroom, serenading a boy I liked—who was lying on my bed—with a song entitled "Bedroom Eyes" by a boy band called Climax. But what was most mortifying was that it wasn't like that at all.

"Oh—hi, Ma," I said as the backup Dales kept going without me.

"Hi," Rusty managed to chime in as he sat up, shaking with laughter.

"I was just—singing a song," I explained. "To show Rusty some of my recording techniques."

Ma stared at me like I'd spoken to her in a language she'd never encountered before. "Supper's ready," she said. I couldn't hear her because of the chorus of Dales singing the words "bedroom eyes" over and over in a frantic crescendo, so she had to raise her voice and say it again.

*Ugh.*

And it was just as awkward at the table because of the interrogation. Ma has this knack of extracting information out of people under the guise of normal dinner-table chit-chat. By the time I'd finished my salad I'd found out more about Rusty, his house, his immediate and extended family, and his ancestors than I probably would have in my whole lifetime if left to my own devices.

I could tell Rusty was comfortable with it, because he kept calling Ma and Helmut by name. "The meat loaf's awesome, Helmut." "Dale tells me you work with teeth, Susan." "Yeah, I have distant relatives in Germany, Helmut, but I don't really talk to them except on Facebook." I don't think I've ever called Rusty's parents anything, except in my head.

Fortunately Ma took a break when the doorbell rang and she got up to see who it was.

I leaned over toward Rusty, who was sitting across from me on the chair that's usually Gonzo's. "For some reason I thought you were Jewish," I said.

"No—we're Mennonite."

I was weighing the pros and cons of asking him what that meant when I heard Ma's voice in the distance, greeting Uncle Joe and inviting him inside. Once he'd followed Ma into the dining room, he looked as astonished to see me as I was to see him.

"Kiddo, why aren't you ready?" he asked.

"You're way early," I protested.

"They wanted you there way early—to go over your solos. Remember?"

I stared at him like he was on crack, and then suddenly I did remember. Without a word I bolted from the table, ran downstairs, changed my shirt, got my music together, and repacked Rusty's backpack for him. Rusty and Uncle Joe were shaking hands when I got back to the dining room.

"It's nice to meet you, too, Uncle Joe," Rusty was saying with a friendly grin.

"In case you're wondering how I fit into this family, I'm married to Uncle Scott," Uncle Joe explained good-naturedly.

"Oh—uh-huh," Rusty said without missing a beat. I liked that about him.

"We sing in the same choir," I explained. Then, when Rusty's eyes grew wide, I tried not to crack up. "No—I mean literally. Our big concert's coming up in a few weeks."

I tried to shovel in a few forkfuls of food, but I had to make a decision—be late for my rehearsal and face the wrath of my temperamental choir director or leave Rusty to finish dinner with Ma and Helmut without me there as a buffer. In the end they insisted that Rusty stay, and so I left with Uncle Joe, still hungry and hoping he had some breath mints in the car.

We drove off in silence. At first I thought it strange that Uncle Joe wasn't dying of curiosity about what had just happened. I was still frazzled by the fact that I'd forgotten about this special rehearsal, so I was grateful for the quiet. But after we rounded the corner, the questioning began.

"Rusty seems nice. Where did you find him?" he asked, like Rusty was some trinket I'd picked out at a store.

"In my class at school," I said. I don't know if I sounded annoyed or proud or a combination of the two.

"I thought you didn't talk to anyone at school," he said, glancing at me. "Didn't you call it your shield of invisibility?"

"No—my cone of silence. And we don't talk at school. We keep bumping into each other elsewhere and then he'll start talking to me. Today on the bus he texted me to ask for help with algebra, so I invited him over." I was trying to make it sound like none of this was a big deal, but this was the first time in my life that anything like this had ever happened and we both knew it.

We stopped at a red light and Uncle Joe turned to look at me. "*What?*"

So I started at the beginning, giving him a very bare-bones account of the wedding, the pool, and him jogging by, leaving out anything to do with my feelings. I probably made us sound more like business acquaintances than friends.

"You mean to tell me he leaves you alone at school but keeps seeking you out everywhere else?" he said as we pulled into the parking lot. "Man—he must really like you."

I didn't know what he meant, but part of me was afraid to ask. Since then, I've played that line over and over in my head, and I still don't have any answers.

I've been listening, or trying to listen, to the latest album by some UK singer-songwriter Jordana's obsessed with, even though it has twenty tracks and most of them are super boring; the music's good, but all the lyrics are one platitude after another. Jordana would kill me for saying this, but someone really should have pulled him aside and said, "You know what? No." So now it's time to stop.

Your loving (and frazzled) son,

Dale

## THURSDAY, MAY 5

Dear Pa,

This morning I got caught in that trap where my alarm clock kept ringing every nine minutes, and then I'd press the "snooze" button and fall back asleep. By the time I managed to crawl out of bed, I only had time to take the quickest shower in the universe and to spread some peanut butter on a slice of bread—there wasn't even time to make toast. All day I've been this ball of nerves, threatening to electrocute anyone who gets too close. I rallied a little after lunch, but the only thing keeping me from passing out on my desk was the prospect of killing time after school with some mind-numbing TV.

Unfortunately the gods decided that I needed more drama to spice up my life. Rusty and I chatted again by text message on the bus ride home. Gonzo's at his mother's this week, so when Rusty asked if we could hang out, I invited him to my house again, even though technically it was his turn to host. Turned out Gonzo had left some schoolbooks in his room at our house, and so twenty minutes later he wandered into the kitchen, where Rusty and I were talking.

"Hey," Gonzo said, setting his backpack down. He stood there like he wasn't sure whether or not he wanted to join us, then turned away and started rummaging through the fridge for a snack. I could feel Rusty's eyes on me, no doubt wondering what the hell was going on. I knew the sane thing to do would be to slip some simple explanation into the conversation before moving on to something else. But I couldn't stop replaying in my head the words Gonzo had said to me the first morning of high school three and a half years ago. "Maybe we should pretend we don't know each other." He's probably forgotten all about that, whereas I've taken him at his word with a vengeance.

I looked at Rusty, whose teddy-bear eyes were watching me questioningly, and then the ice in my mind melted away. "You knew Gonzo's my stepbrother, right?" I said.

"Uh—*no*," he said. He seemed far more unnerved by this revelation than he had been to learn that Uncle Joe is married to Uncle Scott.

"Yeah—he's Helmut's son. He lives here alternating weeks."

"The fun of joint custody," Gonzo said with a rueful grin as he finished making a sandwich. When he looked up at us, I'm pretty sure I saw him shake his head a little and suppress another grin. Then he grabbed his plate and said something about homework or whatever before heading upstairs.

Rusty and I sat in silence while I scratched my stubbly face, but I stopped when I noticed his eyebrows were pinched together so tightly that I was half afraid his face would cave in. Finally he turned his head like he was checking to make sure Gonzo wasn't within earshot, then looked at me. "Um—how long have you guys been brothers?"

"Stepbrothers. My mother married Helmut right before I started high school."

"*Really*," he said. "Dude, I had no idea. Does anyone else at school know?"

"I don't think so, except for a few of his friends who've been here." I think I got up at that point, collected our dishes, and set them in the sink to deal with later. The wheels in my head were turning, so I turned back to face Rusty. "And I'd like it to stay that way."

"Why?" he asked. Because of course he needed to know why.

I gestured to the stairs off the kitchen and led the way down to my bedroom. I even closed the door once we were inside. I made my bed before Rusty flopped down on it—the idea of him lying down in my tangled sheets did something to me that was really good and really bad at the same time—and then, because I didn't want to shout across the room to him, I joined him. We lay down on our stomachs, side by side. I knew we were just going to be talking, but I had to let myself enjoy this for a moment—whatever it was. I guess my moment started to drag on, though, because Rusty rolled onto his side, propped his head up with his arm, and said, "Just so you know, whatever you're about to tell me will stay in the vault."

"Oh, I know," I said, and I meant it. But I had a more pressing problem: I was getting massively turned on by the fact that Rusty was lying so close to me. I became so distracted by the heat emanating from his body, like tidal waves, that I started talking without any clear idea of what I wanted to say, and by the time the dust had settled I'd told him pretty much everything. I knew I'd regret it later—I already regret it—but at the time it seemed nice, almost like the warmth I was feeling wasn't from Rusty's body but from some inner peace or whatever that I felt in my heart.

"And that's why you've hardly ever spoken to anyone at school?" he said.

"Well, mainly. I was teased a lot at my old school, and that sucked. And I just—I've always hated our school. I used to think it was because of the people and all this crap they force-feed us about school spirit, but lately I've been wondering if it's me. I keep reading about people who had a shitty adolescence but really came into their own once they were adults, and maybe—I don't know."

At least I stopped myself from telling him I despise everyone else my age.

"Yeah, but there are plenty of guys at school who don't give a shit about all the politics—they just lie low and do their own thing," Rusty said.

"This is my version of that," I said with a shrug. "It works for me. And the funny thing is, no one seems to care that much."

I'd rolled onto my side by this point, so we were facing each other. Then it dawned on me that Rusty and I were lying there almost like clothed lovers having pillow talk. Just as that thought popped into my head, Rusty reached out and ran his thumb along my chin. "You didn't shave today," he observed.

"Yeah—I overslept." He didn't let go of my face. I thought about reciprocating or swatting his hand away, but my arms felt like dead branches inexplicably attached to my shoulders. "Do you shave every day?" I asked instead.

"I do, but it only grows in patches," he said. "I could probably come up with some half-decent sideburns, but my facial hair's even more red than the hair on my head."

I can't remember if I said anything in response. Probably not. Flashes of Rusty's red body hair popped into my head and wouldn't leave me alone. My gut started to churn in a complicated way. The fact is I had a whole list of things I wanted to do to Rusty at that moment and that I wanted him to do to me. I wanted to yank on his tie and unbutton his shirt. I wanted to see if the rest of him looked the way I remembered from my stolen glances that day at the pool. I wanted to know what it feels like to make out with someone you consider hot. I wanted to feel his racing heartbeat against mine, skin to skin. And there's way more that I'm not going to write down, even though you don't care because you're dead.

It's like I was standing at the edge of a pier, and the water in front of me looked warm and inviting, and all I had to do was jump in and be refreshed. But then Rusty let go of my face, and I looked at him, and I didn't know what to do. Surely my hormones were causing me to misread everything—we were just two buddies hanging around and talking about shaving—if I jumped into the water I would get tangled up somehow and drown. I stumbled back, by which I mean I rolled over and sat at the edge of my bed and willed my heavy breathing to return to normal.

Soon Rusty moved over and sat down next to me, then nudged me with his elbow. "You okay, bud?" he said.

"Yeah. It's just—yeah." I knew that if I said something else or even looked at him, he would know everything about how I felt. And he wouldn't want to be friends with me anymore. Or maybe he does like me back—*that* way—but then we'd probably want to do something about it—or talk about it—or *not* talk about it.

I mean, with Jonathan it was simple: he was sexy, but I couldn't stand him. Being friends with Rusty is more complicated, even with my hormones removed from the equation.

Finally he said it was getting close to suppertime. There wasn't anything else to say, so I untucked my shirt as I got up and led the way back upstairs to the front hall.

"I'll see you tomorrow at school," I said as he put his jacket and shoes on. Then I added, "By the way, it's my birthday on Sunday. I'm not having a party, but you could come by for cake after supper if you wanted to." That seems to be the only way I know to invite people to something: to mention casually that I wouldn't mind if they showed up.

It turned out he has a family thing on Sunday. "But maybe we could—I don't know—see a movie over the weekend or something," he said with a shrug of his shoulders. "If you've got nothing better to do."

"All right," I said. It was funny—it almost sounded like he was asking me out on a date, but really we were two friends hanging out, so it wasn't anything to get all worked up about.

He turned away and reached for the doorknob, but then he turned around, set his bag on the floor, walked back over to me, and hugged me. I was too stunned to do anything except hug him back, but part of me was afraid because I didn't want to let go. Then he did let go, grabbed his bag again, smiled at me, and took off. I watched him walk away from our house until he disappeared from view, and when I turned around, missing him already, I saw Gonzo standing there with his eyebrows raised, his arms crossed, and his head tilted to one side. "What the hell's going on?" he asked, sounding more curious than angry.

"Nothing," I said, because it was true.

I got the hell out of there, mainly because Rusty's hug had brought back all the sexy feelings I'd been trying to ignore. I went back to my room, locked the door, took off all my clothes, and lay down on the part of the bed where Rusty had been minutes earlier. I started to imagine what might have happened if, after he'd started touching my face, I'd put my arms around his waist, pulled him close to me, and let nature take its course.

Just for the record, normally I wouldn't share my masturbation fantasies with anyone, and I may delete that paragraph later if my paranoia about people snooping on my computer gets the better of me. But the fact is I don't feel any shame. Yes, it'd be pretty awful to know for sure that Rusty doesn't feel for me what I feel for him, and I know I have to watch myself so I don't do anything that makes him suspect, but that's about it. One day, when I'm older, I'm going to meet a fantastic guy who I have a ton of stuff in common with, and we're going to have lots and lots of mind-shattering sex. If my reality now is having a one-sided thing for the only friend I've ever had, I'll take it.

And you know what? I'm just going to say it: a lot of contemporary piano music just sucks. I have a whole playlist of it on my iPod that I've been scrolling through as I write this, and so many of them are duds.

Your loving son,

Dale

## SATURDAY, MAY 7

Dear Pa,

I just don't get people. Including me.

I ended up in a towering rage all of yesterday afternoon. I was standing around the hallway at the end of lunch period with a book in front of me when they appeared: Rusty and *Gonzo*, walking down the hallway together, both of them laughing. Were they laughing at me? Was Gonzo giving Rusty some juicy dirt on me? Or—and I couldn't decide if this was better or worse—were they talking about something else entirely?

We wandered into our classroom for math class, but I didn't hear a fucking word Ms. Montrose said. I hate to admit this, even to you, but I felt *betrayed*. After school I hid inside my locker until everyone else had left, and then I walked home. It was raining, but my fury kept me warm. And I kept my phone turned off.

I was still wrapped in rage by the time I'd walked through the door, but I needed to get ready for my birthday dinner at Uncle Scott and Uncle Joe's. Since I was soaked to the skin—I caught my reflection in the mirror and thought a wet rat was looking back at me—I took a long shower, shampooed my hair, and put on another layer of aftershave, even though I hadn't shaved again. I even used gel to create that hair wall I sometimes go for on special occasions, the kind of style that's the male equivalent of a Victorian woman putting her hair up. I put on an outfit that made me look like a church organist, which I guess was fitting. I mean, in a way I didn't have much of a choice: Uncle Scott and Uncle Joe are just about as yuppie as ever, and the only reason you'd wear jeans to their house is if you were going to help them clean out their garage. But it was nice to ditch my school clothes. It felt like shedding one skin and putting on another.

It was also a distraction from the headache I felt coming on. I went upstairs and chit-chatted with Ma and Helmut in the kitchen while they made dinner together. Gonzo wasn't due to arrive until after supper, which was great since that meant I didn't need to concentrate on keeping my monstrous fury in check.

And so, as soon as I heard the doorbell, I made a beeline for the front door. But when I opened it, it wasn't Uncle Scott or Uncle Joe waiting on the other side.

It was—you might want to sit down for this—none other than Russell Friesen.

With his red hair flipped up, like mine.

Smiling at me like I was his long-lost friend.

Wearing the jacket he'd worn to Sophie and Jenice's wedding and a shirt that was slightly too tight on him so that it opened at the front, like he knew just how much his chest hair makes me salivate.

I was so stunned that I couldn't figure out how to form actual words to make a sentence that would ask him what he was doing there. It didn't even occur to me to invite him in. We stood on either side of the open door, playing this weird game of chicken. Seconds or minutes later, he jumped in.

"Hey. Did your phone battery die again? I left you about fifteen thousand messages."

"Um—yeah. That's exactly what happened," I said. By this point I couldn't even remember what the truth was. "What—um—what brings you here?"

His eyes bulged out at me as though my question had blown his mind—which it had.

"What are you talking about? Your uncles invited me over for dinner to celebrate your birthday."

I staggered back—literally *and* figuratively. Rusty must have interpreted this as an invitation, because he stepped inside the house and closed the door behind him. I kept backing up and he kept following me, like we were doing this hands-free cha-cha, until finally we were halfway in the living room and I knocked into the edge of the sofa behind me.

"How exactly did this come about?" I asked, trying to sound casual, even though a jackhammer had started to drill away at my skull.

"Uncle Joe friended me on Facebook, and then he messaged me to let me know you were going to their place for dinner tonight and to ask if I wanted to come along," he said with a shrug, like what he was telling me wasn't completely insane. "It was sort of last minute, so I don't have your present ready. But it meant a Friday night with you and not at home with my parents, so I said sure. Didn't they tell you?"

"No. Um—" By this point I had to massage my temples in order to remain capable of coherent thought. "Didn't you find it odd to get a dinner invitation from total strangers?"

"They're not strangers—they're your uncles," he retorted. Then he snickered. "Anyway, what's the big deal? It's not like they're trying to seduce me."

The idea of my uncles putting the moves on a friend of their teenage nephew was so ridiculous that it made me snort, but doing so somehow dislodged some of the bile that had been building up in my esophagus and made me tense up again. If this had happened literally any other day in my lifetime, I would have found it all a fun surprise. But it was like either my uncles or the universe had decided to fuck me over by making Rusty appear on my doorstep after I'd been secretly furious with him for the last five hours, and I couldn't help but wonder what I'd done to deserve this.

So I sat on the arm of the living room sofa to try to calm down, but Rusty was standing over me, which made me start to suffocate, so I jumped up again. I probably looked like a cat who'd just finished a saucer of coffee.

"What's with you today?" he asked, sounding more curious than annoyed.

I told him I had a headache in a tone that even I didn't find convincing, but thankfully he dropped it. When Ma joined us from the kitchen, I ran upstairs to her and Helmut's bathroom, rummaged through their medicine cabinet, and downed a couple of Extra Strength Tylenols. Then I stared at my reflection in the mirror for a moment and ordered myself to suck it up.

"You'll have a great time," Ma was telling Rusty as I made it back downstairs. They were sitting on the sofa like old friends. "Scott and Joe are wonderful hosts, and I know they've been looking forward to getting acquainted with you."

Were they? That was news to me.

At that point Uncle Joe pulled into the driveway and honked, which meant he wasn't planning to get out of the car to ring the doorbell. "Okay, Ma—I'll be home at some point," I said as I got up, trying to sound pleasant. And then—and then!—Ma took out her camera and insisted on taking about seventy-five photos of us. She kept encouraging us to stand closer together and to smile, like Rusty was my prom date. At one point she suggested that each of us put an arm around the other's shoulder and kept badgering us until we did it. From the way she was acting you'd never have guessed that we were two platonic friends going out to dinner together.

So we left the house and made our way to Uncle Joe's car. I made Rusty sit in the front. He tried to insist that because it was my birthday I should ride shotgun, but I climbed into the back seat anyway. Just then the idea of small talk made me want to screambarf, so I thought it would be better for everyone's sanity if I sat by myself in the back and pretended I couldn't hear a word they were saying. Uncle Joe kept glancing at me in the rear-view mirror as he drove, his eyes narrowing at me in a *what the hell is your problem?* kind of way. When I shook my head at him, he shrugged and backed off.

It's strange how well Uncle Joe and I are able to communicate with looks in the rear-view mirror. It's cool, too.

Of course I know I was being ridiculous—I knew it then. The thing is, I don't like these kinds of surprises. I'm not thrilled with losing control of a situation. I like calling the shots, or at least knowing what's ahead so I can brace myself for it. I know you can't control or predict everything in this life; I've been aware of that since the day you died. But the fact remained that I wasn't ready— no—let me be truthful here—I wasn't *willing yet* to forgive Rusty for talking to my stepbrother, something only I would see as a betrayal.

But I could see the bigger picture, too. I mean, Rusty and I are friends. I haven't figured out how to talk to him at school without ditching my Quiet Guy persona. He's obviously free to talk to whoever he wants, including a classmate who happens to be my stepbrother. It's not like he turns into an inanimate object whenever I'm not around. But I was still angry. And I'm not good at putting anger aside because of some crazy situation I have no control over. Years ago Jordana and I had a fight the day before we were supposed to play together in a recital, and I knew that I should forget about the nasty things she'd said about my singing ability and concentrate on our performance. But I couldn't. Pretending nothing had happened felt like such a *weakness*.

I should have been an Aries—like you. Yet I hope I don't end up mellowing with age.

Eventually we made it to Uncle Joe and Uncle Scott's place. They still have their split-level house near the university. Their neighbourhood has been overrun by students, so they often talk about moving, but so far it hasn't come to anything. I'm glad. Some of my earliest memories are of visits to their house when I was little, including the sandbox that they kept just for me. A few of those memories aren't so nice—like getting stung by wasps when I was five—but the rest are.

By this point it was almost suppertime, and as my headache cleared, I discovered that I was so hungry I was probably starting to digest my stomach lining, but when we got inside, we discovered an empty kitchen with several bags of groceries on the table.

"He must be in the study," Uncle Joe said with a sigh. I found out later that he'd picked us up on his way home from work, so he was wiped out and as surprised as we were that dinner hadn't yet been started.

Soon we heard a door click open, and Uncle Scott emerged, still wearing his suit jacket from work. He looked about as jumpy as I had been at home fifteen minutes earlier. Even though he's much more of a talker than I am, as far as personality goes I sometimes think I should have been his son instead of yours. He basically started to unleash what can only be called a block of words. I can't do justice to it, but here's the best reconstruction I can come up with: "Oh my God, Joe, you'll never believe in a hundred thousand years who I bumped into at the grocery store. I was on the phone with Tina—she just couldn't get over it. Happy birthday, kiddo! You look so grown up! I must be getting old to have a nephew who's practically an adult. So I'm standing there in the cheese section trying to decide between two kinds of feta when I notice this guy looking at me, and at first I don't recognize him, but then he says, 'Excuse me, but are you Scott Cardigan?' and it's this asshole who used to pick on me in high school. Oh, it's nice to meet you, Rusty—I'm Uncle

Scott. I used to have panic attacks about this guy, right? Although
we didn't call them panic attacks back then. I don't think we called
them anything. So when I finally piece together who he is, I figure
I'm going to freak right out, because obviously, he won't say anything about it even if he does remember, and he probably doesn't,
right? I mean, if I'd been that kind of douche to somebody as a
teenager I can only assume I would have repressed it by now. Oh, I
didn't make any dinner—I called Tina the minute I got home. But
you know what? He really surprised me. First we did the whole *what*
*have you been up to the last twenty years* routine, as if he reasonably
expects me to give a rat's ass about how his life has unfolded since
high school, and then, just as he's in the middle of telling me about
his company—he builds computers or fixes computers or something like that—he stops himself, then says he doesn't know if I
remember any of this and blah blah blah, but he's always regretted
the way he treated me! And then he *apologized*. I mean an actual
apology, not that *oh, we were just young and stupid back then, weren't*
*we* song and dance you get sometimes. And then he *hugged* me—not
a real hug, of course—just one of those manly half hugs where you
shake hands with your right and whack each other on the back with
your left. I know—it's dinnertime already, so I think we should just
put the groceries away and go out somewhere—my treat. What kind
of food are you boys in the mood for? Oh, let's just get in the car and
drive around till we find something. It might be tricky at six o'clock
on a Friday night, so we'll have to look for those out-of-the-way
places that won't be too busy. Can we take your car, Joe? I forgot to
fill up the tank and I can't remember how long the gas light's been

flashing. I was so amazed to get an actual apology from that guy that I agreed for us to go out for drinks with him and his wife. Can you fucking believe that? Me, going out for drinks with the guy who made my teenage life such a nightmare? I told him the twentieth would work for us, but I know I should have checked with you—I couldn't remember if we have your work thing on that night or on the twenty-first. Anyway, we can reschedule if we have to."

I'm not exaggerating when I tell you that he said all this without stopping or breathing. By the time he was done, we'd already driven away in Uncle Joe's car. He kept talking, and Uncle Joe nodded occasionally as he drove, and both of them seemed to have forgotten that Rusty and I were in the back seat. I turned to Rusty, who was watching all of this with fascination in his eyes, and at that point I realized I wasn't mad at him anymore. It's like the sky in my mind had cleared. Which was great, because I had zero interest in trying to explain why I'd been mad at him in the first place.

His head pivoted toward me in the cutest possible way, and without taking his eyes off my uncles in the front seat, he whispered, "Um—who's Tina?"

"Uncle Scott's platonic wife."

"I see."

Then Uncle Scott turned around in his seat to look at us. "What kind of food are you boys in the mood for? There's a great Thai restaurant that we like to go to. Or there's that new Egyptian–Moroccan–English fusion place that seems promising. Is that the one that's attached to the mall without being *in* the mall, Joe?"

Uncle Joe responded by turning on the stereo. It was playing a choral piece that erupted into the most climactic moment—I think it was something by Handel—and then, after a quick wrap-up and a pause, the choir launched into what was clearly the third movement of something epic.

"Um—either one would be fine," I called out over the sound of two hundred people singing at the tops of their voices. "Right, Rusty?"

"Yeah—sounds great." ·

Uncle Scott turned his head and nodded before falling silent. I couldn't understand what was going on. When I turned in Rusty's direction, he leaned over and said, low enough not to be overheard, "Why does everyone keep calling us 'you boys'? Your mother did it ten times during that photo shoot. And what was up with that photo shoot?"

He looked so appealingly earnest, and I felt so comfortable being that close to him that I unleashed the truth without running it through the filter first. "Yeah—sorry about that. It looks like my whole family thinks we're dating."

What happened next took about two seconds to happen but will need several sentences to describe. First, Rusty broke into a smile, chuckled, and nudged my hand with his knuckles, as though the idea of us dating was hysterical. But then his smile faded and he gazed into the middle distance, looking increasingly puzzled. He started to say something, then stopped himself, looked back at my two uncles, glanced at me again, and then turned right around to look determinedly out the window like I do whenever I'm in the car with Ma. And throughout all this was the sound of a shitload of people singing their devotion to a god that probably none of them believed in.

Somehow we were all back to normal once we arrived at the restaurant, like someone had hit a giant reset button as we were getting out of the car. I caught a glimpse of a cardinal as we crossed the parking lot, which also helped. The restaurant was pretty nice, set up with all these dividers and booths that gave the illusion of intimacy, even though it was so loud you had to shout to be heard. I made sure I was sitting on Rusty's left rather than his right so we wouldn't knock elbows like we had throughout Sophie and Jenice's wedding reception. As we each contemplated what we wanted for supper, Uncle Joe asked Rusty about school and his family, I asked them about work, and Rusty asked about the Fauré concert coming up in a couple of weeks. It was pleasant, but bland. We did that thing that I've never understood where everyone muses aloud about what they're thinking of ordering and comments on everyone else's deliberations. Rusty turned to me and said, "I'm thinking of getting the fish and chips—unless you'd like to split a hen with me." Then, after we'd ordered, Rusty excused himself to go wash his hands. Both my uncles stayed silent, following him with their eyes without turning their heads as he walked away, but as soon as he was gone they became incredibly agitated.

"I really like him."

"So do I. He's so cute!"

"And polite! He has a good heart."

"He's a keeper. Don't you just want to eat him up?"

"Susan and Helmut gave him rave reviews."

"I don't want to be nosy, but seriously, Dale, if you ever have any questions about sex—"

Until that point I'd been kind of amused, but that last comment pushed the entire conversation right over the edge.

"Okay—shut up! Both of you!" I took a deep breath. "I don't know why everyone thinks this is all a foregone conclusion. Rusty and I are friends. We're classmates at school. That's it! We're not having sex—we're not dating—none of that's going to happen."

My uncles seemed stunned by my outburst, as if I'd announced that I was going to be a missionary on Neptune. Uncle Scott recovered first.

"Why not? Don't you like him?" he asked, looking at me kindly.

By this point my heart had started to pound, and when I looked down at my hands I discovered that they had strangled my napkin. "That's not really the issue here."

Uncle Scott and Uncle Joe turned to look at each other before turning back to me.

"Then what's the problem?" Uncle Joe asked. "Is he straight?"

"I don't know. Probably? He likes cars and sports and hiking. He calls me 'dude' and 'guy' and 'buddy.' He sucks at math. His room is so messy it ought to be condemned. He was a Boy Scout. He and his dad won a prize for a wooden birdhouse they made together." I started to tell them about his comment about the woman at the wedding with the side boobs, but it was too complicated to explain, so I gave it up.

At this point Uncle Scott's eyes were still kind, but he also looked like he thought I'd gone insane.

"Dale," he said—and I remember this so clearly because of the way he said it, the way he looked at me when he said it, like he could really see me—"what does any of that have to do with being gay or straight?"

"Or anything in between?" Uncle Joe added.

They immediately leaned back in their seats before I could ponder their question, which I figured meant they'd spotted Rusty on his way back to the table. Sure enough, a moment later Rusty sat down, spread his napkin on his lap, sipped his water, and asked my uncles about work. When the food arrived, we did that obligatory thing of asking each other how everything tasted. Not to pull a Burt and Beverly, but my entree was a bit of a dud.

My uncles seemed to be having a good time, except after a while I noticed that they were speaking more to us than to each other. And Rusty—well, he was acting a bit weird all evening. Or maybe not weird, but off. He'd be pretty quiet for a while, and then he'd revive, only to sink back down again. He was acting like a campfire that was having a hard time staying lit. I saw him check his watch a few times, so I was pretty surprised when my uncles invited us back to their place for dessert and he said yes.

It turned out to be a low-key evening. I was afraid my uncles would start looking at me significantly after everything Rusty said or did, but thankfully they backed off. We ended up sitting in the dining room eating ice cream and playing a board game that required you to crack these alphanumerical codes in the quest for world domination. I didn't like or understand it, but I didn't suck at it either, so that's something.

The only really funny part of the evening that's worth telling you about—or, let's face it, preserving for my own benefit—was that we started talking about nicknames. Uncle Joe is legally Joseph but has always, always been Joe. He didn't even go through a phase of being Joey when he was young. Rusty mentioned that he'd been completely bald when he was named Russell; it was only when he started daycare that he started to be called Rusty, which was fine, except for a group of kids who'd tormented him with the nickname Rusty the Rustificator, even though that didn't make any sense. Then Uncle Scott mentioned that his parents had called him Scooter until he went away to university.

"Oh my God. Didn't I call you Uncle Scooter for a while when I was a kid?" I asked, blown away by the fact that I'd forgotten this.

Uncle Scott started to laugh. "Yes, you did, and your dad and I had a hard time tricking you into stopping," he said. Right after he mentioned you, his face changed, almost like he'd forgotten about you, then remembered. No doubt it's a look that's sometimes come across my face, too.

Someday I'd like to have a serious talk with Uncle Scott about you, but I didn't want to open that can of worms in front of anyone else, not even Uncle Joe. So I tried to keep the conversation going.

"Well, you guys are lucky to have such cool nicknames. 'Dale' is epically unnicknameable."

"I could always start calling you Chippendale," Rusty offered, a corner of his mouth curling up in a half grin. I forget what I said in response or if I said anything at all. He seemed disappointed that I wasn't thrilled at the idea of being named after a gang of strippers, but there wasn't much I could do about that.

You know, this memory popped into my head just as I was typing this: when I was younger, I daydreamed about having a best friend named Chip. We'd be inseparable—interchangeable, even—just like those cartoon squirrels or badgers or whatever they are. There was this one kid back in grade five that I seemed to hit it off with, and at one point I'd daydreamed about pitching this idea to him. Then I found out about Chippendales dancers, and that killed the fantasy.

Finally, once we'd turned into a quartet of yawners, Uncle Scott offered to drive Rusty and me home. We ended up going in Uncle Joe's car. This time Rusty didn't put up a fight when I offered him the front seat. He gave Uncle Scott directions to his house, and by the time we'd pulled up at the curb he already had his seat belt off.

"Thanks for a fun evening, Scott," he said as they shook hands. "Dale, have a great weekend, okay?" And then he got out of the car and headed up the walk.

Something felt incredibly wrong, so I also got out of the car and followed him to his door. Apparently the bulb for the porch light had burned out, so I could barely see anything.

"Hey, Rusty? Are we—um—do you still want to see a movie this weekend?" I asked. I'd also been wondering if yesterday's hug was a one-off because I'd been telling him personal stuff or if it was going to become a regular thing. But Rusty didn't seem that interested even in a handshake.

"Oh—yeah—um—I think I need to take a rain check on that. My dad said something about a billion chores around the house this weekend."

"Oh. Hey—I just thought of something. Unlikely candle scents?"

Part of his mouth turned upward, but he didn't seem that into it. "I don't know. Broken Washing Machine?" He exhaled, shifted his weight from one leg to the other, looked at me, looked away. "I should go in. See you at school."

And then he disappeared into the house, leaving me alone on an empty porch in the dark, with only the sound of a car motor to remind me that reality still existed.

I didn't want to go to bed when I got home, even though it was late. I checked my email, only to discover that Ma had sent me every single photo she'd taken of me and Rusty that evening— each in a separate email message, because she still can't remember how to send multiple attachments. We looked so happy, in spite of how weird Ma had been acting behind the scenes. And now, I don't know what happened, but I think I've screwed things up somehow. This morning, I turned on my cellphone and went through Rusty's texts, hoping there would be a new one explaining what had caused him to act so weird. But the last one was the text saying he was on his way over to be picked up by my uncles. After that—nothing.

I skipped organ practice this morning and went to the pool hoping I'd bump into him, but I didn't. I swam two laps, but I was so discouraged that I could barely keep myself afloat. It's funny: before I had any friends, I didn't mind all the time I spent by myself—I loved it. But now that I do have a friend and all this weirdness has crept up between us, I feel so lonely. And I have no fucking idea what to do about it.

Your loving son,

Dale

## SUNDAY, MAY 8

Dear Pa,

Well, today's the day. I'm seventeen. I don't feel that different compared to yesterday, when I was sixteen and change. By the time Mozart was my age, he was already a court musician in Salzburg, not stuck at some wearisome high school like me, but never mind. I'm also now as old as one of the Hardy boys, which somehow is even more unbelievable.

Do you remember the birthday parties you and Ma used to throw me when I was little? I remember the one when I turned six. You'd decided the theme would be *Toy Story*, so kids and adults had to dress up as their favourite childhood toys. I'll have to double-check this in the photo albums in the attic, but I think you dressed up as a toy soldier and Ma dressed up as Strawberry Shortcake. I do remember that Uncle Scott and Uncle Joe showed up as a pair of Cabbage Patch Kids, and I'm pretty sure, since this was before their wedding, it was around then that I started to understand that they weren't just friends who happened to live in the same house. There were tons of people there, and I was proud, since they'd all come over because of me.

Fast-forward eleven years, and tonight's festivities were as diametrically opposed to the *Toy Story* party as if they'd been planned that way. Today's also Mother's Day, but because Ma had insisted we keep the celebrations separate, mine was especially sparse. Of course I'm not a child anymore, but it was practically the equivalent of Ma giving me money to buy whatever I wanted for Christmas and wrapping my presents in front of me. I had dinner with Ma and Helmut, and once it was over we cleared the dishes and I set the table again while Ma put some candles on the cake. Just as I was letting in Uncle Scott and Uncle Joe, I heard another car pull into the driveway.

Gonzo walked through the front door carrying a package wrapped in colourful paper with a giant bow on top. "Hey—happy birthday, bro," he said, giving me what Uncle Scott would call a manly half hug.

We're always nice to each other on our birthdays, I guess to shake things up a bit.

"Hey—thanks. Did your mother drop you off?" I asked him.

"No. She's waiting in the car."

"Oh." I looked at Ma and Helmut, but neither of them said anything. They just *looked*. None of this made any sense to me, so I said, "Well, that's silly, especially on Mother's Day. We should invite her in for a piece of cake."

I headed back to the front door before anyone could say something to stop me—not that anyone tried to, as far as I could tell. I put some shoes on and walked outside to the driveway. Iliana was sitting in her car, flipping through a magazine, but when she saw me heading her way, she smiled and rolled down her car window.

"Happy birthday, Dale!" she said, reaching out to squeeze my arm. "I do hope you like Gonzo's present."

"I'm sure I will," I said, once again warming up to her immediately. "Um—so yeah. Would you like to come in for some coffee and cake?"

"Oh," she said, her eyes widening, like I'd invited her to go skinny-dipping with me. "I don't know if I should."

"I don't either," I said honestly, "but I'd love it if you would. My uncles are visiting, and I don't think you've met them yet." It was a far-fetched reason, but it sounded better than what was floating around in my head: *It's high time you see for yourself where your son spends the other half of his life.*

Finally Iliana got out of the car and followed me inside. I tried to act like this was the most normal thing in the world, but she seemed nervous and tentative, as though she feared the house was booby-trapped. Once we were in the kitchen, Helmut greeted her with a genuine smile, my uncles were friendly, and Ma looked stunned. As soon as Gonzo and Iliana went upstairs so she could see his room, the tension in the kitchen rose like an out-of-control volume dial.

"Honey," Ma said, still gripping the counter with her hands. Then she said something about me creating an awkward situation without taking her feelings into account or something like that. I can't remember exactly what she said, because it didn't make any sense. But I do remember how I responded, because as far as I'm concerned it's the only truth that matters.

"She's Gonzo's mother. That makes her family."

I heard footsteps on the stairs again, so there wasn't time for anything else to be said. But I did see Helmut smile a little, like he was realizing I was right. Or maybe he was thinking about something else entirely—how the hell should I know?

The rest of the party seemed fine, although kind of flat. But that may have been because I was having a hard time staying chipper. "Where's your friend?" Uncle Joe asked at one point, and I told him part of the truth—that Rusty had a family thing. But his question brought everything back, including the weird turn on Friday night, and it reminded me how much I wished Rusty could have been there.

But I tried to keep smiling and focus on the here and now. It's true that I don't have any other friends except for Jenice and Sophie, who couldn't be there either because they're off on their honeymoon. But at least I have my family. They sang "Happy Birthday to You"—all in different keys, of course—and I was so touched by their gifts. I'm probably not the easiest person in the world to shop for, but they all managed to surprise me. Ma and Helmut bought me a leather binder for sheet music as well as three DVDs of concerts by an Irish orchestra that performs Celticized renditions of the great works of Vivaldi. Uncle Joe and Uncle Scott gave me a boxed set of the novels of E.M. Forster, an author I'd never heard of before. And from Gonzo and Iliana I received two tickets to a concert featuring a group that plays orchestral versions of theme songs from famous video games. I was taken aback, mainly because I wasn't expecting to find tickets in such a huge box.

"This sounds weirdly awesome," I said honestly.

"Great," Gonzo said with a grin. "I figured we could go together." Which floored me even more!

Just as I thought we were ready to start slicing the cake, Uncle Scott said he had another surprise for me. He fished a box out of his jacket pocket and handed it to me. My heart started to pound as I opened it to find a pair of silver cufflinks, each with the letter C engraved on it, and a silver cross on a chain.

"Those were your father's," he said. I tried to focus on my breath as he continued. "The cross was given to him when he was born, I think—I don't know who gave it to him. He never wore it, though. We weren't that kind of family. The cufflinks belonged to your granddad first, and he gave them to your dad to wear on his wedding day. These are some of the things I've been saving for you. I want you to have them now."

I'd kept my eyes on these shiny objects in my hand this whole time, but finally I made myself look up. Everyone in the room looked so sober, like they were half expecting me to crumble to the floor. But I wasn't upset. I was grateful to Uncle Scott for giving me these things of yours. I think they mean more to me now because of these letters to you. I went up to him and gave him a hug—a real one. "Thanks, Uncle Scott." He hugged me back and told me he loved me. And I knew perfectly well what he wasn't saying—that he regretted so much that you couldn't be there with us.

As soon as I felt a tear spill out of my eye I let go of Uncle Scott, turned back to the table, and sliced the cake. Then we sat around the kitchen and chatted until it got late.

Once everyone had left, I sat down at the table again and took another look at Uncle Scott's gift. "I think I'll wear these during the Fauré concert," I said out loud as I put the cufflinks back in their case. The cross was more complicated since I'm not religious, but I liked the idea of wearing something that had belonged to you. I tried it on and tucked it inside my shirt, and so far it hasn't tried to strangle me or stab me, so we'll see how this goes.

I glanced up and saw Ma still sitting across the room, looking at me. I figured she was going to say something about Iliana again, so I sighed a little and waited. But all she did was look.

"What? What is it?" I asked.

"Never mind," she said, and with that she rose from her seat and started to put the cake dishes in the dishwasher. I went out to the front hall, grabbed a jacket, and sat on the front steps for a while, enjoying the cool evening air and the quiet. Nobody was around, but I didn't need anyone else. I was just so glad to be alive. And even though my life is far from perfect—friendless and fatherless— I felt this odd sensation of gratitude.

Finally I decided it was time to go in. As I reached for the handle of the screen door, I noticed something sticking out of our mailbox. It was a small plastic bag, and when I looked inside I found a CD jewel case with the words *Covers and Mash-ups* handwritten across the front, along with a rather artless image of two stick figures standing around wearing headphones connected to each other with a wire. On the liner inside was an amazing lineup of songs and a note: *Happy birthday, Dale! Here are some of my favourite covers and mash-ups for you. Sorry I didn't have this ready sooner. Your pal, Rusty.*

By the time I'd finished reading it, all the blood had drained from my face and settled in my crotch. This gift seemed far more intimate, far more personal, far more intentional, and far more special than anything he could have bought me. I don't know what any of it means, but I'm going to play the CD right now and see if I can find out.

Your loving (and grateful) son,

Dale

## THURSDAY, MAY 12

Dear Pa,

Still nothing from Rusty. On Sunday night, after I listened to the CD he'd burned for me, I sent him an open-ended, slightly guilt-inducing text message. When that didn't budge him, I figured it was better to leave him alone and accept the fact that the CD was some sort of consolation prize. Yesterday on the bus ride home from school I started to let myself hope that things would get back to normal when I saw him texting on his phone, but when I reached into my bag for my own phone and turned it on, there weren't any texts or voice mails waiting for me.

Lately in English class we've been doing a poetry unit, which is okay. I seem to like the *idea* of poetry well enough but the reality of it far less so. Even though I've tried to use my music training to help me see what Mr. Kassam means by rhythm and cadence, I've come to the sad conclusion that when it comes to poetry, I have a tin ear. Anyway, a couple of weeks ago Mr. Kassam told us that not only would we have to *write* a poem, but also, we'd have to read it aloud to the class. I wasn't thrilled about the reading aloud part, especially since he doesn't ever let me get out of it like many teachers do because of my supposed voice training. And the prospect of *writing* a poem seemed really daunting, too, so you can imagine how surprised I was when a poem popped into my head a few weeks ago while I was cleaning my bathroom. I called it "Untitled," partly to be deep and heavy, partly because I had no idea what else to call it, and it went like this:

> When my mother told me
> that my best friend had been brutally attacked
> by a flock of wild geese,
> I immediately telephoned his mother
> and offered my condolences.

I wrote it out once and that was that. Who knew writing poetry would be so easy? True, I didn't really "get" it—I'm still not entirely sure there's anything to "get"—but it seemed witty and clever and I still think I could have received at least a B+ for it, especially compared to the poems I've heard this week from some of my classmates, including one filled with all sorts of semipornographic innuendo about mountains and caves. It wasn't completely terrible, but I'd give him D- for subtlety.

But then, one night before my birthday, partly because of Rusty and partly because what Jordana had told me about her friend's supposedly gay boyfriend still wasn't sitting well with me, I sank into this weird mood. I just started writing, and eventually it turned into a poem. I wrote and rewrote and revised and pruned and moved things around until I was black and blue. And I was pretty proud of it once it was done. So I decided to shelve "Untitled" and read my new poem to the class. It was a risk, like everything at that school is for me, but what was the worst that could happen? They'd shun me? Be my guest.

I don't plan to show it to Ma or Helmut, even if Gonzo brings it up first, but I'm going to paste the text of the poem into this file, and I'll pretend you're reading it over. And I'll try to imagine that you're proud of me. I call it "A Cappella." As I stood up this morning to read it in front of my classmates, I could see a few of them snickering to each other, but that was the least of my worries.

I stand tall at centre stage, eyes open and alert.
Before me, they wait for my first note,
either clear and sound or flat and plain.
There is no music behind me.
I sing a cappella.
Whether I succeed or fail, that first note will show.

I dress all in black save the shiny gold cuffs,
My hair neatly combed and my silver cross
dangling from my neck under my shirt.
Looking my best, prepared for the worst.
A distorted shadow the spotlight makes,
checking and following my every movement.
You are that shadow. But I am me.
I won't forget that. Not today or tomorrow.
I sing without background music. I need no shadow.
Whether I succeed or fail, that spotlight will show.

Wandering down the road. Before me is a highway,
straight and long and dull and flat and plain.

You will follow that route. But I am me.

The difference between you and me is that I'm not you.

I sing a cappella. I take a left at the light.

Whether I succeed or fail, my driving will show.


The straight road's safest, but it's not for me.

Too safe. Too predictable. I've tried to follow it.

But there's another path, the crooked path,

full of twists and turns and forks and knives.

Nothing in sight beyond the first bend.

No signs. No maps. No indication.

I sing a cappella. I take the left turn.

I follow the crooked path.

Whether I succeed or fail, my first steps will show.


I am at the beach. The hot sand feels cool

under my toes and I wear no sunscreen.

I swim near the big rocks under the pier

where the waves are high and I won't be seen.

If I drown, I drown, but I won't, so I won't.

I sing a cappella. I take the left turn.

I follow the crooked path. I don't drown.

Whether I succeed or fail, my first strokes will show.


They grow restless; they have no patience.

My throat suddenly ready, I take a deep breath.

My voice is clear and bright and reaches the farthest depths.

I will not fail.

I swim under the pier and not near the edge.

I follow the crooked path and not the safe road.

I take the left turn and don't continue straight.

I discard my shadow and don't cling to it like a child.

I sing a cappella.

Whether I've succeeded or failed, my voice has shown.

I looked up once I'd finished, and there wasn't a single sound. Nobody moved. At first my blood ran cold when I saw that the most gut-wrenching revelation I'd ever written, let alone read aloud to a roomful of douchebags, had been met with such indifference. But then my body switched gears and heated up, and there was nothing else to do but drop my hard copy on my teacher's desk, walk back to my seat, and hide for the rest of the day.

Just as I started to move, though, one kid started to clap—not Rusty and not the kid a few rows ahead of me who'd apparently written a perfect sonnet. It was Muppet Face, who sits in front of me. Then a few more jumped in, and it just escalated from there. My legs were shaking by the time I sat down, and Muppet Face turned around and said, "Dude, that was awesome! I didn't understand most of it, but it was awesome."

Normally I would have just smiled and nodded, but since I was fairly certain I wouldn't start to cry, I did something I never thought I'd do. I said, "Thanks—thanks a lot." And then Muppet Face—I mean Mark—grinned at me before turning away.

"Thank you very much, Mr. Cardigan," Mr. Kassam said gravely once the applause had died down. "I look forward to reading your hard copy carefully." And I was pleased, because Mr. Kassam is a tough cookie when it comes to our work, and Sonnet Guy and I were the only ones who'd received that kind of response from him.

When I was heading back to class after lunch, Sonnet Guy came up to me and

My phone just beeped. A text from Rusty! *Cool poem. Really moving.*

Then another one: *Unlikely popcorn toppings?*

I need to go—I want to write him back right away. I don't understand what's happening, but as long as we're friends, I'm fine with it.

Your loving son,

Dale

## FRIDAY, MAY 13

Dear Pa,

Today was an okay day, although I can't give it a much higher rating than that. Rusty and I nodded to each other in the hallway, which I guess is an improvement. After my last class, I took my time at my locker and started scouting the hallway for someone who seemed nice and approachable. I was considering walking up to a live person and starting a conversation! There's this guy named Seamus who was in my class last year and who sounds like a leprechaun. But he seems friendly enough, and, more importantly, I've never felt even remotely attracted to him. I started to weigh the pros and cons of having a friend named Seamus, but I figured it couldn't be worse than having no friend at all.

But just as I was muttering the words "Hey—waddup?" under my breath for practice, these three super-popular grade twelve boys sauntered down the middle of the hallway like they owned it. They were practically walking in slow motion, their hair wafting in the breeze even though we were indoors. And the crowd *parted* to let them pass. One of them was carrying a football, and they all looked so full of themselves, with their backpacks and their matching hoodies and their cool names like Andrew and Parker and Justin. (I'm guessing—I didn't know who they were.) The one on the right caught me watching them walk by, and he gave me this *who the fuck are you?* smirk and turned away.

I slammed my locker door shut and marched off in the opposite direction. It's like the universe had rushed up to me, waving its arms and exclaiming, *No! Don't do it!* as a way of saving me from myself. It served me right for coming so close to breaking my cone of silence and ruining everything I'd worked so hard for, but it left me feeling discouraged, too. I mean, why can't I ever meet any normal people my age? But then another thought occurred to me. Maybe all these douchebags *are* normal. Maybe all this time I've somehow failed to understand how the earth actually works and that I'll always be the weirdo. Well, fine. So why can't I meet other nondouchebaggy weirdos to hang out with?

I became so disgusted by my entire school that I skipped the bus again—the idea of being crammed with a bunch of other guys in a swaying vehicle made me want to puke my guts out. I pulled out my iPod and tried to drown out my thoughts with a music shuffle as I walked home. But it didn't work that well. I guess it's a fine line between choosing to be an introvert and having the label of social outcast thrust upon you.

And then, just as I was a few blocks from home, my iPod selected the song that Rusty had played for me on the sidewalk in front of my house—whenever that was. My feet stopped by themselves as I got lost in all those associations of feeling enveloped by the song, of being so physically close to a friend I found attractive, of having to stop myself from leaning my head against his shirt because I knew doing so would cause me to get burned. When I opened my eyes again, I saw that I was standing motionless at a corner and that a car had stopped in front of me, wanting to give me the right-of-way. I was so disoriented that I couldn't figure out whether to keep going or to turn back, so I waved the car through.

I'm alone in the house this evening. Ma and Helmut are off to a dinner party and won't be home till late. Normally I enjoy being alone in a silent house, but I'm in this weird mood right now, which can be both the best time *and* the worst time to write to you. I think I need to stop. Maybe I'll make some popcorn and watch one of the DVDs I got for my birthday. Or maybe I'll read. It's not like I can go out or talk to somebody or *do* something. I guess that sounds pretty cynical, even though it's true.

No—my mood is getting worse—it's time to go.

Your loving (and temporarily cynical) son,

Dale

Wait—I don't think I'm done yet.

Just for the record, just in case you've misunderstood me somehow, I do remember the day you died. I don't like to revisit it that often—once I do, I sometimes have a hard time letting go of it again—but I do remember. In a way it's like my brain was filming everything even before I knew you were dead, because when I play those scenes over in my mind, I see everything, including myself, from someone else's point of view.

It was a Friday evening at the end of February, and we were at the recital hall in downtown Guelph for my school's late-winter recital. I think Ma was more nervous about it than I was—even at nine, I loved to perform in public. I was part of a small group of kids singing Benjamin Britten's *A Ceremony of Carols*, even though technically it's Christmas music. I remember liking those pieces, although I don't think I've listened to them since. Before my voice changed, I'd sung mezzo-soprano, something that suited me fine. I liked being in the middle when we sang in three parts; I found it far more interesting than singing the melody. Jordana sang soprano and had a solo in one of the Britten pieces, but I don't remember how it went. I used to sit with this guy named David, who acted like my friend part of the time and tormented me the rest of the time. But I liked him when we were friends, so I put up with it.

I don't think I realized it then, but Jordana and I were the stars of the recital, even though we were in the youngest grade. Each of us played a piece separately—I forget what mine was, but I must still have a copy of it somewhere—and we also played one together, me on the piano and her on the cello. I don't know how she did it, since back then her cello was taller and heavier than she was. The piece itself wasn't overly complicated, but I remember we played it super theatrically for some reason: Jordana kept swaying her head back and forth as she sawed away at the cello, whereas I made a point of wiping imaginary sweat off my brow whenever I had a hand free. I think there's a video of us on YouTube somewhere taken by one of the other parents on a shitty camera. I came across it once not too long ago, and I think I found it funny before I realized what day it had been filmed.

Jordana came across as a pro when it came time to perform, but backstage she was usually a mess. I remember her grabbing my arm a lot and saying desperate things. She could be all meek and humble if a performance went well, but if she made the tiniest mistake, even something no one else noticed, she'd vow that she wanted to die. And because all the other grade four kids were just beginning to play an instrument, they were happy if they got through their performances without collapsing. Since we were far more advanced than everyone else our age, Jordana and I had only each other to confide in—or to feed our neuroses.

For the grand finale, the entire school got together for this elaborate piece that I'm pretty sure was meant to be an opera, with half the students singing and the other half playing in a makeshift orchestra. Jordana and I were the leads, her the soprano and me the alto. Even though I remember the performance well, I can't bring to mind the actual song, but seems to me every line included the words "lads" and "lassies" and everything about the piece was overdone. I mean, it was pretty ridiculous for a couple of nine-year-olds to sing the leads in a love ditty, but we didn't think about that then.

When finally the audience erupted in applause, Jordana and I laughed and hugged each other, and then we turned to bask in the glow of our adoring public. That's when I saw Ma in the audience, sitting next to an empty chair. She was applauding but looking down at her cellphone at the same time. And although we didn't find out until later, you were already dead at that point.

Once the recital was over and Ma and I were in the car, I asked her why you hadn't been there. "I don't know where he is," she said. But she didn't seem too worried about it—at least, not until we pulled up in the driveway at home and two police officers approached us as we got out of the car. I couldn't figure out what was happening when they pulled out their badges, said your name, and asked us if we were related to you. I looked up at Ma, saw her face go pale as she nodded and invited the two women inside.

And then—well—then we knew.

I don't remember much after that. I remember one of the officers telling us about the accident and some of the words she used, but not how I reacted to it. At one point I was lying down on the sofa with my head in Ma's lap as she telephoned Grandma and Uncle Scott in turn. I remember seeing her hands shaking as she dialled and sensing her ragged breath and her racing heartbeat, but I can't recall anything she said. I didn't want her to leave me with one of the neighbours while she went to the hospital, so she took me with her. In my mind I see a flash of a traffic light not too far from our house, but nothing more. I remember sitting on a bench in this antiseptic hallway, and even though Ma didn't tell me what she was doing I'd watched enough TV to know that she was about to go to the morgue to identify your body.

The next day, Ma made me stay in the basement while she and Uncle Scott and Grandma sat at the kitchen table and talked. I wanted so desperately to know what they were saying, especially when I could faintly hear their voices rising, but I couldn't eavesdrop because Uncle Joe was sitting with me, trying to distract me with a card game.

Then came the funeral—another hard day. The service didn't make much sense to me. I had too little experience with religion and too little energy to concentrate, so now it's all a blur. And then the reception at home—I watched Ma and Grandma work together as best they could, though looking back on this now, I wonder what it was like for a mother-in-law and a daughter-in-law to share this experience. It was like one of my birthday parties, in the sense that the house was full of people and I was the centre of attention, but everything had taken a creepy, melancholy turn. Part of me wanted to hide in my room, but I didn't.

Ma and Grandma and Uncle Scott had decided on a private burial, so they scheduled it for after the reception. As soon as I reached for my coat I started to cry, because it hit me what we had to do next, and Ma sighed and said maybe it would be better if I stayed home with Uncle Joe. Which made me cry even harder.

"No! I have to go!" I said, or something like that.

Now I'm crying as I type out these words. I can't seem to stop. But I don't want to stop. Tears don't hurt like the ache does.

We drove to the cemetery, just the five of us, in a single car. The five most important people to you: your wife, your son, your mother, your brother, your brother-in-law. Your family. Uncle Joe drove, with Ma in the passenger seat. I sat in the back between Grandma and Uncle Scott, each of whom held one of my hands. I was used to being the only child in a family of adults, so this felt safe and comfortable.

The cemetery people were waiting for us. I'd never been to this part of the cemetery before; your plot's in a different spot than Grandpa's is. We parked in front of the hearse and got out of the car. I remember walking with Ma and Uncle Scott. It was a sunny afternoon, but cold. I remember approaching the open grave, waiting as the cemetery people wheeled your casket out of the hearse. Uncle Joe read a poem that I couldn't understand—something about a hungry bear. Grandma and Ma stood together, almost holding each other up.

All this time, I felt this depthless sadness in the pit of my stomach, like a toxic balloon. But it was only once they lowered the casket into the ground that I really started to cry. Because I understood then that it was *final*—that you wouldn't be coming back— that the void in my stomach would never go away completely. Uncle Scott kneeled down next to me and put his arm around me. He was crying, too.

And when it was time to go, even though I was nearly ten years old, Uncle Scott picked me up and carried me to the car. I let him— he reminded me so much of you, and it almost felt like I was giving you one last hug. I can't remember if I said it out loud or inside my head, but it was at that moment that I said goodbye.

The five of us returned home, sat around the table, and ate leftover food from the reception for supper—at least we pretended to. And then it was time for my uncles and Grandma to drive back to Waterloo. "I'll call you over the weekend, Susan," Uncle Scott said as we stood on the porch. "Let us know what we can do. Rides, visits, food—whatever you need. I mean that. We're family—I don't want that to change."

"I don't either, Scott," Ma said, and they hugged each other again.

It took me years to understand what Uncle Scott was afraid of, but it didn't happen. Ma has stayed close to your family all this time, even after she married Helmut. She still refers to Uncle Scott and Uncle Joe as her brothers-in-law. She continued to visit and talk on the phone with Grandma and helped take care of her after she started to get sick. I know this was done mainly for my sake, but I like to think it benefited her, too. Her parents died when she was so young, and she's an only child besides. Looking back now, I think it would have been too hard on her if she'd lost her husband *and* her family in one day.

You know, this is probably small potatoes in the grand scheme of things, but do you know what really hurt me throughout all this— or, rather, what *else?* When I finally went back to school, no one said anything. Not even Jordana—especially not Jordana. My teacher smiled sympathetically my first morning back, and then he set me to work getting caught up with what I'd missed. Nobody even made fun of me when I'd start to cry in the middle of class, like on your birthday, or my birthday, or your wedding anniversary. Not that I would have wanted them to, but at least it would have shown that they fucking knew I existed. Maybe that's where my cone of silence came from—but I made this one, rather than let other people shove me into it.

Well, it's getting late now. Writing all this down has wiped me out. But I don't mind that I still feel sad that you're gone—that the ache in my stomach is still there. It's because I miss you. But I remember you in my heart all the same.

Your loving son,

Dale

## TUESDAY, MAY 17

Dear Pa,

I have two things to say about what happened at school today. The first is *Aaaaaaaaaaaaaargh!* The second is more complicated.

This morning my media studies teacher, Bruce—who makes us call him that because he thinks he's cool and who seems to be making up the curriculum as he goes along—announced that for the next few weeks we're going to work in pairs to create a major project that's part creative and part analytical. But when he wandered into the hallway to give us a chance to form teams, no one started brainstorming project ideas. All I heard was guys ranting about how they had no idea what we were supposed to be doing. I even heard the phrase "what the actual fuck" from more than one direction.

I stared out the window and wondered what it'd be like to have the ability to fall into a coma voluntarily. None of my teachers seems to realize that making a group of twenty-five students work in pairs always leads to the same end. I just wait till everyone else in class has teamed up, and then—surprise!—I'm the odd man out. No one wants to work with the guy who never says anything, so that's no problem. Half the time my teachers don't even notice that I'm working by myself, and if they do, they don't care because they love my projects. Last year I figured out what my English teacher's favourite TV show was and diagrammed the hell out of it. She still raves about it whenever I bump into her in the hallway—apparently she had it framed.

It's kind of nice that I'm responsible for such a highlight in her career as a teacher. Even though it was all for the sake of not having to talk to anyone.

And so I was surprised and then alarmed when Rusty—who, since my birthday, has acknowledged my existence solely by nodding at me in the hallway—marched over to my desk, his eyes dancing. "Oh my God—I have a great idea for a project," he exclaimed. "I'll tell you about it later. You in?"

Everyone seemed to be staring at us, so I nodded just to get rid of him. At one point I heard some guys talking about how they couldn't remember ever having a three-person group before, but I just stared at my fingernails and let them wonder. Breaking my cone of silence at school was a giant leap in my friendship with Rusty, and for the rest of the morning, I was both frazzled by and curious about this unexpected plot twist. I figured I was doomed to spend the rest of the day in suspense, but right before lunch, while I was in my jail cell practising the violin, I had the overwhelming sensation of being watched. I turned my head to see Rusty's disembodied face peering at me through the tiny window in the door. I nearly whacked myself in the head with my violin bow, then used it to wave him in with.

"Sorry about that," he said sheepishly as he entered the room and looked around.

"No worries. How did you find me?"

"Process of elimination. I'd heard about this part of the base-ment but thought it was an urban legend. After a while I knew I was getting closer because I could hear the violin, so I figured it was either you or some mermaids being held in captivity."

He asked about the piece I'd been practising; I ran through part of it for him and ended with a few high-pitched chords from *Psycho*. I asked about gym class; apparently they're playing volley-ball now, and as Rusty said, it isn't the most manly sport in the world, but a lot of the guys in our class do everything they can to make it look like it is. "You should see some of the he-men," he said with a laugh, naming one or two people who have a pretty lethal case of Alpha Male Fever. "All they ever do is spike."

I grinned or giggled or something, but I didn't know what to say after that. Finally Rusty asked if I wanted to eat lunch with him. When I told him I usually ate in the jail cell and kept practising until the start of afternoon classes, he shrugged and took his lunch out of his bag. We sat cross-legged on the floor and ate while Rusty laid out his idea.

It turns out that when Bruce told us about this assignment, Rusty remembered watching TV one night and being amazed when a commercial for a high-end cruise line included part of a song whose lyrics pretty obviously glorify drug use. So he wants us to create either a video in which a song is completely out of sync with the images—like a Disney tune about the delights of frolicking under the sea alongside footage of excessive marine pollution—or a mash-up of two or three songs whose messages are completely at odds with each other, like an anti-materialism folk song and a

Christmas carol about all the presents waiting for you under the tree. Basically, he wants us to create something that's equal parts parody, political protest, and total silliness, all while featuring me singing and playing the violin. He told me that his dad's side of the family is obsessed with home movies so someone always has the latest equipment, and apparently he knows all about shooting digital video and editing it together since he's in charge of converting old movies from VHS into digital format and burning copies for everyone. "It gives me the opportunity to edit out all the embarrassing footage of me when I was younger and to highlight all the embarrassing footage of my cousins," he said. This process apparently includes slow-motion replays and sound effects.

I leaned back and felt all these song titles dancing in my head like a slot machine, but parts of his idea seemed far-fetched. "Why do you want to film me doing all the parts?" I asked.

Apparently when I sang my Climax cover at Sophie and Jenice's wedding, the overdubbing had given him the weird impression that there were multiple incarnations of me singing as one—which is great, because that was exactly what I was going for. "There are all these anti-establishment songs from the sixties with a group of people singing in one voice as a form of protest, but now you see those songs being used in commercials to sell products—they're the same songs, but their meaning is totally the opposite of what it used to be."

I thought it over. "How long do we have to pull this off? Three weeks?"

"Yeah."

"That's not a lot of time," I said, even though I wanted to smack myself for being such a wet blanket.

Fortunately Rusty didn't seem to find this timeline nearly as daunting as I did. "Then we'd better get started," he said with a grin. He reached inside his bag, pulled out his iPod, and handed me one of his earbuds. I grabbed my day planner and a pen, and we spent the rest of the noon hour shoulder to shoulder, listening to music and putting ideas together. We couldn't have been physically closer than if he'd been sitting on my lap. But it was fine—for once, the closeness was so wonderfully uncomplicated.

I can't believe I'm writing this, but for the first time I'm excited about a school project. Usually school is the stuff I have to do on weekdays that gets in the way of everything else in my life—similar to Uncle Scott's dead-end job. Last weekend, when I had nothing better to do, I started rummaging through the piles of paper in my desk drawers and came across an essay I wrote for English class two years ago on "An Adult I Admire." I have no recollection of doing this, but it looks like I made one up: a neighbour in the house across the street (where there's actually a park) who supposedly played this grandfatherly role in my young life. He had a name and a backstory and everything. I got a fantastic grade and it was all lies.

But this? This is new. Rusty and I each spent the afternoon after school going through all our music and emailing lists to one another. That's bound to continue until we figure out the perfect combination. And, of course, the fact that I'll need to be perpetually in contact with Rusty is certainly a bonus!

It's hard to believe that I found this whole idea horrifying at first. As long as I don't screw things up too badly, it should be a lot of fun. Right?

Your loving son,

Dale

## SUNDAY, MAY 22

Dear Pa,

This morning at church, Jenice and Sophie practically ran up the aisle as soon as Reverend Heather gave the benediction and I launched into my postlude on the organ. The postlude is technically part of the service and you're supposed to sit in your pew till it's done—or so I've been told. In reality, everyone pretty much treats it as walking-away music. My two friends stood next to the organ while I played, looking like they were literally itching to talk to me. It was pretty unnerving, so I wrapped up the piece before I was a quarter of the way through and decided to try again next week.

"What's going on?" I asked as I put my music books away, even though I already had a good idea what they wanted to know.

"How was your sleepover?"

"You look tired. Is that a good sign?"

They sported identical smiles and practically spoke in unison, like this was a play and they'd rehearsed their lines too well.

"It was fine," I said. "We got a lot done on our song."

They looked like they were having a hard time believing me. When they asked if I was sticking around for coffee hour, I grabbed my bike helmet and gave them an apologetic shrug. I had two reasons for getting the hell out of there as quickly as I could. One was that I feared people would overhear us and that my sleepover at Rusty's would become the latest chapter in the annals of church gossip. The other was that I've found it's too easy for opinionated people to decide what something means when they didn't witness it themselves—my uncles are terrific examples of this. Besides, I wanted you to have first dibs.

What happened was this: on Thursday night—or was it Wednesday? I forget—Rusty called.

"So, like, there's been a death in the family. Nobody I knew," he added before I could unleash the whole *I'm so so sorry* routine. I forget now who it was—maybe his mother's cousin's father-in-law's half-sister's husband's mistress's rich aunt, or something like that. "The funeral's in Leamington, so my parents are going to drive there on Friday after school and won't be back till late Saturday. I told them I was old enough to stay home by myself, but they still think I'm afraid of the dark, so they wanted me to see if you could stay over."

"Me? Why me?" I asked, partly because it bought me some time and partly because I wanted to know.

"Well, I already called my 750 other friends, but they're all going to a rock concert that night," he said, in a tone so serious that it took me a few seconds to decide he was joking. "Whaddya say? The pullout couch in the rec room is pretty decent, and I figured we could get a lot done on our project."

"Okay—sure," I said.

"Really? Don't you need to ask your mother and Helmut first?"

"I don't think they'll put up much of a fight," I told him.

And I was right. I found Ma and Helmut in the living room watching the news, and at the start of the next commercial break I told them about the situation and basically informed them that Rusty had invited me to stay over. This was my way of asking for permission without asking for permission. Sure enough, they were so pleased that I was finally doing something normal for once, so that was that.

On Friday after school I packed up my laptop, some good earphones, and some blank sheet music. I'd never voluntarily slept over at a friend's house before, but I was barely dreading it at all.

Helmut dropped me off at Rusty's house just as his parents and Maisie and his grandmother were getting ready to take off. My legs started to buckle with impatience as they triple-checked the directions and Mitch finished going through his endless reminders about not opening the door to strangers or leaving the oven on. We waved so long as they drove away that I thought my arm was going to snap off. Finally Rusty led the way inside, took a deep breath, and extended his arms like he wanted the furniture to get up and hug him. "Don't you just love the quiet?" he demanded. He was grinning so hard that he had dimples I'd never seen before—they looked like they'd been stapled into his cheeks. I didn't say any-thing, though, since watching him was plenty for me.

"You know what we should do?" he asked, wagging his bushy eyebrows at me suggestively.

"What?"

"We should take advantage of this situation—do something we wouldn't normally be able to do."

"Oh?" I started to panic—he was looking at me so intently. I shifted my weight from one leg to the other and tried not to let out any of the giggles that were fluttering up my throat.

"Buddy," he said, his grin growing even wider and his voice sinking to a whisper, "*let's have ice cream before dinner!*"

And so, once my heart rate slowed back down, we sat on the sofa with soup bowls full of ice cream with cookies crumbled on top. I teased him about the state of his bedroom; he chuckled and told me that last Christmas his parents had bought him a book called *The Feng Shui of Clutter* and it vanished. I showed him a YouTube mash-up of a song by Coldplay and one by Sufjan Stevens, and he pointed out that the video had had more than fifty-two million views: "That's more than the population of Canada." He told me about an HBO drama with "a real ADHD quality to it," and I told him about a nineteenth-century composer named William Crotch. He told me about a reality show he'd watched about a brooding Austrian whose fiancée had ordered zebras for her supposedly scaled-down engagement party, and I told him about a friend of one of Ma's colleagues who specializes in feline photography. He told me about a novel he'd read whose ending involves two people on cocaine and a sedated parrot, and I told him about the latest composer on my list and the fact that you can totally tell he killed his wife because his music is so chromatic.

When I asked him about actual dinner, Rusty explained that his parents had left him some money, so we could either order a pizza or buy groceries and make something ourselves. I told him I didn't care, so the next thing I knew, we were walking to the grocery store. The ready-made salads looked like literal death, so we settled on a chicken stir-fry, despite Rusty's major hate-on for most vegetables. He was in the middle of telling me about his aunt who has a figurine phobia when we turned a corner and our cart collided into Sophie and Jenice's.

We all did the whole *what are* you *doing here* routine, and then Sophie, speaking to both of us but looking intently at me, added, "I didn't know you guys were friends!"

"Yeah—we've been hanging out since your wedding," Rusty said easily.

I could have punched him. Of course they'd imagine "hanging out" was code.

We started talking like a house on fire, and finally they invited us to spend the evening at their place. Rusty and I looked at each other—I didn't know what *he* was thinking, but *I* was thinking that we really needed to get cracking on our media studies assignment. When we continued to stare at each other and wait for the other to speak, Jenice snorted. "Come on, Soph—they probably want to be alone."

"No!" we insisted simultaneously. And there was nothing to add to that. The truth was just too unbelievable. *You're sleeping over on a Friday night while his parents are out of town so you can get some homework done. Riiiiiiiight.* In the end, we had no choice but to go to Sophie and Jenice's house in order to prove that we didn't prefer to stay in and make out all evening.

So we bought the groceries. We walked back to Rusty's, talking the whole way. Now that our Friday evening plans had changed, we vowed we'd wake up early the next morning and work on our assignment then, even though I knew in my gut that reality would get in the way of our good intentions somehow. We swapped stories while we made the stir-fry and then ate around the charred parts. He told me about an old photo he'd found of his dad in the late 1980s with the most insane mullet imaginable. I told him about the week Ma and Helmut had cooked all-vegan dishes without telling us and all our moods took a terrible nosedive. While I told that story, I apparently referred to her as Ma.

"I love that you call your mother 'Ma,'" he said as he replenished the mound of ketchup on his plate or whatever he was doing. "It's so old school it's almost badass. Hi, Ma. Hey, Ma! Over here, Ma! *Maw*."

"Is it?"

"Yeah. Are you guys big fans of *Little House on the Prairie* or something?"

"No. My mother called her parents 'Ma' and 'Pa.' They died before I was born, so I guess she wanted to keep that tradition going." I shrugged, trying to prevent everything from getting super heavy. "But yeah—I'm probably the last kid on earth who calls his mother that."

"Yeah." And then something in his brow changed, and I braced myself for what would come out of his mouth next. "What about your dad? Did you call him 'Pa'?" he asked in a more subdued tone.

"Yeah. I—I did," I said. I mean, it's the truth, but I stumbled on the verb tense since I still call you that.

We got to Sophie and Jenice's eventually, offering them the bag of chips we'd swiped from Rusty's pantry when I remembered my mother's rule never to show up to someone's house empty-handed. Rusty hadn't been to their place before, so Sophie led the way through every room, including the cozy basement they never use. They pointed out photographs and paintings on the wall, books in their bookcases, and everything else imaginable that had some kind of story attached to it. Rusty's comment after every one? "Nice."

And then—how can I put this? Sophie offered to show Rusty the backyard while Jenice asked me if I'd give her a hand getting drinks ready. It was all done so smoothly that I felt bad for suspecting that they'd planned this in order to quiz us separately about what was going on. But I did suspect them of doing that, so my instinct was to clam up.

"So how are things going?" Jenice asked as she dug out some wineglasses.

"Fine," I said.

I didn't know what else to say, so I asked her what I could do to help. As I washed a bowl that was lying in the sink, I looked through the window at Rusty and Sophie in the yard. From the way they were standing, I had the feeling they weren't talking about the garden at all. Just as I finished rinsing the bowl and turned off the tap, I heard Rusty's voice start to rise. "Look—there's nothing to tell, okay? We're just friends."

I didn't say anything else as I dried the bowl with a dishtowel, placed it on the counter, and filled it up with chips. It occurred to me that if I didn't want to be asked all these questions about my friendship with Rusty, one-word answers weren't going to cut it. So when Jenice tried again as she set the wineglasses on the table, I smiled and started channelling Uncle Scott.

"Things are going really well. Right now we're working on a big project for our media studies class. Have I ever told you about our teacher? He's a nice enough guy but totally disorganized, and I think he sprang this on us because he ran out of material to cover. His instructions were really vague, but then Rusty had the idea for a song mash-up, and blah blah blah blah blah." I kept going with inconsequential details until I heard the sliding door scrape open. "Oh! Russ, I was telling Jenice about our media studies project. Wait till you hear about our teacher, Sophie. Yak yak yak yak yak." And then I went through the whole thing again. By the time I'd completely exhausted the subject of our stupid teacher and our stupid assignment, we were ready to sit down at the table and talk about something else. Which was just as well, because by that point I could feel my heart beating behind my eyes.

"Red or white, guys?" Sophie asked, digging a corkscrew out of a drawer.

"Just water for me, please," I said, already mapping out a plan to rummage through their medicine chest in search of some Extra Strength Tylenol.

"Yeah, me too, for now," Rusty said with a sigh.

As soon as we sat down at the table with our water and our wine, with Rusty and me on one side (me to his left, thankfully) and them on the other, I asked them how married life was treating them so far. That took the heat off of us for a while. They told us all about their few days in Niagara-on-the-Lake right after the wedding and their longer honeymoon in Montreal. That led to us talking about the summer. Apparently Rusty wants to go tree planting up north— this was news to me—and I still can't figure out if he really wants to do this or if he'd just like to get away from Mitch for a while. The subject of choirs came up, so I mentioned the choir school I'd gone to in Guelph. "We sang like angels but acted like little shits" was how I described it.

"You went to choir school? I didn't know that," Rusty said with amazement. I didn't know how to answer him, because really, what he doesn't know about me could fill a volcano.

But I ended up telling them all about it. It's funny—what I remembered wasn't all the times I was teased or picked on, but some of the funnier aspects, like singing all these pieces in Latin and German that we didn't understand, how we learned the words phonetically and gave it our best shot. My class somehow gained a reputation for being demons to substitute teachers. I told them how, even in grade six, boys as well as girls made up the nastiest rumours about each other: who was going out with whom, who was doing it with whom. Really outlandish things, none of which was remotely true or even thought to be remotely true. At one point someone had started a rumour that I was getting it on with the cafeteria lady, even though I was eleven—that one didn't go away for months. I thought of Jordana. Most often we were chosen to sing duets together, so a lot of the rumours were about what supposedly went down when- ever she and I got together to "rehearse." I didn't tell them that.

At one point Jenice left the room and returned with two envelopes of photos. One was a small stack of regular-sized photos from the wedding and the reception, which was great. But in the second envelope, the larger one, were three blown-up photos that I have in front of me now as I type all this. Don't think me incredibly vain or anything, but I find them fascinating.

The first photo is of me at the reception, standing alone with my imaginary backup singers, snapping my fingers with one hand as I belt out my cover of "Bedroom Eyes," sporting my requisite high-E face. What I like about the photo is that it's really close to the way I want people to see me—if that makes any sense.

The second one is of me at the wedding, sitting at the organ, looking out with this expression of awe—it must have been when they were exchanging vows. The photographer they hired should have been a sniper—I had no idea either of these pictures had been taken.

The third one, smaller than the other two, was of Sophie and Jenice. I think they're walking down the aisle or something.

I looked up at Jenice and Sophie to thank them, but they were both staring at Rusty, each set of eyebrows arched to practically ninety degrees. So I glanced at him and caught the weirdest expression on his face. He was smiling, and his eyes were shiny. He looked—well, had the circumstances been different, I would have said that he was looking at those photos of me with love, but since he'd been so insistent that we're just friends, I shrugged it off and figured it was allergies instead.

I don't know what I'm going to do with these blown-up photographs of myself. I have no intention of framing them or even showing them to anyone else. But I'm glad I have them, for all that. Maybe one day someone can use them for a career retrospective.

We kept talking for a while. I thought of Gonzo and the kinds of parties he sometimes goes to, where it's loud and crazy and the term "super trashed" is used to describe what happens there. Compared to that kind of party, the four of us sitting around a kitchen table talking—two of us drinking *water*—would probably seem unbearably tame to most people. I mean, the most insane part of the evening was that we polished off a whole bag of root vegetable chips. But it was exactly my speed.

The walk home was uneventful, but kind of weird, too. I'd been out late before, but this was the first time I was heading home with someone who wasn't a family member. It felt like a sneak preview of what it'll be like when I'm in a real relationship. Except I was going to sleep by myself on the pullout sofa in the family room.

But then the gods intervened, as only the gods know how. (I read that sentence in a book once, and it seems fitting here.)

Basically what happened was that the pullout sofa got stuck halfway to being unfolded and refused to keep going or to fold back. We debated what to do next. Rusty said his parents wouldn't like the idea of either one of us sleeping in their bed, which was fine, because I didn't like that idea either. He said they had an air mattress, but he didn't know where the pump was. As a way to lighten the mood, I told him I could always curl up in Maisie's crib, and he jokingly offered to sleep in the bathtub.

Then we stared at each other. I heard the sound of a clock ticking, but I'm pretty sure it was only in my head.

Finally I said something like "Look—you have a double bed, right?"

"Right."

"So it's, like, made for two people, technically."

"Right. *Oh*—really?"

"I mean, sure. I don't care if you don't care."

"Yeah. I don't care either." But he looked away from me as he said it.

Looking back, I can't imagine what I was thinking. But there was no other option unless I wanted to walk home and subject myself to Ma's endless questions. I followed Rusty upstairs, carrying my backpack and my overnight bag. Usually his bedroom is apocalyptic in its messiness, but that night it looked like the kind of room you'd see in a magazine. I didn't know if tidying up had been Rusty's idea or if his parents had browbeaten him into it, but either way I was amazed.

I dug out my toiletry kit and went off to pee and to brush my teeth, and when I got back Rusty did the same. I turned on his bedside lamp, sat on the edge of the bed, and stopped myself from peeking inside the drawers of his nightstand. I'd brought pyjamas with me—the kind that make me look like a three-year-old accountant—but it was a lot warmer in Rusty's room than it is in the basement at home, so I stuffed them back in my bag.

It turns out Rusty doesn't bother with pyjamas. He just started taking his clothes off and tossed them to the floor till he was down to his boxers. Standing in front of me, he asked if I wanted the wall or the edge. I looked away like I needed to consider it, then forced myself to say "edge" because I figured that if I ended up pinned between him and the wall all night, eventually I'd panic and be driven to fight my way out.

So Rusty moved past me, pulled the comforter and the top sheet back, and climbed into bed. I kept my back to him, unbuttoned my shirt, took off my pants, peeled off my T-shirt and my socks, and tossed everything to the floor the way he had. Once I was down to my boxer briefs, I looked down and discovered that my pants had landed on top of his, making it look like they were going at each other with abandon.

Rusty may have said something at that point, but my heart was beating too loud for me to hear him.

I quickly pulled the covers around me, adjusted my pillow, and tried to get comfortable. The sheets felt weird—I couldn't tell if I was going to be too hot or too cold—and Rusty's bedside lamp looked like a fire hazard. Rusty turned to face me, smiling, like all this was the most normal thing in the world. But strangely it did feel normal. I glanced at the hair on Rusty's chest that's the colour of barbecue sauce, and in an attempt to distract myself from my hormones I forced myself to pretend that Rusty and I were trapped in a sexless marriage.

I love that term, by the way—"sexless marriage." I never want to *be* in one, mind you.

"Did you have an okay time tonight?" he asked me.

"Yeah. I think Jenice and Sophie were disappointed that we didn't have any wine, though." I paused, then decided to go for it. "You didn't need to stick to water because of me, by the way."

He looked at me, surprised, like that hadn't even occurred to him. "Oh, it wasn't that. I was in a grumpy mood, and I figured wine would make it worse."

"Oh." I didn't know what to say about that, so I went with the next thought that popped into my head. "What were you and Sophie talking about in the garden?"

"Nothing," he said in a tone that clearly indicated it was some-thing. But I didn't push it—partly because I didn't really want to know and partly because I was starting to get drowsy. We talked about this and that for a few more minutes, and then we both decided that it was time to sleep.

I rolled over and reached for his bedside lamp, but then I couldn't figure out how the switch worked, so finally he leaned over and got it for me. But of course he practically had to climb on top of me to reach it. I didn't have time to react from the heat of his body brushing against mine before he rolled away and said good night. I lay there in the dark, trying to remember what it felt like to be sleepy, Rusty's voice echoing in my head: "Look! We're just friends!"

And then—

Well, anyway, I woke up Saturday morning when Rusty rolled away from me and dragged 90 percent of the blankets with him. The sun was shining through the window, so I got dressed, fetched the newspaper from the mailbox outside, and helped myself to a bowl of cereal. When I went back upstairs to check up on Rusty, he was snoring away, sprawled out on the side of the bed I'd slept on.

I went back to the family room, managed to fold the sofa bed back into a sofa without too much difficulty, and sat with my laptop and a cup of Earl Grey tea. I put on my headphones and listened to some of the songs Rusty had sent me as possibilities. I also browsed through Rusty's parents' CD collection and ripped a few that seemed promising—I figured no one would care. I was hoping that if I let a bunch of songs swim around in my head long enough, eventually something clever and original would emerge. But nothing did. I sat there, jumping from one song to another, trying to piece them together like a fucked-up jigsaw puzzle, and all I heard was a bunch of sound fragments that refused to cooperate with each other.

I peeled off my headphones when I thought I heard footsteps upstairs and the sound of Rusty's voice. "Dale?" The footsteps suddenly increased in speed and intensity. "Dale!"

He seemed to be panicking, so part of me wondered if he'd woken up with a horse's head in his bed. I hurried out of the family room and took the stairs two at a time. "Sorry—I was downstairs listening to music," I said.

Rusty was still wearing just his boxer shorts, but what amazed me even more was the weird look on his face, like he'd come across a burglar. He tried to laugh but didn't quite manage it. "When I woke up and couldn't find you, I was afraid you'd gone home," he explained.

"Why would I do that? We have a ton of work ahead of us," I said.

Eventually I told him I'd hit another dead end with the song, and we talked through our options. Basically, we're running out of time. I need to record all the audio before next weekend, because on Saturday Rusty is coming over to film me, and he needs all the next week to edit everything together, something that hadn't dawned on me before. We'll be presenting our project in class the following Wednesday—just over two weeks from now.

That meant letting go of our ambition to do something really deep and heavy. I suggested keeping everything in the realm of love songs, ideally with something the guys in our class would already know.

"It's too bad we can't just use that Climax song you did at the wedding," Rusty said thoughtfully. "It's supposed to be this generic love song, but the lyrics have this weird stalkerish vibe to them. All the guys in class know that song inside out, even though they think they're making fun of it."

I looked at him, and it was like a book of ideas opened in my mind to the right page, and suddenly everything was so clear. I don't pretend to understand how this sometimes happens and sometimes doesn't—I just try to roll with it when it does.

"Why don't we?" I said.

The song "Bedroom Eyes" is a pretty typical boy-band pop song, complete with horrendous lyrics—at one point they try to make "rush" rhyme with "touch." But after Rusty's crack about stalking, I started to see their lyrics really differently: "Say you'll be mine," "Never gonna let you go," and "Because I said so." It seems shocking that I didn't pick up on this before—I mean, hell, their debut album was called *We Have Spoken*.

So what we're doing is this: I'm going to use the arrangement from the ballad version I did for Sophie and Jenice's wedding, but redo it in a minor key—I've spent the whole day working it out in my head and so far it sounds monstrous, which is to say it sounds amazing.

Anyway, I'm getting really sleepy, so I guess I should get ready for bed. I don't remember the last time I was so excited about a homework assignment, and that's saying something!

Your loving son,

Dale

Fine—so I lied. It isn't time for bed—it's 4:30 in the afternoon. And that's not all that happened at Rusty's house.

For all these weeks, I've been writing letters to my father, pretending I'm talking to him in a way I have zero interest in talking to anyone who's alive. I mean, my usual answer to my mother's daily question of "How was school today?" is "Fine," so writing letters in which I can be more or less totally honest has been good, since it's given me a sense of what it'd be like to have someone I could count on. I know Uncle Scott and Uncle Joe and even Jenice and Sophie have my back, but all four of them seem to be big on solving my problems for me. It's like they view me as this little kid who's too stupid to see things clearly or too immature to make good decisions. But here I can let myself go in a way that's possible only because I'm writing to someone who can't judge me or tell me what to do. Even though I'm not really sold one way or the other on what happens to us after we die, no part of me has any faith that what I'm writing to my father has any way of reaching him.

But even so, there've been a lot of details I just couldn't bring myself to include in these letters—or that I went back later and took out. Like the way my balls started to tingle when I saw Jonathan again, even though I wanted to kick myself for it. Or the way Rusty started to chub up the day we were at the pool and I took off my towel. Or the times I've caught him looking at me with his face flushed. Or the time he mentioned some rock star who's apparently bisexual and he seemed to be studying my reaction. Or the fact that Jonathan broke up with me before I could break up with him only because I'd thought—and still think—it was more polite to wait until we'd finished putting our clothes back on first. When I wrote the letter to my father about my sleepover at Rusty's, I told him that Rusty and I had climbed into bed together and behaved like castrated angels all night. But even I didn't find that believable and I can't imagine he would have either.

The truth is Rusty and I sort of fooled around—accidentally. I know I'm making it sound like I tripped on a branch. We didn't have *sex* sex like anything I've seen in porn, but we got to where we needed to go, if that makes any sense. I can't write any of it down in a letter addressed to my father, but I need to write about it just the same, because, being me, I'm a little freaked out by what we did—at least, I figure I ought to be. I'm going to save this file as "Algebra notes" so no one will think of opening it, and I'm going to reserve the right to come back later and delete this, but here goes.

Things had been building between Rusty and me for a while now, but for the most part I tried to fight it. Ever since the debacle with Jonathan, I guess I've been gun-shy about dating or "hanging out" with someone, as Jordana would put it. True, Rusty doesn't infuriate me nearly as much as Jonathan did, but then again, Jonathan and I had far more to talk about. I didn't know how to explain all this to Uncle Scott and Uncle Joe when they were grilling me at that restaurant, since they don't know about Jonathan, and I don't know if I can explain it any better now. I've liked Rusty for a while—like, *really* liked him—and although it was easier to tell myself he was straight and everything I thought I saw was only in my imagination because that helped me draw a pretty firm line in the sand, I'd picked up on enough skewed eyebrows and flushed faces and nervous giggles to piece together that him liking me back is at least not outside the realm of possibility. But honestly, the fact that we have so little in common always held me back. Say we got naked together—no doubt that would be good in some ways, but what would we talk about afterward? Unlikely ballet moves? Unlikely reality show concepts? What would we do when, inevitably, we ran out of those kinds of topics?

And so, when Rusty and I stripped to our undies on Friday night and hopped into bed together, I felt dread mixed with hormones and sensed that falling asleep was going to be a chore. Everything felt backward. I liked him, but we hadn't said anything out loud about how we felt about each other. Did we really like each other romantically or were we just two friends with a case of the hornies? I was turned on, but I didn't know if I was supposed to be. Filling the awkward silence was the sound in my head of Rusty insisting to Sophie that we were just friends and the memory of him ignoring me for days after my uncles took us out to dinner. And yet he was lying on his stomach with a look in his eyes that was almost of hunger. We talked a bit, the blankets kicked off because it was a warm night, the sheet covering only part of him, but as my eyes wandered, my mind was racing with questions I couldn't answer. What did I *want* to happen, both that night and later? What did I *feel* for this guy anyway?

I couldn't figure out how his lamp worked, so he leaned over and snapped it off, his—well, I guess the right word would be "protrusion"—poking my thigh as he did so. I glanced at his bedside clock just in time to catch the transition from 11:59 to midnight. I kept hearing a rustle that sounded like Rusty looking over his shoulder at me, but I tried not to look back. Eventually I grew bored lying on that side, so I rolled over and watched Rusty's bare back as it rose and fell with each breath.

Finally he rolled over and faced me.

"Can't sleep?" he said sympathetically.

"Nah. You?"

"Me neither."

He smiled at me. I returned the smile.

"Is everything okay?" he asked.

"Yeah. You?"

"Sure. It's just—um—" Somehow I knew he was blushing, even though it was so dark I couldn't see colours anymore. "Sorry if this is too much information, but I usually rub one out when I go to bed. It helps me fall asleep."

He looked at me in a way that was kind of drool-inducing, like he was offering me step one and it was up to me to decide if I wanted to unleash step two. "Yeah—me too," I said—except I had to clear my throat and say it again. When it dawned on me that he'd admitted something incredibly private about himself, like he trusted me, I rushed ahead with the compulsion to do the same thing. "Although when I do it in the morning, it helps me wake up. Isn't that weird?"

And then—well—we went back and forth a few more times, moving on from *when* to *how*. I guess not surprisingly, the more we talked about jerking off, the more *not* jerking off became physically unbearable. Eventually we came to the conclusion that we both had a problem we needed to take care of, so we went through the whole *I don't mind if you don't mind* routine again. We agreed to pull our underwear down on the count of three, and once that happened we just lay there and giggled, like the sight of each other naked was hilarious.

"Remember the portmanteau you came up with a while back, about the novelty of seeing someone naked for the first time?" he said. "What was it again? 'Newdity'?"

I chuckled and fought the instinct to fold my arms across my chest. "Yeah. Except this isn't the first time. The locker room at the pool, right?"

"Yeah. That was fun—but not like this." He paused and squeezed his junk for a few seconds, then used the same hand to prop up his head. "Just so you know, I've never done anything like this before."

"Oh—okay."

"Have you?"

"Um ... sort of."

But I really didn't want to talk about Jonathan, because if I did I'd have had to admit that the three of us had sat together at Jenice and Sophie's wedding reception, and I didn't want to go there. For once I didn't want to think about anything except my immediate reality: the sight of Rusty undressed after I'd daydreamed for weeks about what he looked like that way, the catch in his voice that showed he was nervous, the feeling of unfamiliar sheets against my bare skin, the heat from his body next to mine. And even though this wasn't my first rodeo, there was a glow in the pit of my stomach that I'd never experienced with Jonathan, and I wanted to lean into that as much as I could.

Rusty responded by reaching for my hand and placing it against his furry heart, which made mine start to beat even faster. "Then maybe you can show me what to do," he whispered.

So I did. We lay side by side on our backs and started to touch ourselves, me with my left hand, him with his right. We were basically doing what we normally do on our own, except with an audience, which meant it would have been a shame for me to close my eyes. I figured this was plenty, but gradually we seemed to be turning toward each other and the gap between us got smaller and smaller. At one point my right hand brushed his thigh. He responded by leaning his head against my shoulder. And then, just as the sensations in my body started to build toward something stronger than I'd ever imagined, we switched hands or switched dicks or whatever you want to call it and kept going, first slowly, then with increased urgency, until, seconds or minutes later, we both crossed to the other side and I finally discovered for myself why people call it "afterglow."

After catching my breath and letting go of him, I turned to look at Rusty, whose eyes had glazed over and whose head was rolling back and forth like he was having a seizure. "Dude," he whispered. "Buddy—" And then his eyes closed and sleep overtook him.

I got up once I was able to control my legs again, tiptoed toward the bathroom down the hall even though we were alone in the house, grabbed some toilet paper, and went back and tried to clean Rusty up as he slept. I couldn't find my underwear, so I climbed into bed again without putting them back on and pulled the sheet over us. After pausing for a moment to feel proud, I slinked my arm around his stomach—he was so warm and toasty—and closed my eyes, figuring I'd stay that way for just a second before rolling back to my side of the bed. But I must have fallen asleep like that, because the next thing I remember is waking up the next morning.

What happened after that is pretty much what I told my father: I was listening to music with headphones on when Rusty woke up and couldn't find me, except that once he'd got over his fear that I'd flipped out on him and gone home, he stood there at the top of the stairs in his boxer shorts and asked me if I was okay. "I mean, with the whole—" And then he did a jerking-off motion with both his hands that made me laugh.

"This may come as a shock, but I'm fine," I said. "I mean, I wasn't expecting that, but it's all good." I couldn't help but notice the splotches of red stubble on his face. It made him look like he was in the first stages of leprosy, but it totally worked for him.

Rusty seemed relieved that I was being such a good sport about it, and then his smile morphed into a mischievous grin. "Wanna go again?" he asked, like this was some sort of ride.

So we did. And you know what? It was *fun*. We wrestled and horsed around. We gave each other noogies and nipple twists. We played sword fight. He taught me about foreskin. We shampooed each other's hair. We had a contest where one guy smacked the other guy's bare ass as hard as he could and the other guy tried not to flinch. We compared techniques. We touched each other and measured each other and talked about everything. We kept saying the word "jizz." He's a lot hairier than I am and I couldn't stop petting him for some reason, so sometimes he'd make this purring sound. We paused to eat something before going back at it. It was like our shenanigans at the pool, except we were naked and we didn't have to look away because that was the point. And through it all we laughed and laughed and laughed. It was only once we were in the shower the second time that I remembered our media studies assignment and suggested redoing that awful Climax song in a minor key.

None of this was like anything I'd ever seen or read about, which made me think this wasn't really sex at all. It was something else—something I couldn't name, except maybe with the word "jizz." At one point, when Rusty was amusing himself by lathering my testicles with so much body wash that you couldn't see them anymore, I decided I could totally get on board with having a friend like *this*.

I ended up staying till early evening, partly because I was having such a good time and partly because I couldn't stomach going home to face my mother's interrogation at the dinner table. But once I was standing in the front hall with my shoes on and my bags packed, I didn't know how to say goodbye. Rusty blushed as soon as I turned to face him, then grinned. "You okay?" he said.

"Yeah," I said, but I think I sounded surprised. "You?"

"I can honestly say I've never felt better," he said with a laugh. A handshake seemed pretty pathetic after everything we'd spent all day doing to each other, so he gave me a bear hug, kissed my cheek, and whispered something about being glad we were friends. Even though my body literally ached from being manhandled so much, I held on as tightly as I could, neither one of us letting go until we heard the sound of car doors slamming shut in the driveway.

"Oh, *fuck*," I said, and because the idea of having to face Rusty's parents at that moment filled me with panic, I swung my bookbag around my shoulders, grabbed my overnight bag, and fled through the house and out the back door. I ran to the end of their backyard, hopped over the chain-link fence onto their neighbours' property, and kept running. At one point I caught sight of a cardinal in a tree as I ran past it, and without even thinking about it I called out, "Hi, Pa!" and started to laugh.

Ma and Helmut were cleaning up the kitchen when I got home. I managed to keep a straight face when I told them I'd had a good time, but I quickly made a point of yawning and telling them I needed to hit the hay so I could go to church first thing in the morning to practise. They took this as a good sign that my new-found social life wasn't going to impact my work responsibilities, so they left me to sit in my room and think everything over.

I lay down on my bed and started to text Jordana, not to give her a play-by-play of what had happened but just to check in. But as I typed in her name and the several unanswered texts I'd sent her in the last few weeks filled my screen, I changed my mind and texted Rusty instead. I didn't want to be too explicit since Mitch strikes me as the type of guy who'd rummage through his kid's phone, so I wrote something only Rusty would understand. *Thanks for a great visit, buddy. Let's do this again sometime!* I started to add something about unlikely cartoon show crossovers, then deleted it—we're definitely past that now.

I figured that once I was alone in my room I'd start to freak out about what had gone down between us, but instead, I read a book for a while, slept like a log, showed up at church an hour early, and managed to dodge Sophie and Jenice's curious questions after the service without cracking up. This afternoon I put together a rough piano score of the Climax song in a minor key—I got so immersed in it that I even managed to forget what had happened between us yesterday—and sent off a demo to Rusty.

And now I've typed all this out and I haven't lost my mind after all. And I've just looked up at the photo of my father on the wall above my desk, and he's still smiling. So maybe this is just what best friends do at sleepovers and it isn't something to get all worked up about.

I told Rusty in my text message yesterday that I'd be up for doing that again, and in his reply he said the same thing. Which is great!

But I just thought of something else.

When?

And *where?*

Dear Pa,

The strangest thing happened yesterday. All week I've spent every waking moment at home working on the Climax song. I finished my arrangement sometime on Wednesday afternoon, so last night at supper I asked everyone not to go downstairs for the evening because I'd be recording. Ma and Helmut knew about this assignment, but Gonzo seemed surprised by what Rusty and I are planning. "Why? What's your project?" I asked.

"We're doing a skit about politicians trying to find their way out of an art gallery," Gonzo said with a shrug.

"Oh." Actually, compared to some of the ideas I'd overheard in class, that sounded pretty clever, although it didn't occur to me to say so.

I figured that would be the end of it, but after supper, as I was doing scales to warm up my voice, I turned to see Gonzo coming down the stairs. "Hey," he said, pausing halfway down like he wasn't sure if he should continue. "I just wondered if you needed some help with the recording or whatever."

I looked around at how I'd set up the room so that everything I needed was within reach: the mixing board, the microphone, the headphones, and my music stand. I'd always done everything myself, but something about the way Gonzo was looking at me stopped me from telling him that. "Yeah—that'd be great."

So I showed him how everything worked, gave him the fairly straightforward task of hitting the "record" button and the "stop" button, dug out a second pair of headphones for him, and moved some of the equipment around so that I could focus on singing. Then I went back to the piano. There's something about the way singers warm up that seems normal when you're in a group but becomes vaguely humiliating when you're by yourself. Singing "ma-may-mee-mo-moo" over and over again isn't all that dignified, somehow. Gonzo didn't seem to care that much, though, and finally I figured I'd do a few practice runs of the lead vocal line to finish warming up.

I got everything ready, explaining that I'd set up a metronome to help me stay on tempo and a rough piano track to give me something to sing to. I went through the lead vocal part once, but halfway through the second verse I saw Gonzo shake his head, so I stopped.

"What's the matter?"

"You're speeding up."

"I am?"

"Yeah."

This annoyed me, especially because Gonzo isn't supposed to know anything about music, but I figured his merciless comments would help me get it perfect, so we started over.

At one point, when we took a mini break, Gonzo said, "My mother wants to invite you over for dinner sometime. She says she'd like to get to know you better."

"Yeah—that'd be great."

We recorded all the vocal parts that evening, including the harmonies for the crazy tag at the end of the song. I did all the backing parts twice and the lead part three times to give me a few options when I edit everything together. I'm glad we got that much done, since I've found that my voice doesn't always match if I try to edit together tracks that weren't recorded on the same day.

Today I snuck my laptop to school and spent all of third period and the whole lunch break mixing the vocal parts, sitting on the concrete floor even after my butt had fallen asleep. Rusty came by after gym class, and I waved him in, silently handed him the headphones, and played for him what I had so far. Then he sat on the floor against the opposite wall, dug out his lunch, and started to read. We didn't say a single word to each other the whole time—only when it was time to go did we break out of our silence, and that's only because Rusty had to give me the lowdown on a novel I hadn't had time to read for English class.

After school I marched home, ate a sandwich standing up, and went downstairs to start recording the violin tracks. Gonzo was already there with his headphones on. With him, too, there was no need to say anything. I offered to print another copy of the strings parts so that he could follow along, but he said not to bother since he can't read sheet music anyway.

By the time we were done, we went upstairs to discover that Ma and Helmut had already eaten but left supper on the stove for us. We sat together at the dining room table and had what was probably our first ever substantial conversation. There wasn't that much to say about the song, but we talked about the assignment and school and didn't seem to run out of things to say. And when Iliana arrived to pick him up and he explained why he wasn't ready yet, she wanted to know all about it, so while Gonzo was packing I showed her around my little recording studio. And then, once they'd left, I recorded the piano track and the drum track by myself.

Now it's after midnight and I've finished mixing and editing the instrumental tracks. I just exported the file as an MP3 and emailed it to both Rusty and Gonzo. I'm so fucking tired! This is probably the most boring letter I've ever written to you, but I don't have the energy to jazz it up. I wish I could sleep all weekend, but Rusty will be here first thing in the morning to film me playing and singing all the parts again. There were times this past week when I wished I'd never agreed to do this, but now that my share of the work is finished, I guess I've been having a lot of fun all along.

As a way to get that song out of my head before I go to sleep, I've been listening to the latest single from a Scandinavian samba band whose name translates into English as "Porn Widows." All the vocalists in the music video are dressed in puffy snowsuits and smiling super aggressively, so whatever it is they're singing about, they mean business.

Your loving son,

Dale

## SUNDAY, MAY 29

Dear Pa,

Yesterday turned out to be such a full day. I would have written to you after Rusty left, but I was so wiped that the prospect of trying to put together coherent sentences filled me with dread. This morning I headed to church at some ridiculous hour to make up for the fact that I hadn't had time to practise this week's hymns. The service went as well as it could under the circumstances, which is to say it didn't go well at all—at least from where I was sitting. But a few people came up to me afterward to tell me that my organ playing keeps getting better, so I was relieved to know that people were too polite to say anything about all my mistakes.

I also had a cup of coffee with Sophie and Jenice—well, I sat across from them with a glass of water while they drank coffee. I told them about the song, and they said they definitely want to see the video once it's done. They told me about their plans for a camping trip to Algonquin Park, which doesn't appeal to me personally but sounds fine in the abstract. In short, it was the kind of chat we used to have before they started bugging me about Rusty, and this time, thankfully, he didn't come up once.

Rusty rang the doorbell on Saturday morning while I was wolfing down a bowl of cereal. We hadn't been able to spend a lot of time together because of the song and homework and Gonzo being home this week. He and Mitch carried in the equipment we needed: a video camera, a tripod, and two huge spotlights. After Mitch left, Rusty and I debated about what I should wear in the video. I suggested putting on my school uniform, but he liked what I had on, which was a pair of beige corduroys and a T-shirt with the old CBC logo from the 1970s on it, the one that looks like an exploding pizza. Before I could ask Rusty what the spotlights were for, he asked if I had any heavy blankets to tape over the windows, since we needed to eliminate any natural light to ensure that the lighting stayed consistent throughout the day. I didn't understand why that was necessary, since I figured it'd take maybe an hour to film everything.

Well!

It ended up taking us all fucking day and a good part of the evening to get everything done, with about fifteen minutes for lunch and another fifteen minutes for supper. By the end of it I was sort of ready to die, but overall I enjoyed myself. Normally Rusty's a laid-back, happy-go-lucky guy, but as soon as he started setting up he became this artist who knew exactly what he wanted and what he needed to do to get it.

Most of his instructions sounded like they ended with question marks, but they were orders. "Move over a bit?" he'd say, or "Sit up straight?" or "Look slightly happier?" He had me sitting on a stool in front of a blank wall, and once it was in the position he wanted he asked me to tape all four legs to the floor so it couldn't move. "We're filming everything from the same angle, so everything has to be exactly the same," he declared. That meant, among other things, that I couldn't scratch my head or touch my hair at any point during the day, and when I stopped to have something to eat or drink Rusty made me cover my shirt with a dishtowel in case I spilled something all over myself.

So most of the day was spent filming me doing everything I'd done for the audio, but this time for the camera: I sang every single vocal part and played each part on the violin twice, and once Rusty was sure he had enough good takes of everything, he moved the camera to film my hands playing the piano and the drums. Rusty said I could lip-synch, but even though we weren't recording the sound I wanted it to be more authentic—I can always tell when people are lip-synching in music videos. All in all, we ended up listening to the finished song about eighty or ninety times, so now I don't want to hear about bedroom eyes ever again.

Rusty's a great director. I can see why he's in charge of home movies in his family. He has high standards, but he never lost his patience. Early on, after a couple of takes, he told me I needed to smile more as I sang. "I was going for a melancholy look, to match the song," I argued.

He shook his head. "When you don't smile at all, you look like you're towering with rage," he said. I didn't believe him until he showed me, and oh, man, he was right. Good to know, by the way.

Once we were done, Rusty thanked me for being such a good sport and gave me a hug.

Now Rusty has to take those hours of footage and create a four-minute video out of them. I have no idea what kind of work is involved or even what he's aiming to do. He tried to describe it to me, but finally he shrugged gleefully and told me I'd understand once it was finished. I guess I can relate to that. I offered to help, but I have the feeling that film is for him what music is for me and so he needs to do everything himself.

Even though my part in this assignment is done, I still have an insane week ahead of me. We perform the Fauré *Requiem* next Saturday, which is also the day of Uncle Scott and Uncle Joe's anniversary party. It'll be an intense day, but at least I'll have Sunday to get some rest.

Your loving (and exhausted) son,
Dale

I've been shivering with rage for the past twenty-four hours. I know everything, Pa—*everything*. I just came home from church, where I botched every single hymn. Jenice and Sophie came up to me afterward and asked me what was wrong, but I couldn't tell them. I knew I'd fucking lose it if I tried to say anything.

Everything I thought was true turned out to be a lie. Not because anyone actually lied to me, but because they left out so much of the truth. Ma, Grandma, Uncle Scott, Uncle Joe—

You know what? Fuck this. I have a whole lot to say to you and I'm going to say it in person.

## MONDAY, JUNE 6

Ma wouldn't let me borrow her car yesterday. She didn't want me to drive while I was upset. I mean, fair enough, but what it boiled down to was that she didn't see the point in me driving forty-five minutes each way just so I could yell at your tombstone.

"I need to talk to him," I explained, even though the words sounded crazy as soon as they left my mouth.

"But honey—your father's dead."

She wouldn't let me stay home from school today, either. I told her I felt worse than if I'd had the sniffles or a fever, but she didn't—or wouldn't—understand. "I don't want you to fall behind," she said, as if school mattered.

So I tried: I put on my uniform and made a lunch and went out. Even though it was barely eight in the morning, I knew it was going to be one of those days when wearing long pants and a jacket was going to be an ordeal, and not just because of the heat. Gonzo kept looking back at me as we walked to the bus stop, but he didn't say anything. As soon as we were standing at the corner, this earthquake of panic started in my gut till I thought it was going to choke me. That feeling of my heart beating in my throat reminded me of the time my grade six bully told me at a dress rehearsal that when I sang my solo in some Bach cantata I sounded like a hundred-year-old vampire choking to death while trying to suck my own knob—except it felt much worse. I didn't know what to do. When

I turned to Gonzo, he reached for my arm. "Look—go home," he said.

I don't know if I said anything in reply, but I did walk back. Ma and Helmut were still in the dining room reading the paper, but they didn't seem surprised to see me again.

At that point I was done asking for permission. "I'm not going to school today," I said, unknotting my tie and looking at the wall between them. "I will tomorrow and the next day, but not today." I nearly added something like *I have spoken*, but I figured that would just set them off.

Ma sighed a little, but rather than fight me on it she offered to call the school to let them know I'd be absent. "But just for today," she added, like this was a great concession on her part.

"Thanks," I said. Then I made myself look at her. "Ma, I'm angry at what happened—not at you."

"Oh, honey. Sit down. Let's talk everything over," she said, holding out the chair next to her and gesturing to it. Instead, I shook my head and backed away from the table.

"Maybe one of us should stay home today and keep you company," Helmut said, and when I turned to look at him, I saw that his eyes were wide, like he was alarmed.

I didn't have a lot of energy left in me, but I managed to reassure them that all I wanted was to be left alone. I couldn't help smiling, too, in the back of my mind. Ma and Helmut have this weird way of parenting. It's like life to them is this great big pond of FINE, and every once in a while these buoys of BAD come up in the water, but as long as we manage to dodge them, we're still

FINE. It's like they keep consulting this checklist on a little pad of paper on their dresser. Are the boys doing something BAD? Are they drinking or doing drugs? Are they shoplifting or sexting? Are they cutting themselves or attempting suicide? No? Then high-five! Everything's FINE.

Maybe I'll understand them better when I'm older. But I doubt it.

I went downstairs and closed the door to my room. I took the framed photo of you from the wall above my desk and set it face down in a drawer. I texted Rusty, thanking him again for being a friend to me yesterday and telling him I'd see him tomorrow. Then I turned my phone off, lay down on my bed, and listened to the footsteps upstairs like they were a private percussion recital for my enjoyment. Soon enough I heard Ma and Helmut leave the house and go to work. I continued to lie there, staring at a dot on a ceiling tile and wondering if at some point it would start to move.

I must have fallen asleep like that. I don't remember dreaming anything. When I opened my eyes, it was almost eleven and I felt dull and overtired. The worst part was that for a moment I'd forgotten everything, but then I remembered again. I went upstairs, checked all the rooms in the house to make sure I was alone. I cued up some ambient music on YouTube to keep me company, but an upbeat cappuccino commercial came on, so I turned it off. I tried to make tea using the impossible contraption that takes up half the kitchen counter, then gave up and proceeded to boil water in a saucepan on the stove and found a tea bag so old it probably came from our old house. So now I'm sitting at the kitchen table with my laptop, and unless Helmut or Ma comes home early, I should have about five hours of silence ahead of me. There are a number of parts to what happened over the weekend, but I think I'm ready to start at the beginning.

It turned out that when Uncle Scott planned his anniversary party for last Saturday, he'd forgotten about the Fauré concert that Uncle Joe and I would be singing in that evening. By then it was too late to cancel, so he moved the party up to early afternoon, even though they ended up with lots of leftovers because half the guests had already eaten lunch. The plan was that I'd get changed for the concert at their house, Uncle Joe and I would leave early for the university, and Ma and Helmut and Uncle Scott and Gonzo would join us later. And that's technically what happened.

The party was nice. I like a lot of Uncle Scott and Uncle Joe's friends, except for one guy who keeps asking me how old I am with a laugh that can only be described as a guffaw. I've always loved everything about Tina: her scratchy, Peppermint Patty voice, her *oh, if only you were twenty years older* routine, her knack of summarizing people's looks as beautiful, ugly, or "beautiful in a weird way," and her funny stories about her mother-in-law, who apparently only wears green, except at Christmas, when she wears green and red. Nearly everyone was in the backyard enjoying the sunshine. Rusty kept texting me with vague *It's finally coming along!* updates about the video, and I'd send him encouraging replies using emojis because I couldn't think of any more words to use. I was in a good mood then—it was one of those days when making small talk with people I hardly ever see wasn't unmitigated torture.

But I sensed something was off between Uncle Scott and Uncle Joe. I kept looking for them while I was mingling after I'd noticed that Uncle Scott was spending most of his time in front of the barbecue while Uncle Joe was milling around, speaking with everyone there except his own husband. Finally I saw Uncle Joe walk by Uncle Scott without looking at him and caught the defeated look on Uncle Scott's face. "You remember my sister-in-law, Susan, and her husband, Helmut, don't you?" I heard Uncle Joe say to someone. It didn't occur to me till later that he'd jumped right over you in that sentence.

I went inside and found Uncle Scott in the kitchen. "What's going on?" I asked.

"Nothing," he said, wrapping up a plate of samosas like doing so required all of his concentration.

"I mean between you and Uncle Joe. Is everything all right?" I asked as I got closer. I didn't want this to come across as an inquisition, so I got some plastic containers and started to help pack up leftover food in them.

Uncle Scott let out a sigh and leaned the top half of his body against the fridge like he was looking for a hug. "Oh, Uncle Joe and I are just going through a bit of a rough patch right now, kiddo," he said. But it seemed like a lot more than a rough patch, especially when some of the things I'd noticed at my birthday dinner started to flood back into my mind. I didn't know what to say—I mean, the idea of problems in their marriage scared me. But Uncle Scott didn't need a whole lot of prompting. "Sometimes," he said, "when two people have been together for as long as Joe and I have, they start to grow in different directions. They start to want different things." I don't know if he was talking about careers or the house or money or sex, and really, I didn't want to know. I mean, if I'm completely honest, I have to admit that even though I was the one who'd got this conversation started, all I did after that was stand around holding a plastic container of potato salad while he kept talking—first about him and Uncle Joe, then about couples in general. Once he stopped, I figured I had to say *something*.

"Well," I said, trying to make it sound like I somehow knew what I was talking about, "I mean, probably all couples go through rough patches at some point. But that doesn't mean they can't be worked out. Right?"

Wait—was I still holding the potato salad at this point? I guess I wasn't. I must have put it down. I'm fairly sure I had a bottle of ketchup in one hand and a jar of relish in the other by the time we got to this part. You know what? It doesn't matter what I had in my hands or where we were standing or how either of us looked as we were talking—none of that is remotely important. What *does* matter is that then Uncle Scott said something like "Sure, with some couples. But with others—I mean, just look at your parents."

At first that was fine. I'd heard his reply—he was agreeing with what I'd said, sort of.

Then my brain computed his words and what they sort of implied. I felt all the sensation drain from my face. Uncle Scott was still rummaging through the refrigerator, like he wasn't aware of

what he'd just said. It looked like it was up to me to decide whether
or not to drop it. I started to sway a little—I was in the middle of
the kitchen and there wasn't anything to hold on to—I dropped
the bottles of ketchup and relish, but they didn't smash since they
weren't made of glass. Uncle Scott looked up and saw my face, and
then his expression changed, too. I thought about retreating, but I
forced myself to speak.

"What do you mean?"

We stared at each other. He opened his mouth to say something, but only dead air came out.

"What do you mean, Scott?" I asked again as the numbness
started to fade.

Uncle Scott bit his lower lip and closed the refrigerator door.
His hand was shaking as he pushed up his glasses. He shook his
head—kind of at himself. Then he exhaled. "You'd better ask your
mother," he said.

Nothing happened for a few seconds, until my legs and my
arms started to move of their own will. I headed outside to the edge
of the back porch, scanned the yard for my mother, and headed over
to where she and Tina were talking.

"Ma, I need to talk to you—alone, please."

"Oh, but honey, I'm in the middle of getting caught up with
Tina. What is it?"

"Were you and Pa having problems before he died?"

Ma's eyes widened, but she stayed calm. She and Tina glanced
at each other, and then without a word she grabbed my hand and
led the way back inside. I hung back a bit, almost like I was afraid of

·what I'd find out. Scott and Joe were in the living room, and when we walked in Scott took a step toward us, looking aghast.

"I'm so sorry, Susan—it slipped out. I'd forgotten that he still doesn't know—"

"Scott—it's all right. I should never have kept it from him all this time."

They all turned to look at me. I felt my legs buckle and pricks of tears start to collect behind my eyes. I looked from Ma to Uncle Scott to Uncle Joe and back again, only dimly aware of the sounds of thirty people enjoying themselves outside.

"Sit down, honey," she said. And I did. She sat next to me on the sofa and took my hand, looking like someone who'd run out of options. And then she told me. *She told me.*

I know everything now—about the affair, the woman you were leaving us for, what you'd planned to tell me after my recital. Ma was calm and matter of fact, like she'd been practising this for years—which I guess she had. I started to shake all over. I was having such a hard time understanding what she was telling me that I started to second-guess everything. "You mean he wasn't killed by a drunk driver?" I asked.

"Of course he was. Honey, what we told you was the truth. We just didn't tell you everything."

"*Why?*"

"Because you were nine years old and I didn't see the point. You were already going to lose so much with your father dead—you didn't need to know that he'd died driving home from seeing his girlfriend. When it happened, I decided I'd tell you more about it when you were older, but as time went on it didn't seem that—oh, I don't mean that it wasn't important, but I started to wonder if it'd be better to leave it alone unless you started asking questions. He's your father—the last thing I wanted was to damage your memory of him."

"And you all knew?" I asked, glancing at Uncle Scott and Uncle Joe.

"Yeah, we did, kiddo," Uncle Scott said, holding Uncle Joe's hand. "We agreed with Susan that you were too young to know everything, and we both thought that when it was time for you to be told it should come from her. And even if we hadn't agreed, it was her decision to make. I'm sorry, Dale—I didn't mean for you to find out like this."

"No. I meant—did you know before he died that my father was cheating on my mother?"

Out of the corner of my eye, I noticed Ma turn her head like she was as curious to hear the answer as I was.

"*Oh.*" Uncle Scott shook his head and leaned forward in his seat without hesitation. "No—he never told me anything about that. But then again we hadn't seen each other since the holidays, and we'd never got in the habit of talking much on the phone. We were both busy—something I regret now." He paused and glanced at Ma. "But if he *had* told me he was having an affair, I wouldn't have been willing to keep that secret for him. So no. The first I heard about the—about the relationship is when your mother told me, after he died. Right, Joe?"

Uncle Joe looked thoughtful for a minute as he stared into the middle distance, and finally he shrugged. "I guess. Don't misunderstand me—he never told me anything either, nor even hinted that something like that was going on. But when we saw him at Christmas I'd noticed some—signs." He and Uncle Scott glanced at each other, then looked away. "He'd been—jumpy, I guess you could call it. I remember thinking his energy seemed a bit off. I didn't think too much of it at the time, but later, when Susan told me—"

His words brought back the memory of sitting with him in the basement the day after you died, while Ma talked in the kitchen with Uncle Scott and Grandma and hearing their voices rise. But before I could ask about that my mind fixated on something else.

"So Grandma? She knew, too?"

"Yes," Ma said with a sigh, touching my shoulder. "I had to tell her the truth—it was just too big to keep from her—but I felt awful for her sake. She was devastated. Her son's death, of course, but—everything else on top of it. And she was worried, too, about losing me and her only grandchild as a result. But there wasn't any need for her to worry. I didn't want to lose my family either. I mean, yes—your father's death was especially complicated for me. I was angry—I felt humiliated—for a time I thought my life was over. And I had to keep it all to myself. But I wouldn't have found the strength to keep going without your grandma, and your uncles, and *you*."

She started to cry, but after a moment she rallied, wiped her eyes, and turned to face me again.

"Honey," she said, "your father loved you very, very much." And it's at that moment that I started to lose it. "He wasn't leaving *you*—he just wasn't happy in our marriage anymore. It was his decision to leave and I didn't see it coming. I'm telling you that not because I want you to blame him but because you're old enough now to know what happened. But what *hadn't* changed were his feelings for you. I can't say for certain what our lives might have looked like now if he'd survived the car accident. We'd probably have joint custody of you, like Helmut and Iliana with Gonzo. It would have been a very different struggle—that's for sure. But not a day goes by that I don't wish he were still alive, for your sake—that I don't regret the fact that you've grown up without your father."

I stared at my lap because I didn't know what to say. As far as she knows, you're a distant memory to me. She has no idea that now, in a way I probably wouldn't have felt before I started writing you these letters three months ago, I, too, feel betrayed.

"And the woman he was planning to leave us for," I said, because in spite of my anguish I was curious, too. "Did you know her?"

"I met her once at an office party, but that was before the—their relationship started. He—your father felt awful about leaving. It's not like we'd turned against each other or were fighting all the time. It's just that he'd met someone else and wanted to move on." She paused, and I felt her hand tighten against mine. "I met up with her for coffee once—two or three months later."

"I didn't know that," Uncle Scott said.

"Yes—well. I wanted to close the book, so to speak. I thought she would, too."

I reached out with my other hand and squeezed hers with it. All of a sudden, it dawned on me how awful this must have been for her, not only for having to mourn a husband who'd died while in the process of leaving her, but also for shielding me from it for so long.

Even though she asked me not to, I do blame you for that.

We sat there in the silent living room until finally, Uncle Joe shifted in his seat and glanced at his watch. "I'm sorry," he said, "but Dale, we really need to go."

"Oh, *fuck*," I said out loud. I propelled myself upward and marched up the stairs to the second-floor bathroom, where my suit was hanging in the shower—the same suit I'd worn to Sophie and Jenice's wedding but with a grey shirt and a different tie. I yanked off the crucifix that had been hanging around my neck since my birthday and barely flinched when it ripped out a few of the hairs on my chest. My hands were shaking so badly that I couldn't get my tie on properly, and when I looked at my reflection in the mirror all I could see was agony. I left the room with my tie still hanging limply around my neck and walked up to Ma. "Could you help me with this, please?"

She did, and when she was finished, she wrapped me in her arms for a hug. And she told me she loved me—more than anyone in the world.

I mean, how could you do this to us? What were you thinking—that I'd just forgive you for leaving us for someone else? Were you so unhappy with Ma that this seemed like the only solution? I don't get how you could be so fucking selfish.

Just as I typed out that last sentence, the reality came crashing down on me: I'll never get to understand.

Uncle Joe gave me a pep talk in the car, and that helped, but I had to work hard to repress the feeling that my tie was going to strangle me to death. This was our only dress rehearsal with the orchestra, and while normally I love seeing a piece of music we've been working on for months come together in the end, I could barely pay attention to what was happening. I sang my two solos mechanically, less than amused when I remembered that the title of one of the pieces—"Libera Me"—means "liberate me" in Latin. Fuck you, Fauré.

There was a light supper for the choir and the orchestra, but I couldn't eat anything. Then Marty, our director, walked up to me, asked if we could talk, and led me down several hallways till we reached a small studio room with a piano. At first I thought he'd read my mind and was going to give me ten minutes alone in a quiet room, and I was filled with gratitude. But it turned out to be something else completely—and it was the last thing I needed.

Basically, the situation was this: the soprano who was supposed to sing the central solo in the piece had been rushed to the hospital—they suspected it was a kidney stone. There was no understudy, and it was such a central part of the *Requiem* that we couldn't skip it. Would I learn it and take her place, singing an octave lower?

"Fuck," I said, wiping my forehead with my hand. I mentally smacked myself when I saw the look of shock on Marty's face and added, "Okay—fine."

I had no intention of telling him that anything was wrong. I like Marty—he's far more good-tempered than a lot of choir directors I've worked with—but everyone knows he's a notorious blabbermouth.

We only had enough time to go through it once. It's a gorgeous solo, and Anne-Marie sings it beautifully, but I hadn't paid nearly as much attention to it during rehearsals as I would have if I'd known I'd have to sing it. I didn't have any room left for panic, though, and that helped.

The concert was split in two: a children's choir performed a selection of pieces by Saint-Saëns, almost like an opening act. I'd been looking forward to this and had asked Marty if I could sit in the wings and listen from there. The first piece was so unbelievably dissonant that it sounded like the nightmare I was living through had come to life, but it mellowed after that. Sitting there meant I could listen to the singing and try to collect myself for forty minutes, but it was hard, too, because the kids reminded me so much of my own choir when I was younger—especially the recital on the day you died. There was a little boy in the group, maybe nine years old, who looked uncannily like me—or at least my frazzled mind made me think he did. It was like watching my younger self. And I started to envy him, because he didn't know yet all the terrible things I knew.

We had a short intermission after that, at which point one of the altos in my choir came up to me and said, "I didn't know you had a little brother!" Which made me panic. What if the woman you were leaving us for had been pregnant and that kid *was* my little brother? For once in my life math came to the rescue when I realized that the dates couldn't possibly line up. But at least I wasn't imagining the resemblance if other people could see it, too.

After a final warm-up, it was time for us to head upstairs and take our places onstage. I tried to lose myself in the music or at least in the experience of performing in a large choir with an orchestra, but I couldn't. It finally dawned on me that the word "requiem" means "Mass for the dead."

Somehow that reminded me that I'd forgotten your cufflinks in a drawer in my room.

And then the other shoe dropped in my mind and I finally figured out why Uncle Scott and not Ma had given me these belongings of yours from the things he'd been saving for me.

Fauré's *Requiem* contains all the components of a traditional Catholic Mass—apparently—and consists of seven motets. My bass solos were in the second and sixth motets, so Marty asked me to stand at the edge of the first row of basses so that I could move upstage when I needed to without being a pain in the ass to everyone else. Anne-Marie would have done the same among the sopranos. Thankfully Marty had told the rest of the choir that I was taking Anne-Marie's place, but I guess he forgot to tell the audience, and as I approached the edge of the stage a second time I saw a couple of people glancing at their programs in confusion. I figured it was people who knew Fauré's work and were expecting either a woman or a boy, not a nearly grown man singing an octave lower. *Great,*

I thought as I stood there and waited for my cue. *Everybody who knows this piece must think I've turned into a eunuch.*

The piece with the soprano solo is called "Pie Jesu," which literally means "Pious Jesus." Basically it starts with a sustained B-flat major chord, and the soloist jumps in a bar later. As soon as I heard that chord, I glanced down at my score and started to piece together what some of the Latin phrases mean: *Pious Lord Jesus, give them rest. Give them everlasting rest.* I thought of you—not the you in the framed photo in my room, but the you I remember. And you were smiling at me. I looked up at the audience, leaned into the music, and started to sing.

I have no idea what I sounded like to everyone else—parts of the piece are a bit out of my range, and it's hard to be expressive with something you've practised only once. But to me it sounded like I was crying—like I was mourning. Because I was. The first verse was just me and the electric organ, and that was fine. I glanced at Marty as he conducted; he was looking back at me, waving his arms slowly, keeping everything going with the organ, and that made me feel like I could trust him. And then the rest of the orchestra came in behind me and I was surrounded by the music, almost sheltered by it.

I continued to sing, the second verse louder than the first for emphasis, followed by a softer bridge, my vibrato starting to run away from me and my eyes blurring with tears as we crescendoed to the final refrain. Even though I'd practised it only once, I knew this song—I knew it because of you. And what I was mourning wasn't just the father I remembered—it was the flawed human being I never got to know. It was the truth that had been kept from me for my own good. It was the death and the grief I'd experienced as well as the divorce and the aftermath that I escaped. It was all the loss that I've felt for so long underneath all the love.

I'm not sure whom I was addressing in the song—pious Jesus, God, the gods, the universe—but the message was the same: *Give him rest. Give him everlasting rest.*

I'd managed to keep everything together throughout the piece, but I couldn't help but shed a tear once it ended and I made my way back to my spot in the choir. I was annoyed at myself for that. I thought for sure everyone would think I'd moved myself to tears by my own performance.

I felt marginally better afterward. My third solo went well enough—I barely noticed it. And when the *Requiem* was over and the audience was applauding, Marty turned around and waved me over. I was prepared to ignore him, but someone behind me gave me a little shove. I felt embarrassed by this. It didn't seem fair: after all, the only reason I'd sung so well was because I was heartbroken.

I made my way around the orchestra again, and as I got closer to Marty's podium, clutching my music binder to my chest, the applause swelled up, making me take a step back as I faced a standing ovation. But just as I started to feel pleased, I thought of you and remembered what Ma had said: *Your father loved you very, very much.* I flinched, bowed once, extended my arm to Marty, then fled the stage.

My head was pounding—I needed a glass of water—I wanted to sit down in a quiet room so badly. But disappearing right after a standing ovation wasn't something I was willing to do. Once, when

I was in grade six, my choir put on an all-Mozart benefit concert that featured four soloists and an orchestra. The soprano and the alto were friendly and approachable and didn't take everything so fucking seriously, but the tenor and the bass were total dickheads. I tried to ask them about their training and what it was like to be a professional choral singer, and they basically acted like the top dogs at my high school. I vowed then and there that I'd never get so full of myself, no matter what happened, and I've done everything I can to keep that up. Besides, I'm *part* of this choir. Even though Marty thanked me afterward for saving the day, what pleased me more was that the entire concert had gone over well. So I forced myself to smile and be as gracious as I could. I was also ravenously hungry, and that helped, too. I stood around and inhaled some leftover Nanaimo bars, endured a few compliments, and made small talk with people about what Marty's planning for next season.

I even managed to forget about you for a while.

Finally Ma and Helmut and Gonzo found me and we stood around talking, with Marty explaining what had happened with Anne-Marie. Ma nodded and said it was nice that I could step in when I did. Marty gave her an incredulous look and tried again. "Your son is an amazingly gifted singer and musician. No one else in the choir can sight-read like he does. No one else could have learned a solo piece that quickly and performed it with such nuance and precision. And his abilities as a singer are on top of him acing his piano exam at sixteen! I hope you realize how incredibly unique that is. Dale has an amazing future in music, and if he wants to, I can see him having a lot of options in terms of a profession."

I'm sure Marty was baffled by the fact that Ma looked about as surprised as if she'd just figured out I'd been secretly playing the bassoon for years. All I felt was annoyance because of the timing. But Marty had no idea what kind of afternoon we'd just lived through, and I had no intention of telling him. It's just as well nobody had a chance to say anything after that, because the strangest thing happened.

"Excuse me. Mr. Cardigan?"

I turned to see the little boy from the children's choir standing there with a woman who was clearly his mother. She was the one who'd spoken, but I reacted only when Ma nudged me and whispered, "She means you."

"Oh. Hello," I said, trying to sound like something other than a dork.

"Mr. Cardigan, my son was in the children's choir, and we ended up staying for the rest of the concert. We're sorry to bother you, but he enjoyed your singing so much and he was wondering if you'd be willing to give him your autograph."

I couldn't understand how any of this was happening, but this kid was staring at me like I was an apparition. He looked even more like me close up, making me wonder if my grief had somehow caused me to travel through time. When Helmut handed me one of the clicking pens he keeps in his shirt pocket for some reason, the boy silently held out his concert program to me.

"Of course—I'd be happy to," I said, kneeling down so I could face him. "What's your name?"

"Dale."

I swear I'm not making this up. "Really? That's my name, too. I don't know if you saw me, but I sat backstage to watch your choir. You all did a great job. Do you like being in a choir? What part do you sing? Oh, I was in a choir like yours when I was your age. Blah blah blah blah blah." And as I was blathering on I found enough white space on the program to scribble out *For Dale: keep singing! Your friend, Dale S. Cardigan*, or something equally idiotic. Then the boy and his mother thanked me and walked away.

"Am I on crack, or did that kid look exactly like me? And does anyone else find it strange that he was also named Dale?" I asked once we were all in the car, driving home.

Nobody answered me, so maybe I hallucinated the whole thing after all. When I leaned back in my seat, everything that I'd learned about you that afternoon came flooding back, along with the headache that had been brewing since the afternoon. I glanced at Ma's profile for a moment, then gave up and stared out the window as my headache returned.

It was late by the time we got home. I figured I'd go to bed, but Gonzo stopped me. "Hey—I thought I'd stay up and watch *Saturday Night Live* for a while. You in?"

I glanced at the clock, thought about how early I'd need to get up in the morning, and shrugged. "Okay."

"Great. You want some ice cream?"

"Yeah. Let me get changed."

That meant he knew about you now, too. And eventually I pieced together that Helmut has known all along. That's fine.

I mean, really, the only problem in this family is that there've been too many secrets.

When I went downstairs I decided to check my phone, and I found a text from Rusty: *How'd it go?*

I sighed as I changed out of my suit, hung it up in the closet, and put on my pyjama bottoms. I sat down on my bed and decided there wasn't any point in trying to tell him everything in a text message at 11:30 at night. So my reply was true, if impossibly vague: *As well as could be expected.*

After I tossed my phone aside I thought about writing a Facebook message to Jordana, but since I didn't know where to begin, I decided not to bother.

I'm stopping now because I need to stop. I haven't written all this in one sitting, by the way. I haven't even written it in order. I've made lunch and more tea and snacks, put on music, turned it off again. Both Ma and Helmut called the landline, and I forced myself to answer because I knew they'd drive home to check up on me if I didn't. My shoulder ached from sitting in front of my laptop for so long, so I rubbed it against the towel rack in my bathroom until it felt better. Now it's nearly 3:30 and Gonzo will be home from school in a little while. But I'll continue as soon as I can—because of course there's more.

It's after supper now. I needed a break, to move around and take my mind off things. I played the violin for a while and listened to a duet I'd recorded for fun sometime last winter. Gonzo came home with some of my schoolbooks and told me what homework I've got for tomorrow. I made a point of flipping through it so at least I'd know what it is I have no intention of doing.

Supper was an ordeal. I tried to smile and act like all was within the realm of FINE so Ma and Helmut wouldn't insist on making me talk things over. Rusty texted me to let me know that the video is nearly done, which is great. And now I'm sitting at my desk with my laptop again, with the door closed and my phone off, ready to finish up my account of this roller-coaster weekend while listening to a playlist I put together that's basically a lot of piano-based gloom.

I ended up watching about half of *Saturday Night Live* with Gonzo before calling it a night. I slept better than I'd expected to but woke up with a headache that got worse as the morning wore on. As I think I mentioned before, this meant my organ playing was pretty incoherent, to the point that I was afraid the congregation would think I was hungover—or still drunk.

All this time it seemed like everything was more or less okay, in the sense that finally I knew everything there was to know about you and Ma and your marriage, and I felt myself start to calm down as I got better acquainted with this new knowledge. But there was one part of Saturday's news flash that still didn't sit well with me, so as soon as I got home from church I made a beeline for the kitchen, where Ma and Helmut were preparing a nice brunch of pancakes and eggs and bacon. "Ma," I said without any kind of preamble, "what did you mean when you said that as time went on you started to wonder if it'd be better not to say anything about what happened with Pa unless I started asking questions?"

She stared at me for a minute, then set down her spoon or her spatula or whatever she was holding. "Well—it was seven years ago. You don't talk about your father that much. I didn't want to upset you."

"*Of course* I'm upset," I said, and not surprisingly, that upset me even more. "I just don't understand. What questions did you think I'd start asking you about your marriage to Pa?"

"I'm not sure, honey," she said. She didn't seem upset or defensive, just concerned. "When it happened, I decided I'd tell you once you were an adult. I thought you'd understand better once you were old enough to be in a relationship yourself. But as the years went on, there were times when I wished I'd told you sooner and times when I thought it'd be best to leave it."

I started to cry. I don't know why I was so fixated on this part of it, but I was. Ma reached for my hands and waited for me to speak.

"I don't understand," I said again as I started to shake all over. "Why would you never want to tell me? What made you think keeping me in the dark forever was *good*? Obviously I'm upset, but now that I know what happened, what's hardest to accept is that I might never have known if Uncle Scott hadn't let it slip. That everyone's been watching me all these years, knowing something I don't about my own family—"

"But everyone *doesn't* know," Ma said, rubbing my hands with hers, "precisely because I didn't want you to hear it from anyone else. It's just been me, Scott, Joe, Beverly and Burt, and your grandmother—possibly Tina. And I told Helmut when we started to get serious. There's no one else! Not my friends at work—not any of your teachers. We kept it in the family—for your sake. It's what I decided for you, as the adult."

"I know you did what you thought was best. I just—"

But I didn't know how to explain how I felt. I still don't. So I cried.

It's at that point, I'm pretty sure, that I asked Ma if I could borrow her car so I could drive to the cemetery and she refused. "Let's sit down, and we'll have some lunch and talk about it," she said, and I know she was trying to be kind, but I didn't want kindness. It seemed to cement the fact that I'm just a kid, that I have no power, that decisions are made for me by well-intentioned people who don't understand and don't listen. And then I remembered that I *had* asked her about you not that long ago—not about you exactly, but about Mike 1 and Mike 2 and Gary and why we never saw them after your funeral—and she'd shut me down. So I turned and walked out of the house. I heard Helmut calling after me from the porch, so I started to run. I didn't have anything on me—not my wallet, not my keys, not my phone—but I kept running.

I didn't have any destination in mind, but soon I realized that unless I was prepared to run all the way to Uncle Scott and Uncle Joe's, the only place I could feasibly go was Rusty's—maybe Jenice and Sophie's if I needed to. But when I reached Rusty's house, his whole family was in the driveway getting ready to go somewhere. I felt bad about intruding, even looked around to see if I could hide behind a tree until they left, but Rusty saw me and jogged over, full of concern.

"Dale? What's wrong? What happened to your face?"

I'd been crying and sniffling all this time without a single Kleenex in my pocket, so no doubt I looked my grossest. It was such a nice day that the sun was probably baking my snot to my upper lip. "Something happened," I said through the tremors in my throat. "I mean, I just found out about something." I glanced at the car behind him and stopped myself from blurting everything out. "This is a bad time, isn't it? You guys are heading somewhere."

"We're going to my grandmother's for brunch. It's a big family thing for her birthday. But tell me."

In the distance, his father called out to him, but Rusty waved him away as I gave him the lowdown.

"*Shit.* And you found this out only yesterday?"

"Yeah. The concert last night was a fucking nightmare. They kept it from me all these years—for my own good or whatever."

"Ugh—I hate when people do that. What are you going to do now?"

"What do you mean? Plot revenge?"

"No. I meant this afternoon."

"I sort of had a fight about it with my mother," I said with a shrug. "Not really a fight, but—I don't want to go back yet."

"Hold on a second." Rusty turned around and jogged back to his car. I saw him speak to his parents through the driver's window, and soon he turned around again and waved me over. "Why don't you come with us? You're more than welcome. It gets a bit chaotic on that side of the family because of all the kids, but it's totally cool. Anyway, Oma likes you—she won't mind at all."

At first I backed away from this invitation, but the idea of returning home appealed to me even less. At any rate, I proved once again to be powerless in the face of Rusty's coaxing. So I climbed into the car and found myself pinned once again between his leg and Maisie's car seat. Pam turned around from the passenger seat and smiled at me sympathetically. "Rusty told us you received some upsetting news yesterday," she said. "I hope everything's okay." She silently handed me a box of baby wipes so I could clean up my face.

"It isn't right now, but it will be," I said. I thought about telling them actual details, but I noticed that Mitch kept glaring at me in the rear-view mirror as he drove. He could have been just checking the traffic behind us, but I decided to stay quiet anyway.

We drove in comfortable silence to a neighbourhood at the northwest part of town that I don't know very well, filled mainly with old 1950s bungalows, the kind you see sometimes in old TV shows. I turned to look at Maisie, who handed me her doll but immediately wanted it back. Throughout the drive, I was hyper-aware of Rusty's presence on my left, especially his bare, furry, overheated arm against mine.

By the time we got there, I was more or less okay again, and as we pulled into the driveway Mitch suggested that I call home to let them know where I was. When I told him I didn't have my cellphone on me, he unzipped his ridiculous fanny pack, reached inside, and offered me his. I thought he was trying to be nice.

When they all stood around next to the car as I dialled, I wandered down the driveway so they wouldn't overhear every word I said.

"Ma, it's me. I'm sorry I ran off."

"Dale! Where *are* you? Are you okay?"

"I'm fine—or I will be fine. I just need time to process everything."

"Of course I understand that. I really do. But where are you? Whose phone is this?"

"Rusty's dad's. I'm at Rusty's oma's house now—they're having a family brunch for her birthday."

"Oh, honey. You can't just show up to someone else's grand-mother's brunch."

"Well, they invited me, and I'm here, and I'm hungry. I'll be home in a couple of hours, okay?"

Ma sighed and gave up arguing with me. I ended the call, walked back up the driveway, and handed Mitch his phone. Then we went inside, where I was confronted with about thirty strangers, which made me wonder if I'd been insane for thinking this was a good idea.

"Everybody," Rusty announced as we entered the jam-packed living room, "this is my friend Dale from school. Dale, this is—" And then he named every single aunt, uncle, great-aunt, and cousin, all of whose names I was incapable of retaining.

"It's so nice to meet all of you," I said, trying to fight the urge to wrap my arms around myself. "Um—which one of you has the figurine phobia?"

At first I was afraid they were going to tar and feather me, but then a woman with the same red hair as Rusty stepped forward and raised her hand. "That would be me," she said with a good-natured smile.

Thankfully that broke the ice, but I started to panic again when I kept getting swallowed up by the chaos of a ginormous family trying to move around in a tiny house. Every time I turned around there was someone new to talk to, making me wonder if they were cloning themselves.

We had a bit of time before brunch was ready, and nobody would let me help with anything, so Rusty offered to show me around the rest of the house. I followed him down the hallway, where we looked at a montage of photographs on a wall and crossed paths with a Muppet-like lapdog. I'm fairly indifferent to dogs, but I figured I should say something as Rusty knelt down to let it sniff his hand. "What kind of dog is this?" I asked.

"This is Oma's Shih Tzu–poodle mix. I call her a shit-poo." I think it was named Buttons or Muffin or something like that. The dog turned to me, so I held out my hand for about a second before we both lost interest in one another. Rusty steered me toward the bathroom, and as we washed our hands he started telling me about the house.

It turns out that this was where Rusty had spent most of his early childhood. His parents had had him when they were still in university, so they'd all lived in that house while Mitch and Pam finished their degrees and went to teachers' college. His earliest memories are of his grandparents taking care of him. He didn't say it straight out, but it was obvious to me that he'd got along with his grandfather far better than he does now with Mitch. "Opa always made a point of listening," he explained, "and that made me want to listen to *him* when he had something to say." He died four years ago in August. Rusty mentioned that the family had gathered not only for Oma's birthday, but also because she'd decided to sell the house and move into an apartment. By this point we were standing in a combination music room / playroom, and I found out later that this was the room Rusty had spent the bulk of his time in as a child.

"I'm really going to miss this house," he said. He wasn't crying or trying not to cry, but his eyebrows were quivering a little. I didn't know what to do except try to put myself in his shoes, so I walked up to him and gave him a hug. And he hugged me back. We ended up staying that way for a while. The heat from his body seeped through his T-shirt. I could feel his cheek against mine, his toes against mine, his stomach against mine. Whenever he breathed out, I breathed in, and then we switched. And in that moment, it didn't matter that it would never work out between us because we have so little in common. He's my friend. He'd been there for me, and now it was my turn to be there for him.

I let go only when I opened my eyes and saw one of Rusty's young cousins, the one who's the spitting image of the aunt with the figurine phobia, staring at us from the doorway. I stepped away from Rusty and smiled at her like this was the most common occurrence in the world. "Oh—um—Mom wanted me to ask your friend what kind of drink he wants with lunch," she said shyly, looking at Rusty, trying to suppress a smile. She named some options that were in the fridge in the garage, so I offered to go fetch the drinks for me and for Rusty—partly because I wanted to be helpful while a guest in someone else's house and partly because I wanted to get the hell out of there.

And then—well—I opened the door to the garage, took a step inside, and saw Mitch with his back turned to me, leaning against a snow blower, talking animatedly on his phone. As soon as I heard what he was saying, I knew he was talking to Ma.

"—but in all my years as an educator, I've never seen adolescent behaviour like this. It isn't normal. Apparently he hasn't said more than a dozen words to anyone at school in three years. I understand he's a gifted singer and he needed to preserve his voice throughout puberty, but that doesn't account for the more recent outbursts—no, not violence, but he's been known to sob or laugh uncontrollably for no reason. No, I'm not a teacher at his school. But my wife and a close friend of ours—I appreciate what you're saying, but he's been a guest in my home enough times for me to have a good sense— yes, as a matter of fact, I do. As a parent and as a teacher, I have enough experience working with young people to know that this level of anti-social behaviour is extremely troubling. And, to be perfectly honest, I've been wondering if the root of his abnormal behaviour might be found in some serious problems at home."

"Dad, what are you doing?"

I heard Rusty's voice behind me, but I didn't turn my head. Instead I watched as Mitch spun around and his face changed in two noticeable ways: first, a moment of *oh shit they caught me* panic, then a more deliberate look, like he was still convinced he was doing the right thing. His eyes fixed on me.

"I am on the phone with your mother, young man, because I thought it was high time someone tried to help you."

We stared at each other in a silence broken only by Ma's agitated voice through his phone. I'd only ever heard her sound so upset due to events that I don't like to think about.

I felt Rusty's hand on my shoulder, and then I heard him say, "Um—I never told my parents any of those things."

"I know," I said. I think I sighed. If Mitch had jumped to the conclusion that crying or laughing or being angry were signs of being troubled or imbalanced—that they couldn't possibly mean that I was sad or happy or angry for damn good reasons—how could I convince him otherwise? I couldn't help but remember a line Jenice had used once when telling me a story about someone she knew: "It's a matter of perspective, and yours is rather fucked at the moment." But I didn't think telling Mitch that would help my cause.

As I walked closer to Mitch, I could hear Ma through his phone more clearly, and I realized that she wasn't upset because Mitch had basically accused her of being a negligent parent—she was defending me. I heard phrases like "introvert" and "artistic temperament" and "kind and caring and responsible." I silently held out my hand. Mitch hesitated before handing me the phone, and as I pressed it to my ear Ma said, "It's true that I don't always understand him, but he seems perfectly happy with his life the way it is. I've always *encouraged* him to live life on his own terms, rather than force him to fit some narrow idea of what a normal teenager is—"

"Ma, it's me," I said, turning away from Mitch.

"Oh, thank God, Dale. You wouldn't *believe* what that man has been telling me for the last fifteen minutes."

"I'm sorry. I didn't know he was going to call you."

"I don't understand. Why have you been crying in class?"

"That only happened once. It was because I was sad."

"And is what he said true—that you've hardly spoken to any-one at school the whole time you've been there? That doesn't sound like you at all, honey."

"It's what I wanted. I know you're not going to want to hear this, Ma, but high school's stupid. I didn't want to bother." That made Mitch flinch, although that wasn't the only reason I said it.

Ma and I continued like that for a little while. She wasn't *angry* at me, per se—just shocked. Probably about as shocked as I had been to hear her news about you. I looked over at Mitch and then at Rusty, aware that they could hear every word both of us were saying, and finally Ma and I were able to agree that we'd talk it over once I got home. I ended the call, handed Mitch his phone back, and tried to decide what to say to him. It's funny, in a way: he'd pictured me as someone who had these wild swings of emotion, yet now I felt nothing. If anything, I was kind of amused, but I wasn't going to let him see that. Plus I was so hungry by this point that I thought I was going to barf. So I decided to ask him a question, the answer to which I really wanted to know.

"No offence, Mitch, but who the hell wants to be normal?"

It's late now. All I want is to go to bed. That's not where the story ends, but I don't have the energy to continue. Basically, I had a nice enough brunch, if only because Rusty and I sat as far away from Mitch as humanly possible. But all hell broke loose yet again as soon as I got home. Ma was upset about me staying silent at school, but I think what upset her more was that I'd never intended for her to know about it. I said I hadn't told her because I'd known she wouldn't understand, but not surprisingly, she couldn't understand that either.

"Why have you been silent at school all these years?"

"Because."

"That isn't an answer."

"Fine. I never wanted to go to that stupid school, Ma! You made me go because Gonzo was going, and you said it'd be easier if we were at the same school, but really it's only ever been easier for *you*. I wanted to go to a high school that had an arts program, not one that churns out scientists and lawyers and diplomats. Instead the only music I'm getting from school is when I sit in a tiny room near the boiler, wasting my time playing the same old violin repertoire for years!"

Ma found this shocking. I guess she'd figured that since I hadn't openly complained about the school once I'd started and my grades were good, I must have grown to like it. Which shows she doesn't know me at all.

I didn't throw Gonzo under the bus, though—not because I wanted to protect him, but because my cone of silence stopped being about him a long time ago. I wanted to be left alone. I *still* want to be left alone.

It got pretty chaotic as we stood around the kitchen. For one thing, the discussion lasted from about four o'clock in the afternoon until it was time for bed. For another, some of Ma's comments and

Helmut's questions provoked me into saying a couple of things that I didn't really mean. But I managed to stop myself from saying one thing that probably would have really crushed them: *I've been writing letters to Pa for the last three months because I just can't talk to you!*

It's all fine. We'll just keep going with our lives, and soon we'll all forget—or pretend to forget—that any of those things were said. That's the kind of family we are.

As for you, I don't think I'm ready to forgive you yet. But at the same time, I'm well aware that you're long past caring about my forgiveness. And that's probably what I find so fucking difficult to forgive.

Your son,

Dale

## TUESDAY, JUNE 7

I guess technically it's Wednesday, since it's after midnight. The idea of writing to my father right now makes my arteries clench, so I started a new file on my computer. Something happened—or, if you want to point fingers, I did something—and I can't tell yet if it was stupid or not. I was reading in bed when I heard my phone buzz, so I picked it up and saw a text from Rusty. *Video done. Wanna see?*

I texted back something affirmative, figuring he'd send me the file. But then he texted back. *File too big to email. I'll be at your house in ten minutes.*

It was pretty late, but now that the video was finished I knew I wouldn't be able to sleep until I saw it. So I texted him back to say I'd wait for him at the kitchen door. I put my pants back on and crept upstairs to wait for him, hoping Ma or Helmut wouldn't wake up and wonder if they had a burglar on their hands. Soon Rusty emerged through the darkness and walked up the steps to the back porch, still wearing that red hoodie that has this bewitching effect on me. I slid open the patio door, put a finger to my lips, and waved him in.

We tiptoed downstairs, where he dug his laptop out of his bag. Even though it's a pretty long sofa, we sat hip to hip, with his laptop—a Mac that looked far more sophisticated than mine— resting partly on my lap and partly on his. When he plugged in his earphones, stuck one earbud in his ear, and offered me the other, I felt this weird intimacy between us that was both cool and unnerving at the same time. But I forgot all about that as he got the file going.

The video was mesmerizing. That sounds like I couldn't keep my eyes off myself, but I barely registered that it was me I was watching. Basically, Rusty had created a set of split screens to show four, six, or twenty versions of me singing or playing. Sometimes the images formed a square, and other times they were scattered or overlapping against a black background. The cuts from one shot to another always matched the beat of the music. What can I say? The design was simple—the editing was flawless—the synchronicity was uncanny. He did tell me later that there were a few times when the video and the audio hadn't quite matched up, but because he'd shot multiple takes of everything, he was able to work around those problems. I was so taken aback by the overall quality, though, that it hadn't occurred to me to look for mistakes.

The tag at the end showed four versions of me singing "bedroom eyes," then nine versions, then sixteen versions, then twenty-five versions, until the screen was a mosaic of thumbnails of me. Once the song ended, we stared straight ahead for a second or two, and then the screen faded to black.

"So? What do you think?" he asked, a giddy edge to his voice.

I started babbling—the only coherent word I could manage was "again." Without taking my eyes off the screen, I reached for his earbud and stuck it in my other ear so I could hear the music in stereo.

I think I watched the video three or four more times before I recovered from my initial shock. "Rusty, that was fucking *awesome*," I said, folding the laptop closed as a way to stop myself from watching the video yet again. "This is literally going to knock their socks off."

Rusty snort-laughed. "Yeah—it'll literally blow them away."

"They'll literally have kittens over this."

"Their brains will literally explode."

"You literally have filmmaking in your veins."

"Your comments literally put a spring in my step."

We kept going like this until I was laughing so hard I literally farted—except I really literally farted. That just made Rusty laugh even harder.

Then our laughter evaporated, and I realized we were sitting close together on a sofa and it was past midnight and we had school tomorrow and all I wanted to do was curl up with him and go to sleep. So I thanked him for everything he'd done and said it was getting late. We tiptoed back upstairs and lingered by the patio door while he put his shoes back on. He whispered something. I couldn't hear what it was, so we each took a step closer till there was less than a foot between us. "I said, this is going to be great," he whispered.

"Yeah. It will," I whispered back.

Then—well—I leaned over, put my hands on his waist, and kissed him. On the mouth. In my kitchen. After midnight. In the dark. On a school night. His mouth tasted like drool and toothpaste and sunshine. Looking back now, I don't know what I could have been thinking. But at the time it seemed like the most logical thing to do. *Good to see you. Thanks for stopping by. The video's awesome.* Followed by smooching.

And then—I guess this isn't too surprising, since we'd already spent the better part of a day ejaculating together and a few more times since then—he kissed me back. His mouth moved and opened with mine, and then he had one arm around me and the other hand clutching mine, and my other arm was around his neck, and most of me was totally in the moment, except for the part of me keeping my ears peeled for any footsteps coming from upstairs.

It was—I guess the best word would be "delicious." Unlike kissing Jonathan, making out with Rusty was far more engulfing than anything I'd ever imagined, almost like it wasn't happening with just our mouths. But it was terrifying, too, because I couldn't figure out for the life of me what I'd say to him once we were done.

Finally we broke away from each other, and the way he was smiling at me prevented the panic in my throat from gurgling out. "That was awesome, buddy," he whispered. "Listen—there's a lot we need to talk about. But I should go. I don't want my parents to find out I snuck out of the house."

"Okay."

He leaned over and kissed me again, briefly this time, before escaping through the patio door. I tiptoed to the living room and watched him saunter down the driveway and up the sidewalk until he'd vanished into the night.

I'm wired now—I have no idea how I'm supposed to sleep. I can't pinpoint how long it lasted, but the whole make-out session was wonderful. Even now I can taste him on my lips, and when

I close my eyes I can bring back more of the sensations that I've stored away in my memory. But God only knows how I'm supposed to face him tomorrow. What if he wasn't really that into it? Oh, for fuck's sake, Cardigan, of course he was into it. You think he was sucking your face just to be polite? Well, no, but on the other hand—

Another text from Rusty. Holy fuck. *Thanks for that special good night. See you tomorrow!*

Huh. Well, that's definitely a better reaction than *Ew—gross*. Still, it leads to an opposite problem: how am I going to manage *not* to make out with him again when I see him at school in the morning?

Something in my gut tells me tomorrow isn't going to go well. Not because of Rusty, but because of something else. But what?

No music this time—just silence.

## SATURDAY, JUNE 11

The last few days have been one hell of a whirlwind. Well, that's not quite true. Wednesday was one hell of a whirlwind, but the effects of that day have been reverberating ever since, like some vaguely explained sonic thing in a terrible movie. I started to write to my father a few times, but the fact that I'm still pissed off at him kept getting in the way. Eventually I figured that by the time my pissedoffedness runs out I'll have forgotten three-quarters of everything that happened, so I'm going to stick everything involving him in a little compartment in my mind and ignore it for a while. I don't know if that's healthy, but here we are.

On Wednesday morning Rusty texted me as I was waiting at the bus stop to let me know he was getting a ride to school with his mother, since his parents wouldn't let him bring his laptop on the bus. By the time I saw him our first class was about to begin, so all we could do was nod to each other from opposite sides of the room. Not the kind of greeting you'd expect from two friends who'd spontaneously made out with each other less than nine hours earlier, but I guess it couldn't be helped.

All day long, butterflies kept pecking at the insides of my stomach. Not because of Rusty and me—I figured that since he'd kissed me back, he couldn't be too horrified by what I'd done—but because the words "bedroom eyes" kept flashing through my head in pretty unpleasant ways. My leg was shaking, and I guess I was breathing kind of heavy, because at one point Mark turned around in his seat and looked at me with skewed eyebrows. "What's the matter with you?" he asked in a whisper, sounding more concerned than suspicious.

"Nothing," I said out loud, and I guess the fact that I'd interrupted Mr. Kassam's English lesson to answer him made him turn around in a hurry and pretend he'd never asked me in the first place. But for once I didn't feel my face turn red, so that's something.

Still, the heart palpitations didn't go away, and by the time I was alone in my jail cell with my violin, I'd turned into a mess. I couldn't practise—I couldn't sit still—the idea of food was revolting. Rusty found me pacing in the hallway, on his way to fetch his laptop from his mother because it was nearly time to set up.

"You okay?" he asked as I struggled to swing my backpack over my shoulder.

"Just fine," I said. It seemed more polite to keep him in the dark about the clouds of doom that were hanging over my head.

I followed as Rusty marched into the teachers' lounge, greeted some of our teachers by their first names, and made a beeline for the table where Pam was sitting, in the middle of lunch with Mr. Kassam and Ms. Montrose. While Pam was making Rusty swear on the graves of all his ancestors that he would guard the laptop with his life, I saw an opportunity to show my math teacher that I wasn't nearly as insane as she thought. "Oh, hi, Ms. Montrose," I said, donning my best choir boy smile.

She looked about as shocked to hear me speak as if I'd just shattered a light bulb by belching, but she managed to ask me how I was doing.

"Pretty well, thanks," I said. "Rusty and I are presenting our media studies project for Bruce during fifth period."

"Oh—right," she said as she stirred her soup or whatever she was eating. "I heard about that assignment."

She clearly had a whole lot more to say about it, but I couldn't tell if she wanted me to prompt her.

Then I looked up and discovered that the room had gone silent and that all the teachers were staring at us—or, rather, at me—like they expected me to burst out laughing or burst into tears. I tried to keep smiling, even though this time I knew my face had turned purple, but I didn't have the courage to say anything else as Rusty slid his laptop and its charger into his bag and I followed him out of the room. As we headed down the hallway in silence, he made eye contact with me, looked away, and gave me a quick pat on the back.

The door to our classroom was unlocked, so we walked in and started setting up, with about fifteen minutes to spare. I didn't know how anything worked, so I sat around like a groupie and tried to ignore the pangs in my throat while Rusty tried to play the DVD he'd burned with our movie before giving up on that idea and proceeding to link his laptop to the projector and the speaker system. We were both acting like us making out in the dark had happened in some different reality.

Somehow, we lived through math class and waited for Bruce. Five groups were presenting that day, so Bruce decided that the only democratic way to figure out the order we'd go in was to pick names out of a hat, even though to me that seemed like the exact opposite of democracy. Rusty and I ended up having to go last, which ticked me off because I wanted to get it over with. As the hour wore on and I sat through four other presentations, my gut started to churn. Even though this was a media studies course, we were the only ones who'd bothered to use any media in our assignment. Everyone else did some sort of semi-funny skit making light of something sort of topical, like political opponents hanging out at a baseball game and hoping they wouldn't get recognized, whereas I'd arranged and recorded a four-minute song and Rusty had shot and edited a short video of it. At one point I looked Rusty's way, but he was too busy grinning at the spectacle of whoever was presenting to notice me.

Finally it was our turn. Rusty walked up to the front of the room and faced the rest of the class. "Um—Dale and I ended up going in a slightly different direction, but we'll just let our, uh, our work speak for itself."

I seriously thought I was going to barf even though I hadn't eaten anything since breakfast, so I rose from my seat, moved to the back of the room, and leaned against the wall. All background talking ceased as Rusty dimmed the lights and started the video.

Somehow, watching it in class made me see it pretty differently than I had the night before, on the sofa at home. As soon as I saw four versions of me sawing away on the violin, I fixed my gaze on the doohickey that attaches the screen to the wall and reminded myself to keep breathing. Eventually, the sounds of the song were replaced by scattered applause, and in the silence that followed I waited for Bruce's verdict. "Really impressive. Excellent work. You guys did a great job putting the video together."

I was looking at Rusty as Bruce said this and saw the look of delight on his face. Then Bruce turned to look at me and stopped. I was bracing myself against the wall behind me because somehow I knew what would come next. "I really liked the song, too. It was a great cover. Where did you find it?"

And there it was. I let out a ragged breath. It was like the three of us were in a play, standing at opposite ends of the room in a triangle, and our twenty-three classmates were the audience. I kept my eye on Rusty, who looked like he barely understood what Bruce had said.

"Uh—Dale did the song," he explained. "He arranged it and recorded all the parts himself."

Bruce let out a bark of laughter, except it sounded more like outrage. "That's really cute. Look—Dale did a good job with the lip-synching and whatever, but you can't expect me to believe—" He tsked and tried again. "No, but seriously—it's a great cover. Was it on YouTube?"

Rusty looked at me, but at that moment it wasn't my cone of silence that was stopping me from speaking out—I was too stunned to say anything.

"Dale came up with the idea of arranging the song in a minor key. He recorded everything from scratch."

"And I suppose you were there to witness this great achievement?"

"Well, no, but—"

"That's what I thought. You realize, of course, that passing off someone else's work as your own is considered plagiarism, and that will be reflected in your grade." Bruce moved to the front of the room and glanced at the clock behind him. "Well, class, we have about fifteen minutes left—"

"*I* witnessed it."

Nobody could have been as shocked as I was when Gonzo spoke up. There were so many gasps around the room that you'd have thought we were in the middle of some courtroom drama. "I saw him do it—every single take. I even helped him with the recording a little."

Bruce scoffed at that. He was reminding me so much of Rusty's dad that I started to wonder if they were twins who'd been separated at birth. "So you just happened to be at his house at the exact time—"

"Of course I was." He glanced at me, then turned back to Bruce. "I live with him. He's my stepbrother."

Another round of gasps. It seems kind of funny now, but at the time the only thing that felt certain was the wall I was leaning against. The guy in front of Gonzo turned around in his seat and stared at him with something that looked like disdain rather than surprise. "You guys are *stepbrothers*? Since when?"

"Since shut up!"

"That's enough," Bruce said before turning to me. "Well, Mr. Cardigan. It looks like your friends are sticking up for you. What do you have to say for yourself?"

I paused to consider what answer to give. I didn't care that much about our grade. I just wanted the satisfaction of shutting my teacher up. It's not like Bruce had any evidence that we'd ripped the song off someone else—he just thought it impossible that I could rearrange a pop song and record it by myself, and I found that insulting. I guess it looked like I wasn't going to say anything, because the guy sitting next to where I was standing leaned toward me and muttered something loud enough for only me to hear. "Tell him off. He's a dick—we'll back you up."

I felt the corner of my mouth start to curl up into a smile at this weird form of solidarity that I never would have expected from the guys in my class. "It's true," I said, looking Bruce in the eye. "I rearranged the Climax song in a minor key and recorded it. Every single voice and instrument in the recording is me."

"Is that so?" he said.

"Yup. Want me to prove it to you?"

His facial expression changed, and not for the better. "And how would you do that?"

Wordlessly I walked out of the room and marched down the hall. Looking back now, it's a miracle I didn't get caught wandering around school in the middle of class. I'm pretty sure you get flogged or caned for that. I marched downstairs to my jail cell in the basement, grabbed my violin, and marched back. I wanted to wipe that smirk off my teacher's face more than anything I'd ever wanted in my life. As soon as I re-entered the classroom, I set my violin case down on someone's desk, took the violin out, and quickly tuned it by ear. Rusty was still next to his laptop, so I stood under the projection screen and faced the class.

"Hit it," I said.

Closing my eyes in an attempt to block everything else out, I waited until I heard the opening bars and tried to lose myself in the song. At first I stuck to some of the lower violin parts, trying to blend in with the recording, and then I started skipping from one part to the other, playing four bars of low notes and then four bars of high notes and then four bars of notes somewhere in the middle. I made some mistakes because I couldn't remember all the parts anymore, but I figured no one in that room would know enough about music to notice.

Then something shifted in my mind—I don't know if it was the key change after the second chorus, but my anger fell away. I looked up at my classmates, saw their looks of surprise and shock and amusement as they seemed to wonder what was happening. I set my violin down, took a deep breath, and started to sing. I doubled my pre-recorded self on the melody for a phrase, then launched into an improvised descant and tried to make pointed eye contact with everyone in the room in turn.

Bedroom eyes
All I see are bedroom eyes
Gotta have those bedroom eyes
Baby

Most of my classmates seemed to think this was hysterical, so I kept it up until the final bridge, at which point I sang the words "bedroom eyes" over and over with increased anguish, until finally the song ended and the class erupted into applause.

I was so surprised that I started bowing like a chicken pecking at some food in the dirt.

I turned to Bruce, who was staring at me, stunned. And I'll admit here that although I was *hoping* for an apology, I didn't expect to get one. And I didn't. "I really think you should try out for next year's school play," he said in a tone of voice I'd never heard him use before.

Fortunately the bell rang, so I was saved from having to reply. Most of the guys walked out the door without a backward glance, but quite a few of them stayed behind to talk to me. The guy who'd encouraged me to tell Bruce off socked me on the shoulder and laughed. "Holy fuck, Cardigan—did you see the look on his face?" he said before wandering off. A few of them asked me how I'd put the song together and how long I'd been playing and singing and all that, and at one point I said something like, "Hey, well, Rusty came up with the concept and put the whole thing together." There was an awkward pause, and then someone else asked me how I'd come up with the idea of rearranging the song the way I had. But for the most part, these guys just stood around and grinned.

It was like my fifteen minutes of high school fame had arrived, and all these guys who'd never realized I was alive were trying to be a part of it. As soon as I turned to put my violin away the crowd parted like I was an emperor, and wherever I moved, they moved with me. It was so ridiculous that I half expected two guys to start fighting over who would get to carry my violin case for me. I looked at Rusty standing several paces away. "You wanna hang out after school?" I called out.

He grinned, like he knew what I had in mind. "Sure. I just need to bring my laptop back to the teachers' lounge."

"Cool. Meet you at the bus stop?"

"You bet."

And with that, I went back to my desk to get my bag and walked downstairs to my locker. I still had ten guys moving with me like a herd of buffalo, and I had this sudden vision of me playing a lively tune on the violin, leading my classmates outside to the bus stop, like the Pied Piper. But somehow my new-found status as someone who was cool enough to talk to after all didn't have anything to do with the violin. They started talking to me about music and YouTube videos and how satisfying it was to see snotty teachers get what they deserved. Most of my new groupies went their own way once we got outside, but two of them followed me on the bus. This one kid started telling me all about this apparently super-awesome film franchise I'd never heard of and how the latest instalment had ended with this super-awesome post-credits tease—whatever that is. I didn't know what to say, so I told them a bunch of details I invented about Mozart's sex life, some of which involved syphilis *and* gonorrhea, and apparently that was wickedly awesome because both of them high-fived me.

The thing is, I was so overstimulated by this talk with new people that I could barely retain what anyone said or what I said back. I started to wonder if these two guys were going to follow me home like stray cats. One of them asked me if I'd post the video on YouTube so he could watch it again, and I forget how I answered. It was only once I'd stepped off the bus and turned to see Rusty behind me that I let out a deep breath. "Thank God that's over," I said.

"Yeah? I was starting to wonder if you'd forgotten about me," he said with a half grin. But before I had a chance to react to that, he kept going. "Why do you have your violin with you? Don't you usually leave it in your jail cell?"

I looked down in amazement at the violin case I was still clutching in my right hand. At least I hadn't set it down on the bus. I probably would have left it there and never seen it again, like Yo-Yo Ma.

We started walking down the street to my house, talking over everything that had happened in class. But once I let us inside, it was like we'd run out of things to say. We moved through the empty rooms in silence—I didn't offer him anything to drink or eat—and headed downstairs to my bedroom. I closed the door even though no one else was home.

If I was writing about this in a letter addressed to my father, I'd probably tell him that Rusty and I had a long talk, established our mutual feelings for each other, decided to make it official, made out for forty-five minutes, and said all sorts of *I knew I liked you when* mush. Maybe I'd go so far as to admit that we'd untucked our shirts a little, but in that version, we never ventured past what people in '80s movies used to refer to as "second base."

But that's not what happened.

As soon as I turned to face Rusty, I spotted some movement in his pants and watched him toss his tie to the floor and unbutton his shirt. He grinned at me as he started to fiddle with his belt buckle. "I've been thinking about this all day," he confessed with a catch in his voice.

I thought about telling him about my daylong stomach ache that had just vanished, but all I could focus on was trying to keep up with him as he shucked the rest of his clothes, revealing more and more skin and freckles and hair and parts. Once there was nothing left for either of us to remove, I paused to let the anticipation build a few more seconds.

At first, as we approached each other, I figured we'd follow the pattern we'd started during my sleepover at his house and perfected a few times since then, when we probably should have been studying. Then Rusty started kissing me and everything got even better—suddenly what we were doing morphed from naked horseplay between best friends to *sex*. We lay down on the bed, legs intertwining, hands everywhere, and kissed and kissed and kissed. And unlike the previous times, when we'd continued talking, this time there didn't seem to be room for anything but a few scattered words.

Once we'd reached the finish line and cleaned ourselves up, Rusty spoke.

"I really like you," he said, "in case that wasn't obvious before. I like you *a lot*."

"I like you, too," I said, smiling because the feeling of *newdity* hadn't gone away for me yet.

"Okay, but—do you mean you like me as a *friend*? Or as something more than that? I know that's probably a weird question since some of the jizz I'm wiping up is yours. For me it's both, but I'm asking because—because I really need to know. Don't take this the wrong way, buddy, but sometimes you're kind of hard to read."

I snickered, because I knew what he meant. "Yeah, Rusty—for me it's both, too."

And so, part of the real version of this story is that we *did* launch into the *I knew I liked you when such and such a thing happened* bit. "I've been attracted to guys before," he said as we lay back down on my bed together, "but it's only when we were sitting in the back seat of your uncles' car and you told me your whole family thought we were dating that it dawned on me that this was something we could, like, pursue if we wanted to. And it just—it took me a while to get used to that."

"So you *didn't* overhear me yelling at Uncle Scott and Uncle Joe at the restaurant that you and I would never be anything but friends? I thought that might have something to do with it."

"No. You said that? Why?"

"Oh, I don't know. They were starting to piss me off. 'He's so cute! He's so nice! Of course you *have* to sleep with him!' They mean well, but they can be a bit much sometimes."

We laughed and kissed some more, and when we paused again I asked him what had ended up changing for him.

"Dude," he said, his eyes shining at me, "it was the poem you read to the rest of the class—the one about singing at the beach or whatever. I figured if you had the courage to walk the crooked path and see where it goes, I could, too."

And at that moment, only partly because we were sitting on my bed with our clothes off, I felt close to him in a way I'd never felt with anyone—I felt this warm glow in my stomach like that time I took a sip of brandy at Burt and Beverly's house when no one was looking. So I told him what had been going on with me. It felt like I could tell him everything. Well, maybe not *everything*, but most of it. Some. A bit. Okay, very little, but for me it was a beginning.

I think it was at this point that we heard the front door slam. I turned to Rusty and saw his eyes grow wide. "Who do you think it is?" he asked, his voice dropping to a whisper even though there was no way anyone upstairs could overhear us.

"I can usually tell by the footsteps," I whispered back. It didn't take much to figure out that Gonzo had returned home and disappeared upstairs. I got up to lock my bedroom door and thought maybe we should get dressed in case Gonzo had noticed an extra pair of shoes in the front hall and started to wonder where we were.

"I really like you just the way you are," Rusty said, which made me feel good—of course, the fact that we were hugging each other without our clothes on helped. I said something, then he said some other stuff, and then I said something about what Sophie and Jenice would say when they learned of this plot twist.

Then Rusty let go of me, donned his boxer shorts, and sat on the edge of the bed again.

"Yeah—about that. What do you want to do now? Are we going out?" he asked.

"I don't know. Do you want to go out?"

"Like on a date?"

"Sure. I could pick you up on Friday night and we could go to the roller rink and hold hands over hamburgers somewhere," I said. I was kidding, but I don't think Rusty understood that, because the idea seemed to make him shudder.

"Yeah. I don't know if—" He gritted his teeth, like that helped him think. "Dale, I really like you. There's so much I want to try with you. The thing is—" He took a deep breath, like he was afraid of upsetting me. "I've never told anyone that this"—he gestured toward me and back to himself—"was an option on the menu for me. And um—I don't think it'd be a good idea for my parents to find out we're—you know—hanging out horizontally."

"Why? Are Mennonites super conservative about the whole boys-liking-boys thing?"

"Yes and no. It's just—if my parents knew we were dating or whatever, they'd never let us be alone. They both like you, by the way, even though Dad—well, you know what he's like. But everything would change if they found out. Sleepovers with a friend are fine, but sleepovers with a boyfriend would be kind of unthinkable. And they would *definitely* have some questions about me coming over here after school to 'study' when your adults aren't home. Already my dad's been on my case because my cousin told everyone about you and me hugging in the music room at Oma's house."

I nodded as I put my pants back on and looked for my socks. There were two thoughts brewing simultaneously in my brain, and I guess I looked pensive, because Rusty asked me what I was thinking.

"Yeah. I wonder if the same thing would happen at my end, too. My mother's been nagging me to come out for months. My uncles are like Sophie and Jenice: they think that you and me getting together is a foregone conclusion. The thing is—I mean, in a way I'm grateful that all these adults in my life are so supportive or whatever, but at the end of the day—" I looked up at him and grimaced, then figured he might as well get to know me as I really am. "I don't want to give them the satisfaction of being right."

Rusty reached out and hugged me till I started having trouble breathing. "Dale, you're too much," he said with a laugh.

I hugged him back, relieved that being honest hadn't wrecked everything.

"So it looks like we're on the same page here," Rusty said as he reached for his pants. "What then?"

I pulled my T-shirt over my head and looked into those amber eyes of his. What I'd finally figured out since the night I was trying to fall asleep in Rusty's bed was that I want a friend more than I want a boyfriend. Meeting Rusty has completely changed my idea of what a friend is: someone you can count on, someone you *want* to talk to, someone who texts you back! I guess for a lot of people that's a pretty low bar, but it's what I've been missing.

Every time I think about having a boyfriend I start to feel suffocated—like Jonathan all over again, even though no one knew about me and Jonathan. I just don't want the attention or the nosy questions or the excruciating conversations or the drama. Besides, I'm seventeen—next year I'll be figuring out what I want to do after high school. I've read enough books and watched enough TV to know that having a boyfriend right now could hold me back, but hopefully a best friend would wish me well no matter what we decided.

And maybe I'm naive. Maybe it's just a matter of time before someone catches us or puts two and two together and rats us out. But if Rusty and I decide that we're going to call ourselves friends rather than boyfriends, then I can honestly tell that to anyone who asks, no matter how many times we get naked together.

I told Rusty only a small fraction of this because I worried about hurting his feelings, but he kept grinning and agreeing with me as we talked everything over and launched into round two, so hopefully that's all fine.

"You know, I wouldn't mind if you told your uncles about us," Rusty said as we got dressed a second time.

"I've thought about that," I said with a sigh, "but after everything that just happened with the bombshell about my father, I doubt Uncle Scott would like it if I asked him to keep such a big secret from my mother—even supposing he could."

"Are you okay? With everything about your dad?" Rusty asked. "I wanted to ask sooner, but I thought it'd be better to wait for you to bring it up."

"No. I'm not." I concentrated on fastening my belt buckle so I wouldn't have to look at him. "But I will be."

Once we decided we looked semi-presentable, I opened the door to my room and we headed upstairs. I walked him to the front door and watched as he crammed each foot into a shoe without untying or retying the laces. I figured out later that Rusty had donned my tie instead of his by mistake, but when I told him that, he admitted that it hadn't been a mistake after all.

"You really are a good friend—you know that?" I said. I hadn't planned to say that. I just did because it was true.

"You are, too."

After a quick glance around, Rusty stepped toward me and gave me one of his bear hugs. I closed my eyes and let myself lean into the feeling of being so close to him—one of the best feelings in the world. Then we let go, and he grinned at me and winked.

"I'll call you later," we said at the same time. And then I watched as he left the house, headed down the sidewalk, and disappeared from view.

That would be a nice place to end, wouldn't it? But of course that wasn't the end—not by a long shot.

Once Rusty was gone I wandered into the kitchen, where I closed my eyes, enjoyed the residue of him on my lips, and replayed some choice bits of the last hour in my mind as I pulled out some cookies from the pantry and leaned against the dishwasher to enjoy them. Then I heard footsteps again—rapid ones. I really wanted to avoid being caught by Gonzo in the kitchen with a hard-on and my orgasm face, and I knew I wouldn't have time to make it to the basement stairs without him seeing me, so I did the only thing I could think of: I opened the door to the cupboard that houses the vacuum cleaner and slipped inside.

Yeah. I know.

Gonzo entered the kitchen and proceeded to make himself a sandwich. At least that's what I guessed based on the sounds I heard. I tried to help him in my mind—*That's right. There's the mustard. Let's move this along, okay?*—and discovered I was ravenously hungry. He was talking to someone on the phone, but his side of the conversation didn't give me any clues as to who he was talking to or what about. "Oh my gosh," he'd say. "Ugh. Yeah. No—that's crazy. What do you mean, I haven't heard the worst part?"

He hung up after a while, but before he could take his sandwich upstairs, the front door opened again and I heard my mother's voice, which made my heart simultaneously sink *and* beat faster.

I didn't have the nerve to push the cupboard door open even a crack to see what they were doing, but I could hear every word they said. And there was nothing I could do but stand there until they left—or until I got caught!

"How was your day, honey?" Ma asked. I heard the sounds of the refrigerator door opening and groceries being put away. I had to bite my lower lip to stop myself from going insane. Just as I felt a drop of sweat slide between my shoulders and all the way down my back, I pleaded with the universe that neither one of them would develop a sudden urge to vacuum.

"Dale played his song in class today. It was pretty awesome. I'm sure he'll tell you all about it."

"Oh, good. I'm glad it went well. I didn't want to say anything, but I couldn't understand why he and Rusty were going to all that trouble."

They moved on to something else then: Gonzo's basketball game in Burlington. I started to wonder how long I'd be trapped there, especially when the doorbell rang and it was Iliana.

"I know I'm early," I heard her say as Ma invited her inside, "but I wanted to tell Dale how much I enjoyed that program he recommended to me—the docudrama about the life of Beethoven. Is he home?"

"I don't think so," Gonzo said. I heard his footsteps move toward Iliana's voice, so I figured he'd gone over to hug his mother.

"He must be out with Rusty somewhere," Ma said. "Can I get you something to drink, Iliana?"

"Just water, please, Susan," Iliana said. "I get dehydrated so easily when it's this warm."

At this point I gave up hope that they'd ever leave the room. I was still pretty comfortable though, as long as I didn't move or breathe too heavily. But then the conversation took a different turn.

"Rusty," Iliana said musingly. "He's Dale's—um—*little friend*, isn't he?"

"We don't know yet," Ma said with a trace of something like exasperation. "Of course we've met Rusty a number of times, and Helmut and I really like him. And even though he tries to hide it, you can tell Dale's crazy about him. But he hasn't let on that they're anything more than good friends. My brothers-in-law told me he was adamant about that to them. Has he said anything to you, Gonzo?"

"No." To which I added silently, *Why the hell would I?* "But with Rusty, I think he's barking up the wrong tree." That made me grin.

"Have you known for a long time that he's gay?" Iliana asked.

"Oh, I've been wondering ever since he was little." Ma started to laugh. "I remember the first day he came home from kindergarten. He marched off the bus, towering with rage, and as soon as he saw me, he stopped and shouted, 'You mean we have to reproduce!?' We had no idea what led to this."

Everyone laughed. My face started to burn—and no, I have no recollection of that.

"We enrolled him in soccer when he was six or seven, but he screamed so much throughout his first practice that we didn't have the heart to make him continue. Music is where his passion is, although sometimes I wonder if it's becoming an obsession. But I've never really minded any of that. I don't believe in pushing kids into activities that don't interest them." She sighed. "What I've always worried about is the fact that he has such difficulty making friends. That's why we were so happy when he befriended Rusty. I love my son—he's a good kid. I just want him to come out to us so we can tell him that we accept him for who he is."

I could hear that she was tearing up, and then I heard Iliana's footsteps crossing the room, as though she'd gone to hug my mother. I couldn't stand it anymore, so I dared to open the cupboard door a crack. Gonzo was leaning against the counter. Thankfully he turned his head and saw me. His eyes bulged and he started to laugh, but he managed to turn it into a dull cough. "Mom, I just need a few minutes to finish getting ready. Um—Susan, my mother told me she wanted to see your garden sometime. Would you mind showing her?"

Luckily, they both seemed to think this wasn't a terrible idea. Before long I heard the patio door open and close and their footsteps fade away.

"Okay—they're gone," Gonzo said.

I emerged, my face flushed, the rest of me still reeling from everything I'd overheard. Gonzo looked like he wasn't sure whether to laugh or be angry. "Do I want to know why you were hiding in the cupboard?" he asked, sounding uncannily like Helmut.

"Probably not," I said before grabbing a couple of extra cookies from the package I'd left open on the counter and heading downstairs. I sat down on my bed and pondered things—not about Rusty but about how I'm perceived within this family.

I know I'm gay—or queer—or something in that neighbourhood. Of course I know. I've never seen the world through what Jenice would call the "man–woman dyad." I've always had Uncle Scott and Uncle Joe in my life, and now I have Sophie and Jenice, too. And apparently they all think they know. So why do I need to come out? What does liking music more than soccer have anything to do with it? *You mean we have to reproduce!?* So? What does she think that proves?

*We accept him for who he is.* Well, great. But I happen to be a lot of things: I happen to be male, I happen to be white, I happen to be left-handed, I happen to be thin, I happen to have hair that curls a little when it needs to be cut, I happen to be a musician, I happen to be pretty good at algebra, I happen to have perfect pitch, I happen to be an introvert even though I'm comfortable performing in front of hundreds of people, I happen to be an unrepentant nail-biter, I happen to be living in a blended family, I happen to detest several kinds of vegetable, I happen to suck at most but not all sports, I happen to be a virgin technically, and I happen to be gay. These are all aspects of "who I am." None of these components has tortured or confused me. None of them has made me feel bad about myself. And none of them deserves some kind of big announcement, let alone a celebration. Sure—in a lot of ways I'm not like everyone else, but I don't *want* to be like everyone else. I want to do things my way—sing in my own key.

I just don't want to do that thing where I tell my mother and my stepfather I'm gay and then we cry and hug and it's this big ordeal. Because there's nothing to mourn. Gonzo doesn't have to come out as straight; it's clear he likes girls and wants to date them. If it's so obvious to everyone that I like Rusty, why can't that be enough?

I went back upstairs after I heard Iliana and Gonzo leave for his game and I figured my face had returned to normal. Ma was in the kitchen laying out some potatoes and vegetables on a roasting pan. "Oh, honey! I didn't know you were home," she said when she saw me.

"I was in my room reading," I said.

"Gonzo left with Iliana for a basketball game in Burlington and Helmut has to stay late getting ready for court tomorrow, so it's going to be just the two of us for dinner," she said. "I thought we'd do something simple."

"Sounds great," I said, and I went up to her and leaned my head against her shoulder. I wanted to tell her that I'm happy as I am and that I don't need to be defined. But I couldn't figure out how to explain that to her in a way she'd understand. And now, having sat with all this for three days now, I still can't.

Dear Pa,

It's been a while since I wrote to you, so I thought I'd drive to the cemetery today and write you a letter here instead of at home. Ma and Helmut left yesterday after work for some weekend wine tour with Burt and Beverly, dropping off Gonzo at Iliana's on the way, and they won't be back until late tomorrow. So this morning I looked up the location of your grave online, and as soon as I got here I found it just a few rows from where I'd looked for you in February. I'm typing away on my laptop as I sit cross-legged on a blanket in front of your grave, keeping my eyes peeled in case my friend the cardinal decides to pay me a visit and not caring if anyone walks by and wonders what on earth I'm up to. I forgot my sunglasses at home so my corneas are burning, but whatever.

Rusty and I have been spending more time together since my last letter to you. He has lunch with me sometimes in my music room or we study together after school. He's coming over later to hang out, and tonight we're going to a potluck at Jenice and Sophie's. The invitation asked us all to bring a dish whose main ingredient begins with a vowel. Helmut helped me find a recipe for eggplant ratatouille that shouldn't be too complicated, but Rusty decided to play it safe and is bringing a tub of orange sherbet. I've never been to a potluck before and I don't know who else will be there, but I can't wait! Rusty's going to crash at my place tonight, and tomorrow's his birthday, which means I'll get to hang out with Pam and Mitch again for the first time since the shitstorm at Oma's brunch.

You'd have liked Rusty. He's a good guy and a great friend. I used to worry that we didn't have too much in common to do or talk about, but somehow that doesn't seem to be a problem anymore.

Ma and Helmut leaving gave me the opportunity to do something I'd been wanting to do for a while: I dug out your old computer from the storeroom, set it up on the dining room table, and started going through your files. I never asked Ma if I could do this and I have no idea how she'd react if she found out. And I wasn't totally sure what I was looking for. It took me some time to remember how to use a PC again. We became a Mac family when Ma married Helmut, and once you go Mac, apparently you never go back. I hovered the mouse over your email program, then moved it away. I thought about looking at your photos but was afraid of what I might find. In the end I settled on your music program, figuring I might get some clues about you if I listened to some of the music you liked. I spent a nice half-hour sampling some bands like Tears for Fears, Cougar and the Catfish, Simon and Garfunkel, Stevie Wonder, Aimee Mann, and R.E.M. while inhaling an insane amount of ice cream. I kept scrolling until I reached the bottom of your playlist, where I noticed a handful of tracks that didn't name an artist or a composer.

These tracks turned out to be recordings of the two of us when I was little: me at the piano or the violin, you at the guitar. Some of the songs were pretty simple, like "Frère Jacques" and the alphabet song, but the last one was a recording of a pop song I still hear on the radio sometimes and whose name I can never remember. We were playing together as well as singing together, me in my old mezzo-soprano voice, you as a pretty decent tenor. I smiled as I listened, thinking, *Pa was a pretty good singer. At least I have a recording of his singing voice now.*

Then the song stopped abruptly halfway through the first chorus, and I heard the sound of someone—evidently me—banging on the piano keys in frustration.

"I can't get this chord right!"

"Which one?"

"Here—see? *One, two, three, four, five*—it's the fourth one that gets me every time."

"Hey—it's okay, buddy. You'll get there. Look at your fingering—"

I held my breath, because after months of trying to remember what your voice sounded like, finally I *knew*. In the recording, we went back and forth a few more times before trying again from the top. And finally, I managed to get that chord right! We cheered, and you told me you were proud of me. Then we went through the song again, each of us taking a verse and both of us singing the choruses and the third verse together, except this time we made it to the end.

Tears swam in my eyes, but just as my vision was getting blurry I noticed the date of the track in the "Last Played" field: February 26, 2004. The day before you died.

Before I could shake the tears away the track ended and the app adjusted the field to yesterday, but I'm positive of the date that I'd seen.

Which means that you went back to listen to that recording after you'd made the decision to leave Ma. So you *were* thinking of me, after all. Or maybe you weren't and I'm grasping at straws. But it's all I'm ever going to get as an answer, so I'll take it.

That was the last song in your music library, so all that followed was silence. But I'd grasped enough of your real voice to be able to sample it in my head, and in the empty dining room I leaned back in my chair and imagined you telling me all sorts of things: that you and Ma were separating—that you missed me—that you were proud of the way I'd grown up—and that you loved me, just the way I am. It was painful, like tearing a cast off a broken limb before it's finished healing, but once it was over, most of the pain had gone away and was replaced by this eerie sense of calm.

And in that calm, I spontaneously decided to track down your friends and see if one of them would talk to me. I wondered at first how I could do this, but it turned out to be surprisingly easy: I clicked on your address book, found all their phone numbers, and called Mike 1 before I could talk myself out of it. As soon as I heard his voice I smiled, plunged in, and told him who I was. He sounded pleased to hear from me, but when I explained that I was heading to Guelph to run some errands the next day and asked if I could stop by, he hesitated for so long that I figured I might as well come right out with it. "Mike," I said, "I already know that my parents were in the middle of separating when my father died. That's not what I want to talk to you about. I just—I just want to remember him with someone who knew him. Get to know him in a different way. What do you say?"

There was another pause, broken by Mike clearing his throat. "Sure thing, little buddy," he said. My heart warmed when I heard his old pet name for me. "Any time would be fine."

And after putting your computer back where I found it, I went to my own laptop and dug through my emails until I found the list of prospective piano teachers Rita had recommended for me. I started to look them up online, figuring it's time now to get back on that horse.

When I pulled into Mike's driveway this morning, he was standing in the garage with the door open. He smiled as I got out of the car. He hadn't changed much, except, not surprisingly, he wasn't nearly as tall as I remembered him. We sat in the shade in his driveway and drank lemonade and got caught up and talked about you. He told me stories I'd never heard before of you getting drunk at your prom, you playing poker in the dorm, you being a good friend to Mike after his long-time girlfriend dumped him in a really harsh way. In short, what Mike gave me was an idea of you as a person. And although neither one of us mentioned your death or your affair, he did ask me to give Ma his warmest regards. Which I may do someday, if I ever tell her about this visit.

On Thursday after school, I took a different bus and surprised Ma at her dental office. I wanted to talk to her—*really* talk to her—in a way we hadn't since we'd finished unearthing all that stuff about you. I figured I'd sit in the waiting room and get caught up on celebrity gossip until closing time, but the office manager thought that was crazy.

"I'm Susan's son," I explained. "I wanted to surprise her after work."

"Oh—I didn't recognize you," he said. I guess that proved that it had indeed been a while since I'd last been in. Sure enough, he clicked away on his computer and said, "Listen—her last appointment today cancelled, and you're way overdue for a cleaning. Would you like to take that spot?"

Despite being the son of a dental hygienist, I can't stand getting my teeth cleaned. So it made sense to agree to this since I'd have only minutes of dreadful anticipation instead of weeks or months. Normally one of Ma's colleagues sees me, since apparently it's a conflict of interest for hygienists to clean the teeth of their family members, but I liked the idea of quality time with Ma. She wasn't in her cubicle when I got there, so I sat down in her futuristic patient chair and waited. That's when I noticed three framed photos hanging on the wall: one of her and Helmut on their wedding day, a recent one of the four of us, and my school photo from last September, where I noticed a glazed look in my eyes, like I wasn't completely aware that I was getting my picture taken.

Ma was surprised but not displeased to see me. Soon enough I had the bib on and the bright light in my face. In a way, she was in her element, since she could talk as much as she wanted and the only thing I could feasibly do to resist would be to bite her fingers. As she worked, she told me that losing her parents when she was in her early twenties and becoming a widow at thirty-four had made her see that life was too short for resentment or for bowing to convention. That's why she'd never told me that her marriage to you was in the process of ending when you died, and that's also why she tried her best to steer me on the path I was heading toward. "I didn't care at all that you preferred music to sports. I've never seen the point in forcing people to pursue things that don't interest them," she said. Since I had gloved hands, sharp instruments, and a suction tube in my mouth, I didn't have the chance to remind her that maybe sending me to a high school without a music program hadn't been the best way to support my ambitions as a musician. So this time I just let that sit. "The only thing I worried about was that you never had any friends," Ma said. "I know you're a loner by nature, and that's fine. I just thought it was a shame that you didn't have someone your own age to depend on. That's why Helmut and I were so happy when you started spending time with Rusty. We both like him. Your uncles do, too. He's got a good heart. Here—spit into this cup."

I did. She looked at me like she expected me to speak. I wiped the drool from my mouth and ran my tongue against the backs of my bottom teeth to buy myself some time. I knew what she wanted me to say—I could see the reaction she was gearing up to as clearly as if through a crystal ball. It would have been so easy to say those words and to endure the tears and laughter and hugs of reassurance that I knew would follow. But I found myself recoiling. I felt words form deep in my gut and rise up my esophagus like acid reflux, and even though I didn't know what they would be, I knew they'd at least be truthful.

"Ma, I did really well on my piano exam—I got the results in the mail two months ago." I wiped my mouth with the disposable bib while I pondered my next move. The phrase *I guess I forgot to tell you* appeared in my mind as one option, but then I pushed it aside and reached for the truth: "I waited two months for you to ask, but you never did."

Ma squinted as she processed words she clearly hadn't expected to hear. I heard her suck in her breath and saw her rush to say something in response, but then she stopped and looked at me curiously, like I was a painting she was trying to figure out. And when I said nothing more, she exhaled the breath she'd been holding and carried on scraping plaque off my teeth.

I have one more errand to run before I drive home: I need to stop at Jordana's house to return the biography of Joni Mitchell that she loaned me years ago to keep as a memento of her. It's been on my nightstand ever since, but now it's time for me to give it back. I'm going to leave it in her mailbox in an envelope addressed to her. Hopefully her parents aren't around. I thought about leaving a note, but I've decided not to. She'll know it's from me once she gets home in a few weeks.

I'm looking forward to summer. One of Sophie and Jenice's friends might be looking for someone to stuff envelopes and run errands for some politician who's gearing up for a big comeback. It might be fun, and that's one of the reasons I want to make a good first impression tonight. I'm also hoping to spend more time with Uncle Scott and Uncle Joe once exams are over. I'd hoped that our family drama a few weeks ago at their anniversary party would make them realize how much they love each other, but that doesn't seem to have happened. They're okay, but the last time I spoke to Uncle Scott, he told me they have a lot to work through. I don't know about what, but he sounded optimistic, so I am, too.

So now I'm here, in front of your grave. The fact is I have a few things left to say to you. Your tombstone has your name and your dates—nothing more. It doesn't tell any of your life story. It doesn't give any indication of what kind of man you were. And it certainly says nothing about those you left behind.

I know you're dead, and I know you haven't heard or read any of these letters addressed to you. But I couldn't have done it without you, all the same. I needed you so much this spring, and you were there, if only in my mind. Even though you're gone, I like to think that somewhere, in some form, you know that I'm doing all right—and that even though I was badly hurt over the discovery of your big secret, I miss you all the same. I wish I could ask you about it as a way to understand it better, but I'm all left with are bits and pieces.

I'm crying now as I sit by your grave, because it's time for me to let you go. When I think about the future, I think about music, about school, about finding friends I can count on, about having a career and a partner and a home and a family. You won't be a part of that life, and that breaks my heart. But I'm looking forward to it all the same.

Your loving son,

Dale

## ACKNOWLEDGMENTS

Writing a novel is in many ways a solitary activity, but I benefited enormously from the insight and encouragement offered with such generosity by several people along the way. I am grateful to Vanessa Brown, Kelly Norah Drukker, Melanie J. Fishbane, and Rachel McMillan, who responded so generously and with such enthusiasm to drafts of the manuscript. Thanks as well to several friends and colleagues who have supported this book or encouraged me in my writing career, including Jenna Anderson, Brenda Austin-Smith, Michelle Baumtrog, Karine Bibeau, Julie Bruck, James Buchanan, Jennifer Burns, Hélène Champagne, Nina Chordas, Terrence Daigneault, Alannah d'Ailly, Jason Dickson, Jan Draper, Kareem Fahmy, Trevor Ferguson, C.E. Gatchalian, Andrew Hodge, Joanna Jack, K. Lorraine Kiidumae, Bill Konigsberg, Sonnet L'Abbé, Gina Lavine, DeeDee LeGrand-Hart, David Levithan, Jennifer Manuel, Andrea McKenzie, Laurie Myers-Bishop, Kristine Logan Perron, Kathryn Reynolds, Lisa Richter, Wayne Selman, Benoit Simard, Kandala Singh, Naava Smolash, Patti Sonntag, Cynthia Soulliere, Meg Taylor, Susie Taylor, the late Anne Thaler, Candace Webb, Steve Wood, and Lorraine York.

I am especially grateful to my agent, Chris Casuccio of Westwood Creative Artists; to Brian Lam, Catharine Chen, Jazmin Welch, and their colleagues at Arsenal Pulp Press; to my parents, Claire Pelland Lefebvre and the late Gerald M. Lefebvre; to my siblings, Melanie Lefebvre and Jeremy Lefebvre, as well as to my siblings-in-law Éric Lemay and Julie Trépanier and all their children; and to my in-laws, Rudy Letkemann, Walli Fritz, Dave Fritz, Kassi Fritz, and Jasmin Fritz.

Dale's two poems were written by me as a teenager and appeared in student anthologies that I edited, *Spindrift* (jointly with Joanna Jack) and *Spindrift: The Crooked Path*, published in 1995 and 1996.

And finally, thanks to Jacob Letkemann, my first reader, my one and only, for everything.

B.L.

**BENJAMIN LEFEBVRE** (he/him) is the editor of several books, including *The L.M. Montgomery Reader*, a three-volume critical anthology that won the 2016 PROSE Award for Literature from the Association of American Publishers, and an edition of Montgomery's rediscovered final book, *The Blythes Are Quoted*, which has been translated into five languages. He also edits two book series: The L.M. Montgomery Library, which collects Montgomery's extensive shorter publications, and the Early Canadian Literature series, which returns to print neglected works deserving to be reintroduced to the canon of Canadian literature. He lives in Kitchener, Ontario, and can be found online at *benjaminlefebvre.com*.